A CELESTIAL SPHERES NOVEL

LYFT

LISA BORNE GRAVES

AUTHORS 4 AUTHORS PUBLISHING
Marysville, WA, USA

Published by Authors 4 Authors Publishing
1214 6th St
Marysville, WA 98270
www.authors4authorspublishing.com

Library of Congress Control Number: 9781644771938

E-book ISBN: 978-1-64477-192-1
Paperback ISBN: 978-1-64477-193-8
Audiobook ISBN: 978-1-64477-194-5

Edited by Beatrice B. Morgan
Copyedited by Rebecca Mikkelson

Cover design ©2025 Practically Perfect Covers. All rights reserved.
Interior design by Brandi Spencer.
Scene break icon by Lisa Borne Graves

Authors 4 Authors Publishing branding is set in Bavire. Titles and headings are set in Mr Darcy. Handwriting is set in URW Chancery.
All other text is set in Garamond.

LYFT

LISA BORNE GRAVES

Authors 4 Authors Content Rating

This title has been rated 14+, appropriate for teens, and contains:

- Brief intense violence
- Parental emotional and physical abuse

Please, keep the following in mind when using our rating system:

1. A content rating is not a measure of quality.

Great stories can be found for every audience. One book with many content warnings and another with none at all may be of equal depth and sophistication. Our ratings can work both ways: to avoid content or to find it.

2. Ratings are merely a tool.

For our young adult (YA) and children's titles, age ratings are generalized suggestions. For parents, our descriptive ratings can help you make informed decisions, but at the end of the day, only you know what kinds of content are appropriate for your individual child. This is why we provide details in addition to the general age rating.

For more information on our rating system, please, visit our Content Guide at: www.authors4authorspublishing.com/books/ratings

DEDICATION

To CJ Carson and KR Galindez,
thank you for your help with this book.

WORKS BY LISA BORNE GRAVES

CELESTIAL SPHERES

Fyr
Draca
Bladesung

Wundor
Lyft
Water (2026)

THE IMMORTAL TRANSCRIPTS

Quiver
Fever
Shudder
Glimmer

STAND-ALONE TITLES

Apidae
"Dare"

TABLE OF CONTENTS

18 YEARS AGO
LYFT

Nakano's blood ran cold when she entered the bedchamber on her wedding night. The tyrant she must now call husband would not be kind in this endeavor because he was unkind in everything. How she wished she could speak to Shesha, the king serpent, like her mother had. That power bypassed her as well as the power to rule their people. One who cannot command nagas to keep the balance could not rule, so she had to marry one who could speak to the serpents. If she had the power to link her mind with them, she would order them to eat her new husband. Anything, she prayed, to avoid this terrible future that felt like a death sentence. Unlike her warrior-meaning name, reused from her maternal great-grandmother, she was weak, submissive, and a disappointment to her mother, the empress of Lyft. Nakano was forced into this marriage. Over politics. To not lose it all, the *empress* of the Lyft sphere—not a true mother anymore—sold her daughter to the richest serpent-speaker.

The servants, mostly male—her mother's standard, to enforce "equality"—started to undo her elaborate bun, which she found ostentatious. They removed the pins that had held her black tresses in place and all the ornaments from jeweled pins to flowers that ran down the side of her face. She doubted her great-grandmother's people really wore this so many years ago and felt bad her late father's heritage was ignored. But men were nothing but expendable to Mother, and Mother wanted her heritage to stand out as unique and better than the majority who she viewed as common. Nakano saw no reasonable evidence as to why.

Finally, her hair was free, cascading down her back, a burden of femininity falling upon her shoulders. One servant brushed her hair with gentle strokes, being sure not to snag on the sticky wax that had been used to maintain her updo. He applied oil next, the smell of jasmine and lavender giving her a shred of comfort. The oil meant the preparation for her new husband's visit would take hours. Another servant drew a bath, and the aroma of flowers filled the room.

However, once they set out her night clothes, a short, lacy—horrid—thing, bile rose, stinging the back of her throat at the thought of how her future spouse would view her in it. She swallowed hard, the bitter taste lingering.

The other men awaited orders, never meeting her gaze. She was better than them, these "humans" the empress had repeatedly warned her were so vile that they allowed lust to overtake their brains. The more they could control their base nature, the more they had to offer the empire. The more they could offer, the more likely males could rise in society and be trusted. It was "the way of things." Nakano never asked questions. She obeyed. The largest question that burned inside of her was why some women seemed to like them. She often saw hidden kisses and touches between servants and ladies. If men were so vile, then why invite such attention? More so, Nakano could not comprehend why—unlike other ladies her age—she did not like to look upon them or kiss them. To Nakano, the male form was nothing, while a woman's was beautiful, made of soft angles and skin.

Nakano let her mind wander upon these things while her waiting ladies bathed her, a role never bestowed upon male servants. She never found men appealing in any sense. Now, one would rule her—mind, body, soul—and her people. There was so much Nakano did not understand about the idea of lust, or men, to know what to expect this evening. Mother had given her a cursory explanation that sounded pretty simple—weird, but simple. Her ladies had told her horror stories that frightened her. She could not lend credit to their accounts. They were unmarried maidens who were supposed to be innocent.

Once she returned to the bedroom, wrapped in towels, she dismissed the servants, wanting them gone. Only her aide Udaya stayed behind.

Nakano saw her future splayed out in front of her. This vile man, twice her age, could wrestle male-control back, render her powerless, and change the matriarchy that had worked for generations. The Lyft sphere had been founded by Earth's "witches"—accused, branded, or slaughtered—united by their persecution. They, with enlightened warlocks, forged this glorious new world. Nakano's ancestors, as well as many others, followed after them, coming from Asia and then other places around the globe—anyone whose blood sang the charms of their air magic.

Now, at the age of sixteen, Nakano was letting her foremothers and future generations of Lyftian women down.

Nakano's dread was palpable, like a sheet of opaque gloom over the entire festivities.

Udaya sighed. The woman was gorgeous, her beauty and ancestry made Nakano want to give up everything and run far far away with her. Udaya's thick black, wavy hair normally cascaded down her back to her waist, but today it was fastened in a thick braid down her spine, and those almond-shaped honey-brown eyes looked upon Nakano with nothing but adoration. Her golden-tan skin made the vibrant teal sari she wore look decadent. A pang of longing filled her heart as she met her aide's gaze. Udaya should be empress. She *was* the people, was much more charismatic, compassionate, wise, and…her family could speak to the nagas.

Nakano could not do this, marry another, marry a man. There had to be a way out. "I wish it were you."

Udaya's sad gaze met hers. "Your mother would never allow it. You simply breed with him as duty. I will be here for you, in heart. I will always be here."

Udaya leaned down to Nakano and kissed her lips. Nakano's stomach dropped in pleasurable ways. Mother would never approve. She still believed they were only best friends. Only Udaya made Nakano feel this way, and no one else ever had nor would.

"Goodnight, my love," Udaya said sweetly. "Whenever he leaves your bed," she hesitated at the door before opening it, "I will come back. I will care for you. It will be okay."

"And if it's not? If it is everything I fear it will be?"

Udaya's eyes narrowed at the thought of the man being forceful. "I always look out for you. Trust in me." She walked over to the platform bed and lifted Nakano's pillow. Underneath rested a katar. Then she dropped the pillow, ignored Nakano's gasp, and walked out the door, her braid swinging like a pendulum, reminding her that time was ticking away.

Nakano could not take a life. *Impossible. Wrong.* She would give her husband a chance. He had not tried to make himself likable, but if she only had to have relations for progeny—if blessed with a couple daughters—she could survive. She would have the balm of real love from Udaya, always, ever since their first kiss a month ago.

After Nakano changed into the horrid ensemble and slipped into her robe, she sat on the edge of the bed, running her hand along the silky sheets. She felt like an animal on an altar, only this sacrifice would not turn the profane into holy—the other way around. He would sully her. She heard footsteps, boots upon stone. She stood, dispelling that image of herself being ready for slaughter. She would be brave.

Her husband entered, stumbling a little, his body swaying. The stench of alcohol and smoked tobacco wafted in with him. His eyes, squished in his plump, lined face, like almonds pressed in shortbread, greedily ran up and down her body. She felt naked and exposed, despite wearing a robe that covered most of her flesh.

He laughed, for some reason, and then licked his lips. Her pulse spiked and terror pounded in her heart. Hunted, vulnerable. Despite her mother forcing her to train as a warrior, she could not fight this kind of battle. She did not know how to deal with men. Mother was right: Nakano embodied weakness.

Terrified of the prowling beast before her, she fell back onto the bed. She saw a tiger, ready to pounce.

"That's a good girl. Right where I want you." He did not bother to talk softly or flirt with her as men often did, nor did he care about her fear; it was almost as if he was taking pleasure in her terror. She scrambled backward until she hit the headboard, her hand slipping under the pillow. Cool metal touched her hand. Steely resolve formed. Her hand gripped the crossbars, her fingers curling around them.

A sign. All signs pointed to destiny. Not wrong, but right. Not impossible, because it was there in her hand. *Freedom. Power.*

He crept onto the bed like a tiger going in for the kill. His hands were upon what was physically and emotionally hers. No one else's. She would be the empress of her own body, mind, soul, and her sphere.

Without hesitation, she thrust the katar forward in a punching motion, committing an act of sacrifice. She reclaimed her freedom and embraced her future.

Lyft was hers.

No one would take it from her.

Never.

1
AN ANNOUNCEMENT

Princess Alexandra Sapphirian of Fyr—Xandra for short, or she'd throw a punch—chased her cousin Thomas through the palace's orchard. Her more-than-suitable athletic stamina, for a lady, quickly caught up to Thomas's inverse unsuitable lack of soldier status for a gentleman. Although her parents had made strides in changing people's perception of male and female through many reforms in the Fyr sphere, the elderly clung onto traditions with an iron-clad fist. Too much for Xandra's liking.

Xandra tackled Thomas to the ground, then bent his arm behind his back until he cried out in pain. "Mercy!"

"Take it back," she ordered.

"All right! You're not a *complete* shrew."

"Nor unmarriageable?"

"I'm not taking that back," Thomas said defiantly, still fighting back despite being overpowered. "You are obsessed with putting men in a place beneath you, physically beating them up if needed—case in point—and you are obsessed with that crazy man-killing empress of Lyft."

"She is a great woman! Take that back right now Thomas Arlo Sapphirian."

"He is right, you know," a judgmental voice she loved and hated at the same time interrupted the fight. Xandra craned her neck to see her twin sister. She was absolute perfection, dignified and ladylike while Xandra was just the opposite. She envied Tourmaline yet could never connect with her. How could two souls who shared a womb be so different in appearance and personality?

Xandra's momentary distraction allowed Thomas to roll over and push her away with his knees, then feet. She toppled over onto her bottom. Josephine, her cousin and Thomas's older sister by two years, gave a high-pitch giggle like other ridiculous ladies of the court.

Tourmaline shook her head, her sapphire-blue eyes twinkling. She was the epitome of courtly beauty, just like their mother, the queen, who had changed the ideal beauty away from fair features. Tourmaline looked exactly like Mum, dark-haired and tan-skinned, but instead of Mum's gray eyes, they were that vibrant blue Sapphirian color, clashing against her darker flesh. Whatever bloodline she inherited her complexion from was not passed down to Xandra. She looked like her dad, spot on, from the brown hair with subtle auburn streaks to the pale aristocratic chiseled features. The eyes were wrong though. They were gray, which made her an "abomination" on the Fyr sphere. Had she not been a twin, her mother would've been accused of adultery. Paternal eyes were supposed to be dominant. The safety net of being a twin did not spare Xandra at all; she was removed from the line of succession to appease the people. Fyrians ignored her now and simply dealt with her to not appear rude or risk losing favor with the king—the very overprotective dad-king namesake. He had tried to save her through his name. It hadn't fully worked.

Tourmaline shook her head. "Xandra, he's right. You are a *princess*. You cannot go around acting this way if you ever hope to marry."

Xandra stood up, dusting off her pants, ignoring Thomas's hand offering to help her up. His Sapphirian-blue eyes narrowed, annoyed. She did not know why she was always so disagreeable toward him; he was her best friend, her *only* friend. Being a year older than her, he almost felt more like a sibling than her real ones. Tourmaline and Xandra had been inseparable when they were little, until they turned twelve. Tourmaline became obsessed with gentlemen while Xandra could care less about them unless they would let her spar with them. As for marriage? Good riddance to that. "I hope to never marry, but if it is by choice, one should never be called a shrew."

Tourmaline scoffed. "Still think you're going to another sphere to become some heroine like Mum?"

"Dad told me—"

"Dad lies to make you feel better about the people hating you." Tourmaline's eyes were cold. Her sister was embarrassed. Those sparkling blue eyes took in the boy's pants Xandra was wearing with disdain, even though Mum wore similar ones too while sparring and picking fruit.

Her sister's words stung. She tried not to react. It was as if that last connection they had was severed by her vicious comment.

"Out of line, Tourmaline." Thomas defended Xandra—not that she needed it.

Tourmaline's eyes narrowed on Thomas. "You too, Thomas. You are just…weird. Your head is always in a book, discussing stuff no one cares about on Fyr. That's why you two are friends. You're in your annoyingly odd bubble ignoring reality."

"Tourmaline, he's right. Too far." Josephine was clearly disappointed in her. Tourmaline blushed at being taken down a notch and then walked on, Josephine shooting them an apologetic glance before she followed.

"C'mon." Thomas slung his arm around Xandra's shoulder, leading her back to the palace. "She's vile and her husband will suffer for it."

"Oh, did she pick one yet or does she still have them all on reins?"

"Josie said Tourmaline's suitor list has twenty-four men on it still. She is lapping up the attention which is why her head is so big. Just wait till she settles down and realizes only one man will give her attention."

Xandra huffed.

"How many are on your list?" Thomas dared to ask.

"Over my dead body will I tell you. And it doesn't matter. My dad says I will leave Fyr. Every firebrander in this family knows my future disappears, just like yours. We tried so many times to see it, Thomas. You know what that means." She softened her voice at the end, knowing how sensitive her cousin was about the only two outcomes for Sapphirians who could not see snippets of their future in the flames. Thomas had a hard time digesting that no firebrander in the entire sphere had seen Xandra or him in adulthood.

Thomas's jaw clenched. "I do *not* want to talk about that."

"Look, I do not think either of us will die. We will probably go to another sphere. Firebranders cannot see what happens on other spheres, remember?" Most Sapphirians were firebranders, easily seeing the future in the flames.

"You do not know that for sure, and I do not fancy other spheres. I might not fit in Fyr well, but I love it here." He kicked a stone. "Drop it, Xandra."

She scrutinized him. Sometimes they were so alike, and sometimes she did not understand him. She shifted the conversation because he would get more waspish if she kept pushing. "How many girls' lists have you signed?" She nudged him.

"No comment." He opened a door into the palace, letting her enter first.

The answer was likely the same as the acceptable men on her list: zero. Of course, there were poor but ambitious cunning folk on her list after Dad had lessened the nobility-commoner divide. Equality and finances were improving, and Fyr had entered a Golden Age—foretold in the book of edicts—where few went without work, food, or shelter; however, the court's behavior—Tourmaline being a prime example—still stayed snooty rather than humble. Xandra had allowed these men to visit her and pretended to be genteel for her mother's sake, but they all knew it was pointless. The cunning folk men only wanted a leg up in society. She could not dislike them for their ambition. Maybe one day she would find a man she could tolerate who loved disagreeable shrews who had to have their way. Doubtful. The idea of being Bladesung, a heroine like her mother, was more palpable. To ride a dragon into battle and save the kingdom...that was what Xandra dreamed of.

Once Xandra and Thomas were inside, before she could get to her room, she came face-to-face with her mother. Her arms were crossed, those piercing gray eyes, like her own, were reprimanding; the gaze was like being disappointed in yourself. Mum disciplined Xandra, and Dad spoiled her rotten. With the others, it was an even trade of who was the discipliner and who was the sympathetic one. Xandra was treated differently than her siblings—always.

"Running through the halls, beating up your poor cousin, making a spectacle of yourself, all while the ambassador from Water is due to arrive at any moment. We cannot step a toe out of line. Your father—"

"Foolishly thinks he can create peace in the universe since he managed it here."

Her mother's eyes went wide, and her nostrils flared. "Do not test me today, Xandra. All the spheres would be better off if we communicated more, could trade magic and goods, let people emigrate." All spheres except Lyft. The books Xandra read told her that Lyft seemed to have everything, completely self-reliant. "You and I will talk later, alone. In the meantime, please change. You have grass stains on your rump. Dress to impress the Ambassador of Water. Do not wear your brother's pants in company. I had very nice ones made for you that were not too girly." Her mother knew too well that if left to her own choices, Xandra would come down in her younger brother Gareth's doublet as well.

Not wanting to anger her mother in front of an ambassador, she obeyed and opted for her mother's infamous skirt-pants and corset blouse. After all, honoring her mother's style might make her a bit softer with their "chat" later. Deep down, she knew her mother loved her, and she knew why she was hard on her. Xandra often impulsively did things that made her own life harder, made her more of an outcast. No parent would want their kid to feel that way.

Still, she was sixteen. Mum had to stop protecting her. Xandra was going to do something great and daring. She knew it. If only she could foresee what that would be.

Dinner was a boring affair—and, as always, obnoxiously loud. Once upon a time, there had been only one table in the dining hall, and now there were four long tables filling the room. There was the king and queen's table where their elder kids sat; if married, the spouses joined and there was always an extra seat across from Xandra's mum near the head of the table for a guest, like this dark-skinned ambassador from Water. He appeared serious and nervous, unsmiling despite her mother's kind small-talk. Next to him was Xandra's eldest brother, Rowland, and the heir to the throne. He was the brooding type, but he did have the sphere's weight on his shoulders, or he at least he acted like he did. They all foresaw Dad living a long time, so Rowland did not even need to worry about ruling until he was an old man, or he might get completely bypassed, and it would pass to Rowland's daughter Roseland. Rowland was different like Xandra, but in a good way. He had white fire magic like their mum developed from discovering she was a powermender, prompted unconsciously to save Rowland from poison when she was pregnant. She merged her light magic with his fire, and the result gave them electrical zapping powers and white fire. The former was an annoying torture Rowland taunted them with as a child, but with Xandra being eight years younger, he barely picked on her, already becoming more serious as the heir. The people loved *him*. He looked just like their father and his strange color of fire made him seem even more powerful to the people. Dad could beat him still in sword and power duels, but that speaks volumes for real warfare experiences versus training.

The only one who could sometimes best Dad in sparring matches was her warrior brother who taught Xandra all she knew, Aschen. He sat across from Rowland; both had their wives next to them, and Xandra was thankful her brothers chose well—pretty, intelligent, and full of personality. Zigzagging down the table were the rest of her siblings. Grandmother was at the foot of the table, next to Xandra. It was an irritatingly massive family. That was not even counting the kids' table at the back of the room. They got promoted to the adult table at fifteen; it was a condescending system, and who knew what they would do since there was no more room. There was talk of Aschen moving out of the palace with his new wife to maintain his own property. Xandra would miss him but could visit. If her three other older brothers married and moved out, and her cousins did as well, it might not be so loud and chaotic here.

Xandra dared to make eye contact with Thomas at his table with his absurd number of siblings. She swore Uncle Cobalt and Aunt Mary were competing with her parents to see who could have more kids. The person who loved it all, who loved them most of all, was Grandmother. She loved them all with overly abundant enthusiasm, even Xandra, despite her faults. To her, Xandra was no different, no less a Sapphirian for her birth defect.

Thomas met Xandra's gaze and took his butter knife and made a throat-slitting gesture as if the dealing with his family killed him. Xandra laughed but stopped when Tourmaline kicked her under the table. Yes, Xandra should not be out of line in any way with the ambassador here.

The other table had "family" at it. People in their very close inner circle who dined at the palace often who they saw as family were among extended blood-related family: super old "Grandpa" Tobias, and Auntie Madge, Uncle David and his husband Uncle Humphrey, Great-Aunt Edwina, Great-Uncle Gareth, and the other Cobalts who were visiting today.

How could anyone even eat in such chaos or even think? Xandra was not cut out for this big of a family. It made her want to hide away and find quiet. She forgot and mixed up names. Every time a Sapphirian was born, part of her wished to see the wrong eyes, a family member to make her feel less alone, but they were always the perfect sapphire blue. Then guilt would ensue. If any were born, they would be seen as baseborn, shunned. The only thing that saved Xandra was having a legitimate twin and her father's gesture of naming her after himself. She loved her family, and they treated her kindly. How many of them there in one room was simply too overwhelming.

When she turned twelve, she had begged her parents to stop having kids, but no—they smiled slyly at each other and told her she'd understand one day. Then they just kept going. Finally, they were finished after twelve children—she hoped. Xandra's youngest sibling being five, Aunt Mary had her latest just a week ago.

Her father stood up and clinked his glass to gain everyone's attention: an announcement. Did he reach some amazing deal with the Water sphere so soon? Mother stood up as well. Odd. Father was the great orator, and her mother preferred to control things behind the scenes, quietly, and only spoke publicly to put people in their place if needed.

Dad waited for the room to quiet down. "We have an announcement to make. I know we have a guest here and when we have a guest, we have a ball. We wanted to announce this now—because frankly we cannot hide it much longer, and there's no reason to have a second ball to celebrate. We'll be combining the honor of our visitor and peace negotiations with the Water sphere with our news." He took up her mother's hand and they had that pathetic look in their eyes—so sickly-sweet in love. *Barf.*

"We are having a baby." Her mother gushed. Applause reverberated throughout the room and there were hollers of congratulations. Xandra stood up. Grandmother's hand clamped down on hers. Tourmaline's eyes widened, and she shook her head telling Xandra to cease and desist whatever she was about to do. Xandra could not. She never had the courtly gift of playacting, pretending, or even suppressing her feelings. Then her mother's eyes locked on hers, demanding obedience with that cursed gray stare that ruined Xandra's life, made her an outcast for her "mistake" of inheriting them. It did not matter she could perform fire magic; the people only believed in stupid eyes to determine legitimacy.

Her anger boiled up inside her until she felt she might burst. "No!" It came out of Xandra's mouth before she could stop it.

The entire room went silent, everyone staring at her. Her father's face was the worst. When he was disappointed in her, it broke Xandra's heart.

There was no going back. "Why cannot you just…stop?" she demanded. That got a few chuckles and quiet side remarks she could not hear or understand. "Seriously? You two are so old! Isn't it dangerous?"

Her mother's lips tightened. Oh no, too late it dawned on her that she had been epically rude. "Forty-two-year-old expectant mothers are not unheard of," her mother ground, out trying to withhold her anger. Xandra could see the light magic balling up in mother's closed fists.

"It was a surprise blessing," her father cut in, always knowing the right things to say. "And a welcomed addition."

Her Uncle Cobalt stood up. "Cheers to the thirteenth Sapphirian of King Alexander's line."

Everyone ignored Xandra's outburst and toasted in celebration. She sat down and avoided eye-contact, but her mother's angry eyes and father's disappointed ones bore into her with an oppressive weight. As soon as dinner was over, she fled to her room refusing to attend the ball. She was sure her parents were happier for it.

After all, they never sent for her or demanded her presence.

2
MOTHER

Rochan gave his training his all, every time. Today was no different. Sweat trickled down his spine; his ebony hair was plastered to his forehead, dripping salty droplets into his eyes. Lyftian men were not allowed to learn combat, unless they were "expendables"—martyrs for entertainment who fought beasts and each other. Rochan was luckily nowhere close to an expendable in rank. He was one of few men allowed to indulge in this practice since his mothers were Empress and Empress Consort of Lyft.

His trainer Dev—and much more to Rochan biologically—saw his fatigue and called the match. They shook hands. Per usual, Rochan went to pull him in for a half hug, seeking the father-son bond that was denied publicly, but Dev yanked his hand away and grabbed a towel to mop his face. Wondering if he had somehow upset Dev, Rochan grabbed a towel likewise. He waited a moment for an explanation. That was when he noticed Dev's dark eyes dart up into the stands with a hard stony glare.

She must be there, watching Rochan, judging him, always hating him for being born a boy and for inadvertently destroying her womb during his difficult birth. He had robbed her of a chance of a coveted daughter, a future empress. Girls were only coveted because Empress Nakano Jadeite willed it to be so, his "mother."

The empress came out of the shadowed overhang, the light showing the features of her high cheekbones. He did not need to see her dark eyes to know they glared at him with a torturous hatred.

"Have you told him yet?" Her severe voice only ever ordered, demanded—quick words that sounded harsh, intended to intimidate.

Dev bowed his head as all men did. "Your Imperial Majesty, I did not have the chance. I apologize. I will do so shortly."

"Because you played soldiers instead." It was not a question. The empress never asked. She commanded. "He will not need to fight if he marries a warrior wife."

"Marry?" Rochan asked, his tone incredulous. Too late he realized he spoke before being spoken to, showed an ounce of aggression toward the empress's words. He would pay for that later. To insult her words was to insult her personally. A question in an improper tone was an insult.

Head down. Mouth shut. He was forgetting the first lessons of his childhood ingrained in him by the empress's "sheer will."

His mother cocked her head, examining him as if Rochan were a bug that she contemplated squishing. Out of the shadows, Udaya came, the shining beacon in his life—aside from these all-too-short moments with Dev. The tension left Rochan's shoulders, and he dared to feel fleeting relief, no matter how short-lived it might be. Udaya's silky red sari flowed as she walked, the empress's eyes glued to her, taking her in.

Despite the empress being his biological mother, Udaya, the empress's wife, was more of one to Rochan. They had married after the laws were changed to allow marriage between women. In private, he called Udaya "Amma," the word passed down in her family for "mother." Aside from not giving birth to him, every other respect made her his mother, including the love and bond they shared. Udaya, though, was technically his aunt. Dev was his real father—not that Rochan could act or admit it publicly. It had been Dev's duty to give the empress and his sister the closest biological baby possible. He was not sure when the practice of doing such came into being, but it was commonplace in some homes—to use men for their seed and not let them be involved.

"Nakano," Udaya put her hand on the empress's shoulder. "Let me be the one to tell him."

The empress shook off Udaya's hand and said, "Stop babying him. He is practically a man."

Rochan felt pride. At sixteen, his indomitable mother calling him something other than "boy" in an insolent tone was something positive. He hated how the compliment made him feel important. He hated how his confidence depended on the minute moments between his mother's frigid or angry moods.

The empress crossed her arms. Dressed in her typical formidable charcoal-gray qipao for its feminine elegance and reminder of power over the male sex, she was intimidating. Clothing was power, and he had no choice over his wardrobe. Even servants had that. At least Amma won the battle to choose it. She'd always chosen the clothing of her ancestors, not the empress's. Rochan knew that annoyed the empress because she had mandated that he must wear soft soled shoes and to tread as lightly as possible. Everything to make him masculine, powerless, silent.

"You *will* marry," the empress said.

Rochan's blood ran cold at the proclamation. It was an order which meant there would be no say in it for him.

"Your wife will rule as empress."

This was no surprise. He was told his entire life men could not be trusted with power in Lyft, that they were full of violence and lust and could not be logical like women. Men only wanted war and sex. The history books proved the empress right, but Dev secretly had told him that she had books rewritten to hide men's past accomplishments. Plus, Rochan liked the exercise of fighting but could never actually hurt anyone. He would never love the concept of war. As for lust, he did not know what it felt like, not that he got to see many girls, being cooped up in the sandstone and marble palace like a dirty secret.

Who knew what to believe about men? Not that he would ever admit he mistrusted the empress's words. In fact, Rochan's mind spun to what marriage would mean. He would have an empress-in-waiting commanding him too, and then once a female child, an heir, was born, what would become of him? As long as Udaya and Dev were around, Rochan felt safer. Otherwise, he would be scared for his life.

Rochan bowed, waiting for her to continue.

"I'll let your *Amma* tell you more." Disdain and mockery ran through her voice.

Udaya stared at the floor as the empress swept out of the combat room. Rochan did not bow his head to the empress as he should. Luckily, she did not turn to observe his slight.

Udaya's eyes met his. Her features spoke of sadness and regret. She headed toward the stairs to join them.

Dev placed his hands on Rochan's shoulders, bracing him. "Rochan, you knew this day would come, and it is time. You will have to marry. It will not be your choice who will become your empress."

Rochan swallowed hard. Marriages on Lyft, for the history of emperors and empresses, had been arranged until Nakano had changed it all, marrying the woman she loved. "Not at all?"

"I will try to persuade her," Udaya said, sighing as she looked at Rochan with the pure love of a mother. "As much as I can. But your mother—"

"She is not my mother—"

Dev's hand covered Rochan's mouth. "Now is not the time for revolution," he whispered. He pointed to his own temple, reminding Rochan that Dev could read the future off the wind, something Rochan inherited from him. Rochan was not as powerful, though, because he had to hide it from the empress—who had no foresight; if he were caught practicing, it could mean his death. "There are ears everywhere. If any of us misstep, we will die." He let Rochan go.

Dev would not lie. He was telling him not to push his boundaries yet, but Rochan was sick of it. Years of his mother's suppression and disdain built up into bitter resentment that ate away at his kind heart.

"Your mother," Udaya continued, "has set up a tournament, the Empress Games, to 'win' you."

"Win the position of empress, you mean?"

"Yes, and you come with that." Udaya said, her eyes full of empathy. She ran the back of her fingers down his cheek, ignoring his sticky sweat. "I…I'm sorry you have no choice." Her hand dropped to her side. "I tried. She killed to be able to choose me yet deprives you of the same freedom of choice." She shook her head. Rumors were just confirmed. Rochan's head was spinning. The empress was a murderer. He had heard the rumors many times but never wanted to know the truth because… What would she do to him if he disobeyed?

"Enough," Dev scolded. "No talk like this. There will be games. You must go along with this. Foreigners are coming. They can change things."

Foreigners? The term was only used in books about those…from other spheres?

Dev grabbed Rochan by the nape of his neck and pulled him in for that paternal half hug he had longed for—any semblance of feeling gave Rochan strength. Dev whispered, "Trust the flame and no one else. No. One."

Then he patted him on the back smiling like his comment was in jest. He had not let Udaya overhear him. Trust "the flame" over even Udaya? Dev himself? What did he mean?

Rochan forced himself to smile as if it was something good, a joke. Then he looked at Amma and said, "I will do my duty. Assure the empress I will comply— to a point. I want a shred of say in this. I cannot marry a woman just because she can beat the snot out of others. I want to measure their minds and personalities as well as looks. I will help craft these 'games.'"

Udaya smiled. "Very wise. I think she will see it that way as well. Perhaps three rounds? Limit the girls after each. It will give you more time to come to terms with this too."

"More rounds than that, please." Rochan dared to prolong his "prison sentencing" because marriage would be trading one dictator over his life for another.

"Make a list of rounds, and I will try." She patted his face, her umber eyes so solemn, speaking to him of how much she wanted to help him but did not have enough courage or power. To Rochan, those two traits seemed the same, and he lacked them both.

"I can think of many categories to make this lengthy, but I do not want to test the empress's patience." Rochan's mind raced thinking of what the empress would find important other than being a solid warrior. "Aside from two battle competitions, one limiting and then face-offs of the winners until no one is left, an outing together to test social skills, a knowledge round for ability to rule, and…a beauty round for comportment. A warrior wife is one thing, but the people have to like her and if I am expected to have children, she cannot repulse me."

"Beauty?" Udaya grimaced. "The empress—"

"You will present it right, Amma. She must be adored by the people. She must be able to make attractive offspring who will be adored by the people. Battle alone will only expose the girls' powers and brute strength, but we both know power is more important, controlling the naga is more important. You will remind her that these rounds are exactly the same criteria she used to choose your brother to father me. The looks even mattered to her, albeit I admit there was a sentimental value because he has your bloodline. Still, make her see. We both know Dev would have not been her choice if he was not talented in power and fighting, handsome, and intelligent."

Dev shifted his weight uncomfortably. "Sister, give him this at least in his life, a wife he can tolerate; after all we have been through and all we must still endure, he deserves to be happy."

Udaya sighed, clasping Rochan's hand. "Trust me. I will try to get you what you want, but I will have to act like it much of this was my idea and you agreed to it."

Rochan nodded. His mother could manage the empress better than anyone.

"And Rochan, we cannot do the battle competition first. Weeding them out through other rounds will leave us with a handful to fight. She would never tolerate so many battles because they would take too much time." Udaya squeezed his hand and left.

"You should go," Dev said, while putting sparring weapons away. Their conversation was over. Rochan knew when to hide things and when to press for answers. This was not the time. Trust the flame? He did not understand, but he knew asking more would be dangerous for Dev.

He went to his room, pried open the window, and pulled in the wind, letting it wrap around him. He doubted the empress would catch him using his powers, but he could not care less if she did. He had to see something, pull a glimmer of his future off the breeze. Marriage? It was terrifying. He could trade one dictator for another…or did he dare to hope he could find someone who would be a friend, a partner—someone like who Udaya was for the empress. He did not desire control over the sphere, just needed control over his own life.

The wind was not kind tonight, though. He saw snippets only: clashing of swords, gray eyes, pale skin, fire, air, blood, naga—it was too quick and indiscernible. The wind picked up quickly, unnaturally so, meaning someone was conjuring and controlling it through their powers. Rochan gave up and fastened his window. The palace would be hit hard by the cyclone, but not as hard as the

Isle of the Gods—the land of outcasts, runaways, and punished men. The empress was all powerful and she was angry at Rochan, particularly after she realized she would have to give him his request with the games to placate Udaya; the empress would take her rage out on their people. Only they never knew she caused the storms. He wanted to expose her or counter her windstorms with his own, but not yet. He could not, and not because Dev told him not to. The empress was powerful, much more than he could ever hope to be. Rage fueled her power. Rochan should have rage at the life he had been given, but he was weak. It was easier to obey and hold onto hope of an escape.

After the storm ceased—meaning her tantrum had ended—Rochan was summoned to her office. He entered, eyes downcast, head bowed, awaiting her greeting, for one must always show deference for the empress. As a boy, he had seen a man lose an eye for daring to meet her gaze; Rochan learned young to be quiet, mild, and weak. She hated that he was weak, but she hated him even more when he showed an ounce of strength. Now that he towered over her in height, he wondered if she was perhaps as frightened of him as he was of her.

"Sit," she commanded as one would a dog. Of course, she'd demand he sit. She sat upon a small platform, so if he stood, he still would be looking down at her. She wanted to look down at him and upon him. A large mahogany desk separated her from her visitor, a clear divide. It was a well-planned setup to intimidate her guest. And it worked.

Rochan sat down, finally letting himself meet her cold, hard gaze. Her black hair was fastened in a severe bun, her hair starting to gray at her temples. Her face was all hard lines whereas Amma's was always soft and warm. Rochan felt he was a combination of them—hard angles of strength mixed with warm, soft planes of emotion, like rocks in a bubbling brook that were smoothed in time.

"I am going to speak to you about your marriage," the empress started. Her tone was an awkward mix of trying to be kind and sociable but not able to perform it quite right. She never had a way with words, particularly about the important things. "Since I was not blessed with a daughter to become empress, I must select my successor."

This she could do without making him marry the woman but that would emphasize his expendability if he admitted it. Deep down, in her twisted mind, perhaps she was trying to protect him through this union. More like her vanity needed her bloodline to continue.

"I've decided on a contest, a contest to win your hand in marriage. The woman must prove herself in intellect, combat, and social grace. Since every girl in this world would dream of becoming empress—and I am told you are considered very handsome—we must limit the number through questionnaires first. I do want you to be content with whoever wins, as you must spend your life with her, but also to prevent your insubordination. I fought to keep Lyft this glorious matriarchy. I will not have you attempt to usurp your wife's power."

He wanted to interrupt that she had turned a glorious matriarchy into a man-hating, man-slaughtering institution. It had started with his grandmother, he was told, but his mother was the first one to use such severe violence. Saying anything of this nature would be far from wise, so he stayed silent. Giving him any say in his bride was a gift he did not want to lose. Amma must have persuaded her to let him have this little bit of choice and suffered the empress's rage for it.

"Therefore, you will create the questionnaire to try to limit it to compatible women in personality. I suppose it should reflect your interests, preferences, what you might want in a life-long companion."

For how harrowing the situation was, this was surprising leeway. She would let him cull his pool of possible brides. At least if the end decision was not his and came down to chance, he would have something in common with the girl. His mind went to Dev who would tell him about destiny, that his wife was already chosen by the gods, and everything would work its way into balance in the end. Rochan was worried about what he would have to sacrifice or endure to find that balance, something he never had felt was within his grasp. Rochan was on sand that shifted with the empress's moods, never predictable except for its callousness.

A knock at the door interrupted his thoughts.

"Enter," the empress said coolly. He could not leave yet as she had not excused him, so he sat there awkwardly as the servant entered.

"Empress," the man bowed and delivered his message looking at the floor. "The Fyrian ambassadors have arrived."

"Send them to the tearoom."

"They are men, Your Imperial Majesty."

"Men!" The empress snapped. She stood, her fists clenching. "They dare to send *men* here?"

Her hatred of the male gender was completely irrational, but Rochan was used to it. The Fyrians might not know her preferences rather than purposely slighting her, but he would not dare to point out she was being ridiculous.

"A middle-aged man and a meek older boy." At least the servant had the sense to describe them as non-threatening.

"Bring them here, then." The empress flicked her hand at the servant in dismissal. Somehow, without looking up, the servant sensed it and retreated.

"May I stay?" Rochan dared to ask, his curiosity overtaking his sense of self-preservation.

The empress sat down and stared at him shocked.

"I have never met a foreigner before."

His mother smirked. Sometimes, she accepted his outgoing moments and sometimes she did not. Rochan chalked it down to when she recognized herself in him; she could not fully dismiss her pride.

"You'll be disappointed. They're just men, like you, no different."

Rochan ignored her insult. It was acquiescence. He was going to be allowed to see the foreigners, ones from a land where men also had power and people used fire instead of wind magic. He was excited that the empress actually caved in. He also felt a sort of thrilling pulse alive in him, like something might happen.

Trust the flame.

3
A MISSION

Mother did not come to speak to Xandra after the ball. Father did. She'd rather be scolded than to see the disappointment in his Sapphirian eyes. He uncuffed the neck of his doublet and sighed, sitting down on the edge of her bed, his King's Medallion hung from his neck. "You are a piece of work, my darling girl."

"Dad—"

He put his hand up to silence her. "You're old enough to know what you did wrong."

"I offended Mum, embarrassed her…in front of everyone." Now was the time to grovel.

"No, you did worse. You *upset* her. She did not come to talk to you because she's still crying." He sighed, looking so tired. "Xandra, we love our children, all of you. You are a product of love just like your little sister will be."

"It's a girl?"

"Shoot. Do not say anything to your mother. She doesn't know I foresaw it." He smirked, suddenly looking much younger and playful. "I'm hoping to not let this one slip. Every time I have told her too much—more so Aunt Mary—and I hope this secret will make it the full nine months."

"In this family, she'll know tomorrow." Xandra commented. She should beg for forgiveness and yet here she was lashing out at her family size, their foresight, and inability to keep their mouths shut.

Her father stared off at the fire in her grate, "I know how you feel, but—"

"Do you?" Xandra cut in, her anger getting the best of her. "You cannot possibly. You fit in. You're not the gray-eyed abomination. You took me out of the succession!"

His face pinched in pain. "Because you will do amazing things elsewhere. I know it. There was no point in holding you back, keeping you here. You will be your own Bladesung."

Xandra did not know what to say. She let her anger die. He was so hurt by her disregard for her family.

"Your mother would better understand how you feel if you just tried to be kind and apologize. She was raised on Earth, remember? She was completely lost, an outcast in every way. She had to adapt, find a way to fit in and still be her spirited self. She had no one before me, and she doesn't understand how you would not want more family."

Her parents told them the story many times. Tourmaline thought it romantic. Xandra had thought her father tricking her mother into an engagement was horrible, but deep down, the way her mother and father looked at each other—she wanted that one day. A husband sounded awful, but the love that came from a love-match seemed glorious. She'd never admit that aloud, though. And she did love her parents and every single sibling. If it were just quieter at home. Despite living in a palace, there were only so many first floor rooms for entertaining or other activities. Any room you'd enter, there was a Sapphirian, someone else, or both. The only place to be alone was her bedroom—if no one came knocking. Servants and family did constantly.

An idea struck her, but perhaps now was not the time to ask if she could go live with Aschen and his wife when they moved out. Imagine an estate with only two other family members…She would talk to her brother tomorrow, but first she had to make amends. "I'll talk to Mum in the morning," Xandra conceded.

"That's my girl." Her father stood and kissed the top of her head. "By the way, talk to Thomas tomorrow morning too."

"Why?"

"The ambassador of Water is not on board until Lyft is."

Was it because of her outburst? "How come?"

"Water is extremely unstable. The ambassador said there is a princess in hiding, and three baseborn half-brothers who usurped her throne. The princess needs forces from here and Lyft to win the sphere back."

"Will you send them?"

"We have to discuss it with Lyft. I'm not liking the idea of getting involved with another sphere's civil war, but if Lyft will, I will have to send some troops." He took off his medallion with a sigh and rubbed his neck.

Politics seemed so complicated, but Xandra had always been drawn to them, loved hearing about them, but here she was seeing how heavily they weighed upon him. The medallion was a physical reminder of the burden of power.

"Anyway, I was going to send your Uncle Cobalt to Lyft, but now your cousin has also volunteered to go as well. Maybe you can talk him out of it? Your aunt is beside herself with worry." No wonder Aunt Mary was nervous. Lyft was a strict matriarchy.

"Dad, why not send women?"

"Why do you think?"

She pondered before answering, "Would it be seen as a threat? Men are less powerful there."

"Exactly." Her father beamed at her. His smile fell. "I do worry, though, that since men have no power there if they even will negotiate with them. It is a situation your uncle has fought his way out of many times, but not Thomas." Dad was right. Thomas would say something stupid most likely, commit some social faux pas due to his nerves. "He insists on going with his father and frankly, your uncle thinks it's time he spread his wings.

"Thomas will get himself killed. I should go!" Xandra burst out.

Her father was taken aback. "You?" Then understanding dawned across his features.

She knew the expression because it was hers as well. What he understood, she did not know, for she herself had no idea why she had a sudden outburst except her worry over Thomas and a pang of envy that he would get to see the place she fantasized visiting.

"You want to go, but I cannot send you. I promise you can visit if you'd like, when you're older, and we have established iron-clad peace with them."

"But Dad—"

"No." His eyes were hard, and his jaw clenched.

She had never seen him so mad. "Dad, I'm not a child!"

"You *are!* You're my child!" He slammed his medallion onto her desk in an uncharacteristic outburst.

She said nothing but stared at him in disbelief.

He took a deep breath and let it out slowly, composing himself. "In the past, my enemies have found my weakness through attacking the ones I love. They know it will work. Of any of my faults, my heart is the biggest one, and I do not care to change that because it is also my greatest strength. I will not send you there until it is safe."

"I understand." She wanted to protest, to yell and rage at him, but she could not. What he said was true about his kind heart being the worst and best of him. She could grasp that. Instead, she acquiesced and hugged him. He kissed the top of her head again right above her circlet. Then he was off, always busy, but always giving as much time and affection as he could to all of them.

Her father had been through a lot before she was born. Fyr had not been a peaceful sphere when he had inherited it. Grandmother told them many times of what her parents had been through, and Aunt Mary and her mother filled in the romantic bits as the girls in the family had grown older. She could not imagine going through what they did, although she found the idea of fighting a war secretly thrilling. Tourmaline would, of course, lecture her that the death of many was not thrilling and how some threads of the future had foretold their parents would not have lived through it. Her twin would be right, but Xandra found this palace life boring, yet annoying loud. She did not want death, but adventure.

She had to go to Lyft, but how? Uncle Cobalt would never disobey her father. Her mother was furious with her and emotional thanks to the sibling number one hundred growing in her belly. Okay, a wild exaggeration on her part as to the number of siblings she had, but Xandra hoped this was the last one.

All she could do was try to switch places with Thomas.

Instead of waiting for morning, she snuck out of her room and traipsed through the palace to his room. Apparently, when her father was young, he had his own tower. Now, there were too many Sapphirians so her generation each got one bedroom. Rowland had a tower, as the heir, and now two towers became nurseries since there were about ten children under the age of eight, a few being nieces and nephews of Thomas or her own, the rest their siblings. Xandra tapped Thomas's door.

"Go away."

Xandra opened the door.

Thomas did not even look to see who was standing in his doorway. He knew. He was packing a small bag for his trip the next day.

"That's not nice." Xandra frowned.

Thomas rolled his eyes, shoving a shirt roughly in the bag. "I know why you're here."

"Then switch places with me."

"I'm going because I want to, Xandra. I volunteered. I want to learn about the place, observe it. I'm not missing out on this because of your weird obsession with the empress."

"I'm not obsessed." Xandra was sullen. It was her dream to see Lyft. This was her chance. Thomas was stealing it from her. "Thomas, what if you die?"

His head whipped around. "Why would you say that? You think I'm unable? Just because I'm no warrior like you does not make me ill-fit. I have the brains for this, the knowledge."

Her stomach flopped. "I did not mean it like that. I know you're smart, but you've studied Fyr, Water, and Earth more. Lyft is not like the history books now. It is different. One misstep—"

"I'm not going to mess up, Xandra. Stop trying to manipulate me. You're just doing it because you want to go so badly."

"Thomas. Both of our futures disappear soon."

Thomas froze and his spine bristled. "So why would I let you go in my stead, let you potentially die?"

Ugh, he was turning into a noble martyr on her. She would never convince him this way. He would do anything to save her. She would do the same for him.

They were best friends and cousins. To take this from him would be an undercut and selfish thing to do, and yet she longed to protect him.

Instead of protesting, Xandra entered the room and hugged him.

Thomas softened in her arms. "Okay, this is very uncharacteristic of you." He awkwardly hugged her before letting her go.

"You're right. I was just saying goodbye and good luck."

"Thanks." Thomas smiled. "Twins for life, right?"

Xandra could not help but smile. In the years that Tourmaline and Xandra grew apart, and her dear cousin was there for her and often joked about how he and Xandra were supposed to be twins, not her and Tourmaline. "Twins for life."

"I'll tell you all about it when I get back. If all goes well, we'll need ambassadors. Maybe you'll become one and live over there."

"That would be fun. Good luck, Thomas. I have faith in you."

Xandra turned away and left to go to sleep—or to attempt to. She contemplated ways to take his place, but she could not figure out a way. She feared something bad would happen to Uncle Cobalt and Thomas.

Something in her told her she had to go. This was to be her destiny. She felt it in her bones.

4
FYRIANS

Rochan pressed himself against the wall, opposite the servant stationed on the other side of the door. He must, as always, stay small and out of the way, like the man next to him. Anticipation for something to actually happen in his life thrummed through him, but he kept his face stoic and blank. If the empress knew this was a treat for him, she would send him away before he could even see the Fyrians.

She glared at him as if she could read his mind, but thankfully that was not a form of magic on Lyft. "Stop acting excited as a little boy getting a toy to play with."

He dared to meet the empress's gaze in challenge. He thought he had hidden it well. He shrugged. "What else do I have to do?"

She frowned. She'd see his comment as a swipe at her for calling him "prince" in title but refusing him any power. Not that he was interested in power, but he had a deep interest in governments. He knew this system of one gender over another was wrong; even if he had been born a daughter, he would have seen the horror in all of it. If he had been born a girl, he could've changed things.

"You could spend your time finding a wife." She was bristling for a fight. This would not go well for the Fyrian men. He must placate her as best he could, for the other men's sake.

"I am taking the process seriously, I assure you. I am to live with her for the rest of my life and under her rule. I am awaiting the compatibility surveys. For word to get out, send them to the requested homes, and have them returned, we allotted three weeks."

Her anger faded, although she probably was looking for a flaw. "Then what?"

"The most compatible are invited to the games."

"Games? This is a serious matter."

His temper was rising. His intention to be a buffer for the men was fading. "I know that. Would you rather me call it what it is? 'Prince for auction'?"

Her eyes narrowed. "What would you have me do? A woman must rule."

"You could have let me marry for love and selected whatever heir you wanted. You do not want me to rule, but you want your name and blood to carry on." He kept his voice calm, matter-of-factly; his words were insubordinate enough to warrant punishment, so showing anger would lead to something much worse.

"Why did you have to be a boy?" the empress muttered.

"I had no choice in that."

"Still, you suffer for it. Less than others, so be thankful for that."

He did not respond and gazed at the ground because what was on the tip of his tongue would lead him down a path where Amma would not even be able to save him. He should not push her temper. She could force him to marry someone with no say. He had some choice in this. For now.

The doors opened and the herald walked in announcing, "Your Imperial Majesty, a Lord Stephen Cobalt, Prince of Fyr, and his son Lord Thomas Sapphirian, a duke, to see you."

His mother's posture and face shifted in a rigid coldness that spoke of anything but a welcome. "Send them in." Her tone was terse, and it had nothing to do with Rochan being bolder than his usual meekness.

A man with a heavy step entered first, turning quickly to note the servant and then Rochan. He was on the medium side in height, shorter than Rochan, and pale skin. He had light hair, blue eyes, and a scar down the side of his face. Rochan had thought he would look older, but this man was middle-aged with only crow's-feet to show that. The eyes were not impressive. They did not shine like sapphires as the rumors about Fyrian royalty boasted. Checking his back and then scanning the room for threats, Rochan figured he had been a warrior some time ago.

"Why does the King of Fyr send princes into my sphere?"

"Your Imperial Majesty," the elder one said in a cocky-confident tone and funny accent. His tone was highly refined and a bit snobby. Rochan did not know what the preferences for Fyrian men's looks were, but the man was smartly dressed, strong, and his posture showed he knew he was attractive to women. Not that he would have any sway with his mother.

The boy was as tall as his father, much thinner, with brown hair. He bowed awkwardly, his voice full of awe, lacking confidence as he said, "Your Imperial Majesty." He reminded Rochan of himself—unsure, grappling at his position and his autonomy in life. This duke looked to be around his age.

"Sit." His mother ordered.

The boy sat so fast, it was as if his legs gave in. Rochan did not blame him. The empress was an intimidating figure, up higher on her platform, her face always severe.

The father hesitated before he sat, which showed he was in uncharted territory. He thought they would be welcomed. He probably thought he could flirt, cajole an empress. He was wrong. Nothing could thaw his mother's icy hatred; it was in her heart and spread through every vein in her body.

"Your Imperial Majesty, King Alexander and Queen Tourmaline Sapphirian both sent us to negotiate a peace and trade treaty. Water is interested in an alliance as well. Imagine all three magical spheres able to trade much needed magic and goods."

"Lyft has everything we need. Why would we want to deal with refugees of Water or Fyr?"

"If our current news of Lyft is accurate, we could take some men off your hands and in turn women who wish to emigrate or must leave Fyr—"

"Criminals?"

If the prince was affronted by her interruption, he did not show it. "We used to banish our criminals, yes, but these days we have very few that cannot be rehabilitated or imprisoned if they cannot." He was definitely a good ambassador, a negotiator. Rochan had never met anyone who could get his mother to allow them to speak.

"This is a matter that needs some thought."

"Of course. I would not expect less. The king and queen have written up a proposal, one that can be discussed and amended to meet your needs. Shall I leave it with you to peruse at your leisure?"

The man was good, but his mother was scrutinizing him, trying to find a fault. "We do not tend to house men in the palace, even royalty."

"Is there not a prince in residence? My son was eager to meet him."

Rochan perked up. Someone, for once, acknowledged his existence. But this was not good. If Rochan was allowed in the palace, how would his mother explain away the fact she would refuse them rooms.

"Yes, he is right behind you."

The men turned around and then saw him. The father got up and the son followed. They approached him. Rochan felt awkward. His stomach dropped. What were they doing?

"Prince Jadeite, a pleasure to meet you," the father said, not sure what to call him, so he used his surname. The fact his mother did not condescend to introduce him properly should've warned them to ignore him.

Not knowing what to do, Rochan looked to the empress for permission. She nodded.

"The pleasure is ours, Prince Cobalt." He bowed.

The prince bowed and then turned his back, heading toward the empress.

The boy stood in front of Rochan and that was when he saw the eyes: an eerie incandescent blue that glittered like glass, sapphires. He had mixed up who was a true Sapphirian from the start. The duke's face was youthful and his cheeks perpetually pink. Freckles were sprinkled across a proud, slender nose. Fyrian royalty. Rochan stood silently in awe.

So did the boy.

"Forgive my son. He has never left Fyr nor met another royal outside of the family." The father laughed.

The boy was frozen, so Rochan felt he must break their awkward tension. To think, he met a royal who was more timid and awkward than himself. "Lord Sapphirian. Nice to meet you." He bowed.

That snapped the Fyrian boy out of it. "Your Imperial Highness. I'm pleased to meet you." He rushed out his words.

Rochan froze, grimacing. The empress would not allow such distinction to Rochan,

His mother was standing, screeching, her fists balled. "What did you say?"

Everyone in the room just stared at her. Rochan had seen her like this before, but the Fyrians were beyond shocked, frozen as if they had never seen a person act in such a manner. It confirmed what he always knew about his mother: she was unhinged, insane. The worst was that nobody could do anything about it. Except maybe…*Udaya, Amma. My Amma, we need you.* He called for her in his mind. As a boy, she would come. She could sense his distress through her magic.

It took the Fyrian father a moment to defend his son. "Your Imperial Majesty, forgive my son. It was a mistake. He is not used to your customs of addressing male royalty without an honorific. He is young." The man was standing close to his mother, looking up at her. Rochan hoped his negotiation skills and acting were up for the job.

The empress looked at the frightened boy who was shaking now, to Rochan who was sure he looked frightened too, and then to the father. "Very well, punish him."

"Punish him?" Prince Cobalt's amiable façade slipped.

"I would give my son five lashes with a bamboo rod."

Rochan winced at the thought. There was no way this terrified boy could handle it.

Prince Cobalt cleared his throat. "With all due respect, Your Imperial Majesty, we teach our children, through words, to not make the same mistakes again. If they do something a second time, then there is punishment, but we do not use corporal punishment."

His mother, the empress, scoffed and sat down. "Why would I want any Fyrian immigrant then? You all sound soft. You beat him or there is no negotiation."

"I do not understand." The boy said quietly. "What have I done?"

"See, my son doesn't even understand. Surely, he should not be punished for ignorance."

"I punish the ignorant more so that they learn."

"Regardless of your customs, I will not whip my child nor allow any harm to come to him." The father backed up and placed his hand on the hilt of his sword, not in an attacking stance, but his posture loose to not alert the soldiers lining the walls. It was a statement.

"Then we have no deal."

"Please understand, Your Imperial Majesty, that my wife outranks me as *the* princess of Fyr. If I let you harm a hair on this boy's head, she will cross the universe to torch all of Lyft in a heartbeat."

Rochan felt sick. Was this guy asking to die? He watched his mother carefully. She seemed...stunned. She never showed emotion and rarely was shocked. Then to surprise the entire room—especially Rochan—she laughed. He had rarely heard it. Only stolen moments when he came upon Udaya and her having a private moment. It was the only time he ever saw the empress capable of kindness or happiness. It hurt that the love stayed with Udaya only, spread to no one else, not even him, her own child.

The empress sat down and schooled her features. The father walked toward his son and grabbed his arm roughly. "We went over this a dozen times. He is only called a 'prince.' Sit down and keep your mouth shut." He shoved his son toward his seat. The poor boy sat, hunched over, likely trying not to cry.

"I like the sound of your wife. Why is it your rulers decided to send me a boy and man and not her? Surely, I deserve the respect of a female ambassador? I will not negotiate with the likes of men."

"Ah," the father said, sitting back down. "This I can answer for you. It is not out of disrespect, I assure you. My wife has recently birthed our child and would not dare to part from the babe. The queen herself is with child and would not risk the child or her life since nothing was known prior about what sort of reception sudden Sapphirians would elicit."

"I've heard tales of many children. No daughters?"

Rochan knew this must be wearing the man's patience thin. He wondered how others could bear her hatred, merely for their gender.

"We have princesses, of course, yes, twelve—excluding my wife—to be precise. It did take the king and queen time to be blessed with girls, twins actually, who are merely sixteen. The rest are far too young. The male heir is not permitted to leave or the spare, but the next sons are quite the warrior type, as are my eldest sons. We feared it would be offensive to send young male warriors to your door. As for my daughters, I hate to admit it, but since they are far from the throne's line in the scheme of things, they had no interest in politics and were interested in being leaders of their own homes, one married and a mother, the other on the precipice of marriage. The rest of my daughters are younger than Thomas, here, who is seventeen. I brought him," the father's tone turned cutting, "because he is an exemplary scholar and well versed in the studies of Lyft. Or so I thought. Apparently contemporary court life was not something he paid much attention to. He will learn his lesson at home. There is nothing worse in Fyr than shame."

The empress smiled slightly and nodded. "That is something our worlds can agree on."

"I am glad we are in accordance, Your Imperial Majesty. May I suggest, to prevent any more mishaps, that my son could be taken to our rooms, wherever those may be since we will be housed outside the palace."

"No, sorry. I still cannot forgo a punishment. There was a grievous injustice done here. Someone must pay."

The father sighed. "I will take the lashings if you agree to look over this treaty."

"That will not do. Neither boy will learn if there is not punishment."

"Will all due respect, learn from what? My son made a mistake. He has learned not to do so again. Why punish either boy? What has your son done wrong?"

"Been born a boy."

That did not affect Rochan as it did the others.

The boy who seemed so weak and timid stood up. "I will take you ridiculous lashes, because I feel bad for your son and how you treat him, your own child. I will wear the scars to remind myself how truly loved I am by my family."

The father stood and pushed his son toward the door. "This was obviously a mistake. We will return to Fyr and tell the king and queen you do not wish to negotiate. No ill will or word from Fyr again if we leave unscathed."

"Guards seize the boy! For his impertinence, cut his tongue out!"

The soldiers moved off the wall, six of them on each side. Despite being outnumbered, the father withdrew his sword with a stoic look of determination on his face. He grabbed his son and pushed him behind his back. The boy withdrew a dirk from his belt and held it steady. Perhaps he was a fighter in the right circumstance?

"You will touch my son over my dead body."

The empress gave him a Cheshire grin.

Rochan was stuck against the wall, as the servant moved himself in front of the door as the last line of defense, even though weaponless. What could he do? *Amma, Amma, I need you.*

The soldiers attacked. The man disarmed a man in a second, shoved one guard into another, knocking them over, and then turned to stab a soldier in the neck whose sword had been inches from his son's chest. Then the boy ducked under his father's arm, bent low, and got a good stab between armor plates to get the soldier in the gut.

With only two dispatched, ten were closing in. Rochan wanted them to win. He felt some kind of kindred connection to them. He could not watch them die. Something bothered Rochan, pained him. He idolized and was envious of the relationship between father and son, the idea of the parent killing someone who hurt his child. Parents who would die for their children.

The anger at his mother and the desperation to stop whatever was about to happen bashed around in him. He withheld his magic so much and so long, to hide it from the empress, that he was about to burst. He felt the air calling to him, pressing upon him. He was suffocating under the unspent power and the overwhelming urge to save these men. To prevent a war. To overpower her.

"STOOOOOP!" Rochan heard his voice reverberate across the room before he knew he had spoken. In front of him everyone was on the floor including the empress.

What did he just do?

Oh no, he was in for it. He had instinctively used his wind power, quite excessively, to stop the battle, to knock everyone down. The empress stood up, her nostrils flaring, her body rigid and shaking with fury. He did not dare meet her gaze.

There was no way to back down and no reason not to keep going. He'd be punished severely, but maybe he could save the Fyrians. "Have you lost your mind? You will cause a war by killing them! Let them go and let that be the end of it."

The Fyrians scrambled up and headed over to the door. The servant did not want to move, but the door opened pushing him aside. Udaya rushed in and Rochan almost threw himself into her arms with relief. She was the empress's tie to sanity, rationalism.

"What is going on?" The shock in her voice stilled the room. The energy shifted. Udaya had a charisma that warmed a cold room. Amma had come to save them.

It was not the saving he had hoped for, but the best Amma could pull off. The Fyrians were imprisoned without being harmed. But the empress got the flogging she so desired. She watched as her strongest soldier gave him lash after lash until his back bled. The fact it took only six strokes was the soldier using cat-o'-nine-tails to spare a lengthy ordeal.

Rochan tried to sleep on his stomach that night, but the pain did not let him—as well as the empress's windstorm. He did not regret his actions. He saved two lives and stopped a war. Thwarting the empress was just a bonus. The action did something to him, something inside shifted. He wanted to rebel more. He would not dare free the men. That would be a death sentence. Maybe he could find their magically charged stones and get them back to them? Then again, a likely death sentence, even as a Jadeite. Rochan would do something if his mother tried to kill the men, but his growing courage was just a tiny flickering flame. After the windstorm dwindled, Rochan went outside onto his patio and climbed the stairs to the roof above his quarters. The empress could not see him there. He closed his eyes and pulled in the air around him, letting it wrap around him in a soft embrace. He was not great at wielding wind magic, but it sought him out likewise. Reading time off the wind was one power he could improve on in private.

The images came as he tried to harness the future. *Gray eyes, fire, the arrival room, sun shining down from directly above.*

Noon. Someone gray-eyed was coming at noon. But which day in the future it would be was the problem. He hadn't foreseen much, but it was enough.

5
A STONE

Thomas and Uncle Cobalt did not return to Fyr. They were to be gone for a week at most, but two had gone by. Dad dismissed all offers for others to go see what was occurring on Lyft. Xandra understood that he did not want anyone else to suffer whatever fate might have befallen her uncle and Thomas. Even sending a spy could start a universal war.

Princess Mary became despondent, grieving. She took to her bed. A wet nurse was hired to care for her newborn. Xandra's father became strained, and her mother exhausted. Her older siblings were tense. A palpable tension pervaded the castle which previously had felt ready to explode with joy and loving noise. She hated the silence of worry and awaiting mourning.

That's when Xandra snapped. She should've gone all along. She was destined to leave Fyr, strike out on her own, but she never wanted to go to Lyft on these conditions. What if they *were* dead? Even more pressing, what if they were alive and in trouble, needing rescue?

Xandra could not sleep. She had a plan, but could she get away with it in a household of future seers? She had gone to bed after supper and packed. No one stopped her or cared. They were wrapped up in their own worries. As she filled her knapsack, she plotted ways to get around the guards who protected the palace's charged stones used to travel to another sphere. It was a magically protected room, not one she could use dragon's trapdoor magic to disappear and reappear—called "transporting" in modern times. She spent time forging a missive from her father. They had similar handwriting, but it had to be perfect.

She feigned sleep because no matter how old she and her siblings were, her parents would wish a good night to all of them, splitting up the duty. At least they drew the line at her older siblings' engagements. Like clockwork, her mother entered; Xandra could tell from her soft tread, the swirl of her dress, and that lilac scented soap she favored.

Instead of leaning down and kissing her brow and whispering goodnight, as always, her mother paused over the bed. "I know you're awake Xandra and what you're planning to do."

Xandra opened her eyes and rolled over to look at her mum, confused. How could one of the few family members who could not firebrand—read the future— foresee her plan?

"Please do not lie. Your father saw what you will do."

Xandra pushed up onto her elbows, wondering what her mother would do. Her mother waited for an explanation. With the disastrous outburst during supper behind them, she did not want to anger her mother further. She loved her. They had made up after the ball and Xandra's apology, but due to circumstances, their relationship felt unsettled.

"I made him look because I knew what you would do."

"How?"

"For as much as we fight as of late, I thought you would have put it together by now. You might look like your father, but you have my eyes and my spirit. You are exactly who I would've been at your age had I been born and raised in Fyr with privilege and love. I only got that after so many struggles." Xandra could not understand the conflicted look of pride and…something she could not discern but it felt…off.

Xandra also wanted to protest but she had seen her mother equally stubborn about things, bold, and candid. Xandra had to admit her mother was right, and instead of disagreeing with her, Xandra felt pride bloom in her chest. Her mother's comments were positive. She saw herself in Xandra and that made her feel a bit less alone.

"A parent never wants their children to struggle, to face adversity, to have obstacles in their way, but most importantly, they never want to see their child in danger."

"You're going to stop me?"

Her mother pressed her lips together and her eyes teared up in a torn and sad expression, but in which way? Did it pain her to tell her she could not go? Or, dare Xandra hope, her mum was torn up about letting her go?

Xandra held her breath.

Her mother shook her head and grabbed Xandra into a crushing hug. She was letting her go. Her mother stroked her hair as she spoke. "Your father wanted to come, but I insisted it be me. He could not part with you. Your father told me at your and Tourmaline's birth that you'd carve your own destiny elsewhere. Even though he knew this would come from the moment of your conception, he loves you too much to let you go."

Her mother cradled her face lovingly. "Your future. I'm here to give you that gift." Her mother reached into her pocket and pulled out a small pouch on a string. "Do not open it until you have all your necessary things for your trip."

Xandra clutched it tightly. It was her transportation to the Lyft sphere: a charged selenite stone.

Xandra's mouth fell. She could not believe her mother would do this for her. "Mum?"

"I could not let you commit treason on two spheres. You're not allowed to take a stone without royal approval. I think a female queen giving permission to her own daughter to negotiate peace should be more palatable to this zealous *empress*."

"You think she is bad?" Xandra had seen the idea of matriarchy as a dream come true. Was this empress the bloodthirsty man-hater Thomas had insisted?

Her mother gave her a small smile, handing her a missive addressed to the empress in her hand. "I think you need to observe the reality of things under the surface on that sphere, not the polished veneer she will present to you. I fear she imprisoned your uncle and cousin, but for what? Neither would commit a crime. I'm starting to worry that crime is…merely being male. My darling, there is a careful balance needed between genders for a society to thrive. I came to a world where men ruled, but you are in an age where that is ever changing toward equality. Lyft, I fear, is much like the Fyr I was thrust into, just men forced into subordination rather than women. The physical feats most men can accomplish makes me wonder how one woman suppressed them within one generation."

"Violence?"

"Perhaps. Just keep your eyes open, Xandra, and do not anger her and end up in a cell. I am counting on you bringing them home—and yourself. You only have two charges. The stones they had taken still hold a second one. Since they have not returned, it means they do not have their stones. You must find those and them."

Xandra felt so many things but had to say what weighed her down the most. She had said sorry, but those words did not undo the pain she inflicted at that dreadful supper. "I'm so sorry about what I said. I did not mean to hurt you or Dad. I love you, Mum."

Her mother hugged her again, then leaned back and smoothed her hair. "I love you too, sweetheart. Now, hurry and get out of here before your father barges in to stop you out of a change of heart. He was difficult to convince. And please, do not open the pouch indoors." She took a deep breath. "Remember your father's motto: Love. Flame. Draca." He had said that motto after he won the war and the people loved it. With the three of those—love, powers, and dragons—a Sapphirian could do anything.

She stood up. "Xandra, make safe choices. Your father will never forgive me if anything happens to you. I will not forgive myself either." The last part of her sentence was almost a whisper. Then she vanished into her white fire, using her dragon's trapdoor to transport away. To her chambers, likely, where her father would be. Xandra had very little time. Her father definitely would crumble. If her mother started to cry as Xandra expected from her quick departure, the mission would be a bust.

In a mad rush, she grabbed her sack, stuffed the letter from her mother in, and tied the pouch's little loopholes to a necklace chain and fastened it around her neck, melding the eye-and-hook with her powers to secure it better. She shoved her feet into her boots and slipped a sheathed dagger into each. She slipped on her sword belt, making sure she could withdraw the weapon quickly. Last, she grabbed her circlet realizing she needed it to prove who she was. She placed it on her head and not wanting to bother a servant or take the time to fasten it with pins, she wound her hair around it and fastened it behind her head. Good enough.

Then she allowed her fire magic to build up inside her and then envisioned the roof. Opening her eyes, she was there, her fire letting her slip through space. It was her favorite use of her magic.

Lyft had air magic. She did not want to unleash a windstorm in her bedroom as Mum had warned. The draca king, nicknamed DJ by her mother in a dire situation, was in his abode below and peeked his head out to see what she was up to. After the Waterian ambassador's arrival, he came to protect them and be informed. He stayed at the draca "quarters"—a massive eyesore of ash, magma, and bones of past meals on the land in the front of the palace but within the walls. Xandra much preferred the draca queen who told great stories of the past, was sassy and stern, but she passed away a few years ago at an age so old, no one knew the number. DJ was overprotective of his "flesh babies," the demeaning term they called us Sapphirians they thought was cute and appropriate since the legend proclaims the dracas breathed the first Sapphirians into existence. Even after the ambassador left, he stayed. The little kids in the castle—particularly the newborn and unborn baby—were likely kicking in his protective nesting instincts. Luckily, he seemed bored by her presence.

With a deep breath and a heart beating rapidly from anticipation of seeing the unknown, she slipped her fingers into the pouch. She brushed the stone. Instantly, it burned. Instinct told her to yank her fingers away, but they were fused to it. All it had taken was a split second to attach itself to her flesh.

The wind picked up, whipping her hair about. Her mind swirled with the gusts, so many expectations—fear and excitement—warring around with her mother's warnings. It picked up so much she was almost knocked down. It wrapped around her tighter and tighter, winds weaving themselves together in a spinning cone, with her inside. She was forced to close her already dry eyes.

The wind died down. Did it not work? She felt no tickling sensation as she did when she transported, nor did she get knocked out as her mother had accidentally traveled from Earth to Fyr via charged labradorite.

With trepidation, she opened her eyes.

It worked.

6
FIRE

Rochan had gone to the arrival room every day around noon, reading a book near its entrance. He only dared to spend twenty minutes there and then sneak out into the courtyard before the empress could catch him. On the fifth day, he grew bored and vowed to give up. He could wait years for this person to arrive. He waited just a few more minutes.

He felt it. A zing of power, a spark, and then wind swirled the few leaves that had fallen into the open roof.

Rochan leaped up, the book forgotten on the bench, and he hurried into the doorway as he watched the wind grow thicker. It was a strong wind, but hot, like a mix of fire and wind. Rochan closed his eyes to block the dry heat out. When the wind died down and he opened them, a lithe girl, a head shorter than him, with warm, brown hair and pale skin stood before him. Upon her head, she wore a crown in the form of a silver band with a sapphire embedded into it, her hair wound around it pinning it in place.

The girl had a spread of freckles upon her nose and cheeks and the stunning gray eyes he had foreseen, which made what was a pretty face absolutely adorable. She withdrew a sword, pointing it at him, the only other person in the room. Her eyes squinted as she swung. Rochan instinctively swung his blade up to deflect hers. Surprised, her eyes widened, showing off their stormy gray hues, the depth of them so much more than what he'd seen in his visions. *Beautiful.* He almost lost his head being too fixated on them, as she had swung a second time.

Shaking sense into himself, he quickly disarmed her by parrying her sword away and then lunging to grasp her wrist, twisting it. He pulled her into him from behind and pinned her arms to her body, incapacitating her. He shushed her before words could form in his addled brain. All he could think about was how her body was against his.

"Do not torch me, please. They do not know you are here yet. I am the Prince of Lyft. I will take you to the empress." She softened in his arms, no longer fighting, but the feeling was too pleasing, too comforting. He wanted to hold her and spill his unspent affection upon a stranger. What did that say about him? Was he a sullied man, like his mother's servants supposedly were, so crude and full of evil? Of lust and longing?

He let the girl go, now embarrassed, but she sheathed her blade and met his gaze. She bowed her head and said in an accent more refined than the other

Sapphirians, "I am Princess Alexandra Sapphirian, and I demand to see my uncle and cousin. Immediately."

At that moment, he knew she could command him of anything, and he'd comply.

"I take it they are alive, Prince?" She was an impatient sort. Or had he been staring at her too long?

He nodded, which brought sense back to his brain. "Princess, they are alive and in prison as you suspected."

"What for?" She was a bold, demanding type. Would his mother admire that or see this girl as a threat?

"It is not my place to say. The empress jailed them." His mother would be upset if he revealed what they had done. He was sure things were different in Fyr. The other Fyrians had shown they were not equipped for the many changes his mother had made, since a Lyftian hadn't visited since before Rochan's birth. The princess would react to her relatives' crimes. If Rochan prepared her, the girl's lack of shock would be telling. For some reason he wanted to tell her, to protect her, but he did not want another beating.

He led her out of the arrival room. A servant jumped and hid Rochan's book behind his back. Servants were not permitted to read. He approached the servant and whispered to warn the empress that Princess Alexandra Sapphirian of Fyr begged an audience and asked for the book back. His mother could not see it in the man's hands.

The servant ran off ahead of them. Rochan gave the servant a head start so the empress would be forewarned. Plus, he did not mind spending time alone with this princess.

"Please tell me what they are accused of."

To deflect her comment, he asked, "Do Fyrians often beg after being told no?" It should be seen as an insult, but even he recognized the teasing nature in his tone.

"I did not beg," the princess said to Rochan. Her playful smile made his heart pick up in tempo, but this was no joking manner.

"Princess, you must be careful."

"I have studied modern Lyftian culture thoroughly. I have also been warned. I have this in hand."

She put up her arm as if she wanted him to do something with it. Then she dropped it. "I forgot. No gentlemanly propriety here. Of course, you would not take my arm."

Oh no. This was another Sapphirian who would make grievous mistakes.

She took a deep breath and straightened her shoulders. "I swear to you, I can do this."

Rochan was deeply worried she could not. He had to help her.

Figuring the servant had reached the empress by now, he led the way keeping the princess's slower pace. "Men cannot touch women. Otherwise, I would partake in your customs to make you feel welcome. I have studied Fyr as well. Also, do not call me Your Highness in front of the empress."

"Your mother?"

"Yes."

She was confused.

Where to start? "I do not get an honorific except 'prince' and my mother," he changed what he called her to suit the princess, but more so not wanting her to know how he was unwanted, unloved, "is the Imperial Empress, or Empress Jadeite. It was a stone in the culture of my grandparents' ancestors, so the last empress took it on. My mother is also big into honoring heritage when few these days cling to those ties. We are simply Lyftians, a culture of our own."

"Thank you, Prince," she said quietly deep in thought. Her eyes danced over everything, taking in the stone and glass architecture.

They arrived at the doors, the panting servant leaving, giving Rochan a warning look. Rochan slipped the book into his hand stealthily and put his finger to his lips. The man smiled, but quickly suppressed it, and slipped the book under his short, plain kurta.

Rochan put his arm out in front of the princess. "Give her a moment. She must call you in when she is ready."

The princess huffed, not impressed by his mother's power moves. "I had a grandfather much like this. I never met him, and my father took over young and changed the way of royal airs."

"That sounds like a nice environment to grow up in, but she is the empress." He was trying to warn her to tread lightly.

"I understand, Prince. She took over with might and must exhibit that power to keep it." She was a clever and perceptive woman. "Wait, what is your name? I cannot keep calling you Prince, can I?"

His heart almost burst with gratitude from her subtle and kind interest in who he was. "Rochan. Prince Rochan Jadeite." Inadvertently, he made that cringe-face when he said his surname. It embarrassed him and irritated him simultaneously.

"I think it has a nice ring to it. But you do not like it?"

He shook his head. "I like my first name. My other mother gave it to me, but my last name was made up to sound more powerful. My grandmother felt it best to be represented by the most precious stone of her heritage: jade. It had been

Opal." *Rochan Opal.* That name was worse, but he did not want to be connected the empress at all.

"We have that name back in Fyr. Is it bad for some reason?"

Apparently, superstitions were different in other spheres.

"Yes. It is bad luck." It was fitting for his mother. Perhaps fitting for his grandmother whom he had never met as well. She died, or rumors said was killed, before he was born.

"What name would you choose if you could?"

"I cannot, so I haven't thought about it before."

"Dare to dream, Prince Rochan. What last name would you want?"

"Neelam," he blurted out. "It is Dev's and Udaya's surname."

"I do not know that word. Is it a stone?"

"Sapphire."

"Like my last name."

"Yes, Princess."

An awkward silence ensued as she blushed and looked at the floor. He was dying to know what made that rosy flush over her pale skin, for he wanted to reenact it.

"Are languages that important here? You speak English."

Rochan had expected a question about the rumors his mother killed her husband hours after marriage, his grandmother within a year after. Or ask him to explain about his two-mother situation. Instead, she chose language. Either these other things were not important to her, or she already was aware. "Not really, but names are important as well as honoring parents through them. The majority of Lyftian originated in a place on Earth where the English language had permeated the land; since people came from different places, it became the common tongue. Some still speak their ancestor's languages at home, but the empress forbids it in public."

"Why? Why would she want them to lose their connection to their family's culture if it is important to them?"

"Because it isn't *her* culture, the one she is trying to form, and she doesn't know her own family's language well enough. But that, Princess, is a secret."

They shared a conspiratorial smile.

The door opened, but she winked at him to tell him his secret was safe. He should not have chatted so much, revealed so much to her, but she was so easy to talk to. He knew why. It was not her looks—although that helped. She did not view him as lesser than herself or look at him with contempt. Her gaze was open, curious...equal.

The princess took a step forward. He had to stop her but touching her was forbidden and the empress would see it. He threw up his wind shield. Her foot hit it. Confused, she glanced at Rochan. He did not dare speak to her to explain and cast his eyes to the floor, hoping the empress did not notice he used his magic. She hated seeing him use power.

"Princess Alexandra Sapphirian of Fyr," the herald's booming voice announced. Rochan once asked him when he was a boy what his name was. He refused to say. The empress's servants had no name but answered to "Man." It bothered Rochan then, and it still bothered him now. Every human being deserved a name, one they liked that represented who they were.

"You may enter," the empress said in her usual cool, clipped tones.

The princess hesitantly took a step forward to see if his air shield was stopping her, but he had taken it down instantly in hopes to not get caught.

Princess Alexandra walked in, her stride confident in her dressy, flowing pants, like a tighter fitting salwar suit, but the leg bottoms were hidden in her boots. There was also elegance and grace in her walk. Her shoulders were high and back, elongating her neck. Although the tunic type top was not intended to be flattering, he appreciated how the fabric strained against part of her body and how it barely covered her bottom. He could not help but stare but forced his gaze to the ground in subservience. He longed to see the empress's expression but suppressed the urge to glance up.

"Sit." The command came out of his mother's mouth like a bark. She was already displeased. "It seems we have a Fyrian infestation," she muttered purposely loud enough for all to hear.

He dared to look up. Princess Alexandra did not flinch, waited a moment by slinging her bag off her shoulder and looking at the chair placed below the throne for the *goddess* to look down upon her subjects. Then the princess gracefully sat. Waiting.

"At least they sent a princess this time. Why are you here?" Leaving off her title was another textbook move of the empress to put the princess in her place.

"Your Imperial Majesty, I would like to see my uncle and cousin. I demand their release in the name of Her Majesty Tourmaline Sapphirian, Queen of Fyr." She slipped a letter out of her bag. "It also should entail her permission to allow me to travel to your sphere to serve as her voice in this matter, calling on the treaty of 1866 prohibiting the harm to a messenger."

The empress flicked her hand, and a servant retrieved the letter. The empress broke the wax seal upon it, making a spectacle of brushing the wax onto the floor. They must not have the tree-bark-and-resin adhesive Lyft had to seal letters. Still, his mother was so closed-minded and loved to point out that anything different than her way was the wrong way.

The princess took no notice or at least her posture did not show the slight bothered her. He wished he could see her face.

After a minute, the empress asked, "How does your mother know they are imprisoned?"

"It was a meeting in hopes to negotiate a treaty. When an ambassador does not return, it is assumed they cannot. The only other option would be they are dead, but an empress as intelligent as you, with such thorough questions and obvious might, would know that killing them would start a war between our spheres. Fyr uses air to grow. No matter how mighty your imperial army is, the elements would determine the end of that war."

The flattery was good, but the undercurrent of threat was bad, very bad. To suggest fire bested air, well, the empress's pride would be pricked. The empress almost stood up, but refrained, trying to reign in her quick temper. Rochan wanted to intercede, but he would only make things worse.

"Yes, I see you are intelligent as well," the empress grounded out. "How do I know you are truly a Sapphirian? Not some spy. Sapphirians are noted to have eyes forged in the fire of dragons or so your old tales tell." With nothing left, she must be grappling to discredit the princess. In all the commotion and fixation on the steely gray eyes, Rochan had failed to notice the obvious. Her eyes were not blue. Was she an impostor, and he believed her so quickly? *Blinded by lust.* That's what his mother would say.

"Would you like a demonstration?" Not awaiting a reply, she made a sassy demonstration of clicking her fingers. Up leaped a ring of fire around her and her chair. Soldiers pushed off the wall, rushing to attack her. The princess widened the circle so the blades could not reach her. The men slowed to a stop.

"Stop!" The empress commanded a beat too late. "You fools! She just pointed out that the death of their ambassadors would start a war. My apologies, Princess. We have to check these things." Her apology was false, the protest a beat too late, but the princess dropped her flames.

Having a moment to breathe, he found her power quite interesting, almost enchantingly beautiful in the way the flames danced. Strength and grace, like her spirit. Most importantly, it made her a Sapphirian despite her pretty but gray eyes.

"Princess, why did your mother not come? Does she think it above her duties to talk queen to queen?"

Rochan bit back a grin. Like his mother ever would step a toe on Fyr to negotiate. She hardly left her fortress. He knew she was afraid. Despite banishing "uncontrollable" men to the Isle of the Gods where they had to survive among the beasts. These people lived in fear of being devoured by nagas in the sky, weretigers of the mines, and vanaras—humanoid apes—of the forests. On the Royal Isle, the only thing to fear were the nagas if the serpent speakers lost control, but they tended to gravitate around the Isle of the Gods, picking off human and beast alike. The empress feared the people she condemned to this life. There was plenty of unrest in the empire. He had heard the whispers in the hall. She was hanging onto this sphere tenuously.

"Neither the king nor queen will leave the sphere. Plus, she is with child."

The empress laughed. "I heard she is more of a breeding heifer than queen."

Instead of lashing out at the insult, he was taken aback when the princess laughed lightly. "I agree with the breeding part, Your Imperial Majesty. In fact, at an important dinner, I embarrassed my family by shouting at her to stop having kids."

His mother was still smiling. Was the princess growing on her?

"With all due respect, though, she is everything a queen should be, my father's partner in rule and both are loving parents. I'm not sure how they are able to be good at both, since there is always so much to do, but they somehow do it."

That lost the empress's mirth but at least she did not scowl so harshly. "You look so young. How old are you?"

"Sixteen years, Imperial Majesty."

"So not the first in line to rule?"

The princess went rigid. "I'm not in line to rule."

What did that mean?

"So, they send me an expendable? That's only a step above men, even if they are princes." She made a disgusted face, not caring if her hatred of men was so obvious to an outsider.

The princess stood.

Oh no, do not. Rochan held his breath.

"I am not expendable to my parents. I was chosen by my mother because she knew I was up to the task. She has faith in me because I am just like her in personality, intellect, and strength. It was the people who would not accept me, despite having a twin sister with Sapphirian eyes born at the same time, despite me showing my father's powers. My parents always accepted and loved me. I have my mother's eyes as well. In Fyr, sometimes the child does not get the father's eyes. My mother needed to send a girl, and my sister and I are the eldest, but Tourmaline is more interested in dresses and gentlemen than politics. I have been patient and answered your questions, even personal ones. Can I see that my family is well? Then you could summon me when you would like to negotiate their release."

"Sit down." The empress commanded.

The princess held her stance and then sat. It was a power contest between them. Rochan could not believe the princess's nerve and resilience. She did not cower as he would under that dark glare. He was in awe of this girl in so many ways.

"As for their crimes, the boy," the empress made a bitter lemon-faced expression before she continued, "dared to call the prince an honorific."

The princess's head dropped, and she shook her head as if annoyed with her relative's stupidity.

"Then his father refused to punish him."

The princess's head lifted. "With all due respect, my uncle would not avoid punishing a child of his for wrongdoing. What was asked of him?"

"The punishment for any man for any slight or crime, at its minimum, is a flogging."

He had enough of them to know the empress meant it. Rochan's stomach went sour. No living thing deserved such cruelty. It taught Rochan that control overpowered freedom. Hate overpowered love.

"If my cousin was on Fyr, he would be spoken to and denied privileges for such an act and would learn from that mistake."

The empress laughed. "And how does that go in the end?"

"I do not understand the question." The princess looked around, but no guard nor himself could help her. Rochan wondered why she did not understand, and yet what did "spoken to" as a "punishment" mean on Fyr? Merely words made people obey authority? "You beat someone who says the wrong word?"

"The lesser sex." The empress laughed off.

The princess did not miss a beat. "All the same, under the universal treaty, an ambassador must not be harmed in any way. Even forcing an ambassador to whip another ambassador would break this treaty."

"The treaty is five-hundred years old." The empress's eyes narrowed.

He hoped the princess knew to tread lightly.

"But it is the only one we have, so we must abide by it until we draw up a new one, which was the exact reason we Fyrians came here. To help Water and to redraw our terms with Lyft to all become allies, assist each other."

"Why should I help Water?"

The princess stood up, rigid. "It is a fellow woman trying to take back what was rightfully hers, stolen by baseborn half-brothers. Men trying to squash a woman, bullying her into hiding. I thought you would desire to be the Water princess's champion?"

The empress's brow wrinkled. She flicked her hand for a servant who ran to her side and whispered in her ear. Then she folded her hands. "I shall listen to your proposal."

The empress did not know about Water because she kept Lyft self-sufficient. To not know what is going on in the universe was a huge mistake on her part.

The princess sighed, realizing she'd not be able to see her family just yet. Rochan doubted she ever would unless she ended up in prison with them. This was something he could not let happen.

7
AN EMPRESS

The prince was sent away, apparently not involved in politics. Xandra did not ask questions, trying to tread lightly. If the prince would not rule after her, who would?

She'd found the idea of a matriarchy appealing when she'd studied back home. Seeing this powerful, strong, and intimidating woman had left her momentarily dumbstruck. Xandra gathered her confidence and once alone with the empress and her aide, she presented the treaty terms her uncle and Thomas had failed to discuss prior. The empress handed the treaty to her aide whom she seemed to have kind eyes for. It was clear the empress loved her, trusted her—more than her own son. Much more than an aide.

Being so dismissive of the treaty worried Xandra, but the empress was more at ease without her son around. As expected, her severity toward Xandra lessened. "Now, would you like a tour of my sphere, or do you need to refresh yourself in your quarters?"

Xandra of course wanted to see her family, but she must get on the empress's good side first. Perhaps part of the tour would include the dungeons. She would bide her time and find a good moment to broach the subject. Perhaps she should ask the prince first. He seemed more pliable than his mother; there was a kindness in his eyes, a vulnerability that the dark, cold eyes of the empress lacked. For a woman to wield power, she must be aloof. Xandra understood that. A man needed to do the same. Xandra had lost count of how many times she had seen her mother and father happy and relaxed, loving and vulnerable. Moments later, when they would walk into a room of whining lords—smiles dropped, eyes grew severe, shoulders back—they took on personas of impenetrable power. It was something she struggled to master. Xandra's emotions always got the best of her. She could not afford to let that happen here.

The empress left her seat. She was much smaller down on the floor, a few inches shorter than Xandra, but her presence still spoke of great power in her small frame. The empress started to leave the room. "Come."

Ignoring the order more fitting for a pet, Xandra hurried to catch up. She peered back at the aide who was reading the missive. Interesting. Was she the consort? Was this free love like when her father overturned laws that had limited marriages? Was the decision going to be made by this consort instead?

Xandra did not have time to puzzle it out.

The empress had begun her tour, only Xandra had been distracted. She missed something about the stone of the building being dug from the mines on the island. Remembering her lessons about Lyft from her childhood, she knew there was a mainland almost the size of Fyr and then an island to the south. The water that separated it from the mainland was so narrow a bridge spanned over it, linking them.

Xandra touched the smooth white wall, wondering where the mortar seams were between blocks of stone. It was coated with a type of plaster or dried clay that was smooth and bright white. She found the intricate curves to the archways and lack of linear lines cutting through the walls a pleasing sight. Although she had thought she liked Fyr's architecture, there was something more beautiful to these walls. Home consisted of grays and cold, hard lines, while this place was bright and full of elegant curvatures.

The empress's persona was more at ease, but she was far from warm. Did she not trust Xandra yet? That must be it. Surely, she was not this cold, rigid being all the time. "This palace was built by the first queen who brought settlers to Lyft, although generations later, our rulers have made many improvements. Long ago, the favored members of the court were allowed to live within its walls, but men showed their true colors and were banished. Only a select few with husbands who can prove they are more man than beast are allowed to grace the halls during the day."

This was when she should ask about her uncle and cousin. If they were not here...

"That was part of the changes my ancestors made. To protect oneself, a woman must take preventative measures. *I* took that further. No men are allowed inside without my permission. Except the arena. My people do love to see the fighters, and honestly, there is something interesting in seeing men kill each other."

Xandra did not know what to say to that. She enjoyed sparring and the idea of testing her fighting skills, but she did not want to see death or even slay someone herself. She shook off the thought and instead of asking about her family, as she should, what came out of her mouth surprised her as much as the empress. "Does the prince not live here?"

"He is *the* exception, but what is he if not a servant of my reign?" She smiled at Xandra. "He has the seed of my line. That is all. Much like men in history used us women as mere vessels, he is doing his part for the empire. After a female heir and a spare, he is useless to me. The matriarchy must be preserved. In fact, your family came at an interesting time. We are hosting the Empress Games to find the best Lyftian woman to follow in my footsteps."

Xandra looked away to hide her expression. Her parents would never speak of any of their children as useless—even Xandra. Even Tourmaline, who cared for nothing of consequence but her dresses and what lords kissed her boots. Perhaps that was unfair, but it was hard to understand how Xandra and her best friend had grown so far apart from each other, how different they had become.

The fact remained though, Xandra's parents never spoke without pride and love in their voice when it came to their children.

Careful with her words and tone, Xandra asked, "The prince did not get a say in whom he married?"

"Does your sphere not do the same to women?"

"Huh?" Xandra whipped her head around to see the empress's smug expression. Not wanting to offend but having a deep-seated need to defend her world and her people, she responded. "Some Fyrians marry for powers, social standing, money, but many strive for love matches. Regardless, every person gets to choose, not have someone picked for them." Then realizing her words were sliding toward possible insult, she allowed, "There are some parents of course that probably pressure their children into certain marriages, but no one can make a Fyrian say yes at the altar. Women in Fyr are not seen as merely bearers for children. I have heard it was not that way before my time, but it is now. Perhaps Lyft's books on Fyr need an update? I would be happy to help set things straight if you would like."

The empress did not react aside from her cold blank manner, but her tone became chiding. "Well, one might say your mother is sending young women the wrong message by procreating so much. The dwindling Sapphirian line is more than secure, and yet they persist in having more."

Xandra had thought the same thing, but hearing it from a stranger, it made her blood boil. Then it clicked in her head, what her parents had told her. She would understand later the reason they had so many kids. Hearing the absence of any love or feeling from the empress made Xandra realize why. Love. They simply could not stay away from each other. Never thinking of marriage or lords in that way before, a sudden pang ran through her. If she were to marry one day, she would want that: someone she could not resist and who likewise could not do without her.

"My parents are a love match. My guess is they keep having kids because they cannot help but express their love for each other...er...repeatedly." This admittance made Xandra blush. She knew where babies came from, after a reform her mother made to educate women as much as men.

The empress scrunched her mouth in a sour expression. "Love is a weakness."

"My father would agree with you on that one."

"Would he?"

Xandra nodded. "My father almost lost his kingdom and life a few times because his enemies had used my mother as a pawn. He made risky decisions to save her. She did the same for him. He told me it was a weakness, but he has *shown* me it is a strength more than anything."

The empress made a huffing sound. "I think I might actually be able to tolerate a man like your father."

"Enough to create a treaty with you?" Xandra dared.

"That is yet to be seen. I will have my stipulations if I bother to agree. You see, I have the upper hand. Lyft is self-sufficient. I need nothing from Fyr or Water. Why involve myself with Water when it is a crumbling land full of war?"

"Because the princess, a *woman*, is being usurped by her illegitimate brothers. I thought you of all people would champion such a cause."

The empress smiled and looked away, seemingly flattered. "Why did your father not send you in the first place instead of men? I might've let you easily persuade me."

Xandra noted the conditional wording the empress had used. It would take a lot to convince her now. Was it worth it? Perhaps Xandra needed to focus on getting her uncle and cousin home instead—a retreat. The impact of every decision she made would affect several spheres. God and Goddess, how did her parents handle this amount of pressure?

How much to tell the empress? Would the truth keep her prisoner here? Dad had warned her that his enemies had used Mum to tip his hand. Her father would do the same for Xandra—any of his children. Her parents would walk into death-defying situations to protect her. In this case, since her mother was with child, it would be her father or worse, one of her brothers—Aschen was probably beside himself right now, trying to convince their parents he had to come save the day. In a family of a dozen kids—well, number thirteen coming soon—you had your favorites. Aschen and her preferred each other foremost despite the seven-year age gap. Not that any Sapphirian would admit favorites and offend the others.

Xandra realized the empress was awaiting an actual explanation. She fumbled before saying, "My father thought sending men would be seen as a peaceful gesture, that women might be seen as an attack."

"Yet he sent you in the end."

"He did not. I came on my own volition."

The empress laughed. The smile that followed was strange to see on her hardened face. "Oh, I think you and I will get on quite well, Princess."

Xandra was not quite sure about that but listened intently while the empress changed the subject to the history of her sphere, as well as the various rooms and their uses. The décor in each was interesting. While it was different in style than home, with less gold and silver and more simple marble, domes, glass walls that let light in, and warm, vibrant colors rather than dull stone and wood in her palace. Sure, her mother had walls painted and vibrant fabrics to bring some rooms alive, but the smooth walls in rooms, such as the empress's dining room, allowed the yellow color to truly come through, the sunlight assisting from the large flat windows. Xandra smiled to herself how the yellow of that room matched the same hue as the accent wall by the head of her bed back in Fyr.

Thinking of home sparked her ambition to save her family. "Can I see the dungeons?"

"You mean see your family." It was not a question and the empress's narrowing eyes were worrisome.

Xandra decided to be upfront. Like Tourmaline, her twin, she could put on a front. Her sister was so confident, nothing could outwardly crack her mask. Xandra would do the same. Simple. Act like Tourmaline. "Yes. Of course. I must see they are alive to negotiate anything with Lyft. I am already hesitant of our alliance since they are imprisoned in a dungeon rather than rooms. Do you not have a power-blocking room? A noble prison?"

The empress crossed her arms, examining Xandra. "Men cannot be true nobles. All men who do any wrong belong behind bars."

What an awful comment, but Xandra had to play along to stay on the empress's good side. If she angered the woman, she could end up with her family in the prison. What would her father do if she did not send word back about her safety or come back at all? A war of the spheres was on the line if she mucked this up.

Carefully she said, "I cannot argue with that. Regardless of the wrong they have done, I would like to see them, so I know they are alive and well."

The empress glared at Xandra, her lips twitching into a smirk. "I am sorry. I have more pressing concerns than a foreigner's family reunion. Criminals do not have rights in Lyft. I will have you shown to your rooms." She flicked her wrist for a servant to lead Xandra away. The servant was armed, a soldier.

Xandra was a guest but guarded as a prisoner. The look of triumph on the empress's face, delighting in her power over others, told Xandra this was a game to her. She had to be fond of games. She had created one to auction off her son.

One thing Xandra excelled at was playing games…and winning.

8
ENLIGHTENMENT

Rochan overheard his mothers discussing the princess in heated whispers at breakfast. As always, he feigned he was not listening or did not care. It was the only way he could ever glean any information.

Stay silent. Observe. Listen. Learn. Do not act. Plan.

These were lessons Dev had given him as a child when it came to combat—swords or magic—but Rochan was still quite young when it clicked that Dev had meant to do so with everything—foremost when dealing with the empress.

Udaya became pleading, the empress hardened and bitter. Udaya must persuade her to free the Sapphirians or Lyft would be destroyed by fire-breathing dragons—or worse. When Udaya's tone shifted, he knew what tactic she was using next. His presence would no longer be appreciated, nor could he stomach any romance between his parents—not when he could see the love in the empress's eyes, something she bestowed to no one else but Udaya, not even the child she had borne.

With them likely being occupied for a while, he found himself wandering through the guest quarters. He wanted to see *her*. Seeing the princess was not forbidden, since the empress hadn't said anything to him about her, and she was not a prisoner. He could think of no reason not to see her even though the empress probably would not like it. His curiosity outweighed any potential reprimand from the empress.

A soldier was stationed outside her door, but Rochan recognized the nameless man's face.

"Prince. I am to go wherever the guest goes."

Rochan waved his hand, telling him to proceed. The soldier knocked on the door.

"Who is it?" The princess's assertive voice rang out. How strong she was to enter an unknown world, looking for her family, not knowing if it might lead to her death. Her strength appealed to him, but equally came the desire to help her, protect her, despite her not needing it. Maybe he could at least educate her about his sphere, give her the missing knowledge that only comes from experiencing a culture hands-on.

She came to the door, her face guarded. When she met his gaze, those cautiously stoic gray eyes softened. The princess did not see him as a threat. That thrilled part of him, but the other part was irritated because no one ever did. He had to remind himself of the strength he kept hidden from his mother. Dev once told him the story about the stargazer, a fish with eyes atop his head, always watching its prey, buried under the sand. Once its prey was in sight, it devoured the unsuspecting fish. Rochan longed to be a stargazer.

"Yes?" She raised her brows after he took too long to speak, getting lost in his thoughts.

"I wanted to give you a tour."

"Your mother already did."

Rochan gave her a leveled look. "Do you want to sit in your room alone or see places my mother did not take you?"

Princess Alexandra's eyes widened, and then she smiled. To watch her face move from a false front to the real her was adorably transformative. With a pep in her step, she left her room, closing the door. The soldier followed them. She looked over her shoulder then at Rochan. "Am I a prisoner to be followed everywhere I go?"

Rochan made eye contact and quietly responded with the truth he felt deep down to his marrow, what plagued his life more than anything else. "We all are."

"Even you?"

"Especially me."

"But you are to rule one day, no? Something your mother said…I got confused. Your wife and child will rule one day but not you?"

He did not like where this conversation was going. This Fyrian was beautiful, and he wanted to—no needed to—impress her. She was learning how shaky the ground he stood upon was. She would see him as weak. "My wife shall be empress one day. My daughter will rule."

"Congratulations. Will I meet your wife?"

She was confused, but Rochan knew it was a strange situation so how to best explain it eluded him.

He scratched the back of his neck, thinking. "Um…I'm not married yet. There is a kind of—er—tournament that will happen soon, one to win my hand. Symbolically. Really the girls are after the throne, the power." His face burned with embarrassment and shame. He should be in charge of his own future.

The princess did not speak but stared at him, her expression not forthcoming. Was she judging him? Feeling pity? Why did it matter what she thought of him?

Except it did.

"Sorry, the way you spoke of a wife and daughter, I thought…Stupid of me, really. Your mother did say something about games, was that it? Forgive me for not understanding customs here, but it sounds like she is auctioning you off. I have seen this fate back in Fyr, all for power or money. I am sorry you are not free from that. It makes me realize that although I have no power, at least I have a choice."

Rochan was not sure why the princess felt she had no power. She was royalty, a girl, and they had everything. Fyr was different, Rochan had been told, but he had a hard time envisioning a man in power. "We must disagree, Princess. A choice *is* power."

"I suppose you are right." She nodded. She stared ahead, deep in thought.

"Man," Rochan stopped and turned. The soldier stood at attention. At least he had this power, a step above servants. "Take this and ask the librarian to procure these books for the princess's amusement. The bottom one is for you. Remain inside her room while reading. Do not get caught." The nameless man suppressed a smile and saluted him, a gleam of appreciation in his pale blue eyes. Like the Fyrian princess, this servant was not born of this sphere. Perhaps his ancestors were from Earth or Fyr, but such records were long gone. Now he had nothing, not even a name.

"Why would he have to hide in my room?"

"Shhh." Rochan looked around, making sure no one was about. "The empress wants you followed, spied on. I sent him to fetch you some books from the library."

"I could do it myself."

"I sent him because they are not allowed in the library. With my note and orders, the woman who runs the library must let him in and help him. My mother does not let servants learn to read. One of the books is of children's fairy tales. Something he likely can read, but you still might be interested in if he gets caught. You might want to explore our culture."

Her brow wrinkled. "What if he is caught? What if I do not want to lie to the empress because my uncle's and cousin's lives are on the line?"

Rochan's heart sank. He trusted her so quickly, starved for a friend, a relationship that felt on equal terms. He should know better than to trust a woman. Would she turn him in? Tell his mother what he was doing?

Then anger filled him. She did not know. The princess still did not see how truly vile the empress was. He would show her. "Because I'm about to show you the real Lyft, what it costs its citizens to be such a society. If you want to side with the empress after this, there is no hope for you."

She was taken aback.

"Come." Rochan took up Princess Alexandra's hand in his, not meaning anything by it but to guide her down a hall. His grip was too tight to be affectionate. He was furious. How could she be so blind? So accepting of what had been obvious to her male relatives as utterly inhumane and wrong? He needed this princess to see this was no paradise he lived in but a massive marble prison. He reigned in his temper before he could dare to shout at her.

Princess Alexandra stared down at their hands.

He quickly let go. "Sorry." His face burned to the tips of his ears. He was going to apologize further, but she spoke first.

"It's not a big deal." She had no clue how wrong that statement was in Lyft.

He would enlighten her. He had this need, this desire to teach her, show her everything. Why? She would leave soon enough. Why did he even care if a stranger was walking dumbly into his mother's web of deception? *Because she is beautiful.* He dismissed the thought, but another one replaced it. *You're attracted to her, drawn.* This was true, but it shamed him. Was he as crude as some of the men his mother called beasts? *No. The empress was full of hate, wrong.*

"A man does not touch a woman on Lyft unless she asks him to. Me just touching your hand would make me lose mine."

She stopped walking. "Lose?"

"Yes. They would chop off a finger in warning and if it had been a more…a more offensive touch." Rochan's ears burned when discussing such things. "I'd lose my whole hand or something worse."

"What's worse than losing a hand?"

He shot her a significant look and then continued walking. She raced to catch up as he descended the stairs. Her eyes were wide with interest, compelling him to continue. "I do not under—"

"Eunuchs, Princess Alexandra."

She gasped. "Has she done that to you?"

"No!" He could not believe she dared to ask such a personal question. She sure had pluck and might anger his mother. The idea thrilled him until he thought what might happen to her if she truly ticked his mother off. He felt protective of Princess Alexandra. "I do not give her a reason to do such a thing. Plus, she wants her bloodline to continue. I am her only child."

"Sorry. I did not mean to offend, and it was a stupid question. I speak before I think sometimes."

"Be careful when you talk to the empress, then."

The princess looked away, embarrassed, before she glanced back. "Where are we headed?" She was annoyingly headstrong, which he found endearing but was sure the empress would feel the opposite.

"A tour the empress would never show you." He winked at her, too afraid of where he was taking her and how severe his mother would punish him after. She would find out, but he was doing what was right. "Fyrians need to know what they are truly getting into before they sign any alliance with this sphere. If I can manage it, to see your family members as well, but no promises. It's likely she has even barred me from seeing them."

He took her down into the bowels of the palace, not the dungeons. He'd get in serious trouble for that. He took her to the servants' quarters, the dungeons being on the other side of the palace. They passed through the large double doors that had a bar on the outside. The princess's hand touched it in realization it was on the wrong side.

"Servants are locked inside for the evening. The empress takes every precaution."

The princess's eyes were wide. That gray hue gave him goosebumps every time he beheld them. "What if there was a fire or an emergency?"

"She sees them as expendable. I think she is afraid of men and a large revolt, but you did not hear that from me."

"Have they revolted in the past?"

"One or two here and there, but rebels are sent to the island if not killed. Nothing…organized that I know of. The worst fate for prisoners is being assigned to work in the mines." He pushed forward into the quarters not wanting to be there long.

"The mines?"

Rochan met her gaze. She did not know a thing about Lyft—well, she knew a lot about the façade his mother had created. "You do not want to know what lives in the mines. Each one of the stones to build this palace, the noblewomen's houses, and all the magic stones healers use—all paid for in men's blood. I'll show you a captive one of the beasts."

The princess shivered.

He led her through as servants ran out of his path, afraid the empress was with him. He paused to ask a servant, "You, where is my boy?"

The servant bowed and pointed down the hall.

"Your boy?" The princess raised her brows.

He wondered how she interpreted his comment and let her ponder for a moment to see if she'd give him a hint about what she thought. When the silence stretched between them, he spoke, "My personal servant. I give him…time off. Keep that to yourself, please. His mother abandoned him and his father for a widower whose late wife had been wealthy. I let him see his father."

"Surely, the empress would not wish to keep a boy from his parent."

"Forgive me for saying this, Princess, but you do not know the empress as well as I do."

Her brow wrinkled, but he let her stew upon her confusion while he tapped on the door of a room. The door opened and the father stood there bowing his head repeatedly and thanking him, making Rochan feel oddly rewarded for what should be—as the princess pointed out—normal. A child should see his parent.

"Come, Ansh," Rochan prompted.

The boy hugged his father who kissed his head.

Ansh walked to Rochan. While the father nodded to Rochan again in thanks.

"You said an hour. I would've been back in time, My Prince."

"Ansh, you are not in trouble. I simply need you to do something for me."

He awaited the request.

"Where is the boy, the one who was punished today for insulting the empress?" He knew the boy had not insulted the empress, but like the Sapphirian men, he said something she did not like. It mattered not. Insolence from Rochan had to be underhand. He had to go along with her narrative to undermine it.

Ansh looked up to him and said, "The infirmary, Prince Rochan. This way." Then he glanced at the princess and looked away quickly, knowing his place.

They followed Ansh down the hall. Rochan heard the moaning and groaning of the injured and ill before they neared the infirmary. The smell of antiseptic and blood combined assaulted his senses. He hated this place, trying not to recall the times he'd ended up here.

Inside, six patients filled the beds. This was the only care the hundreds of servants received—soldiers were treated a bit better in the castle's actual infirmary. One of the patients was the small boy.

The princess rushed over to him, squatting down to the boy's level, her face etched in concern. "Is he unwell?" She asked the healer.

The healer's mouth dropped. Then he cast his eyes to the floor.

"What happened to him?" The princess looked at the boy who was fighting to stay conscious then to the healer.

The man looked over at Rochan, not knowing what to say.

Rochan motioned with his hand to proceed and said, "Tell her."

The healer looked at the floor as he mumbled, "His tongue was removed by order of the empress."

Princess Alexandra shot up to her feet, her fists clenched, eyes glaring at the healer. "You removed his tongue?"

Rochan intervened before she would torch the man. "He healed him. The servant-at-arms cut it out in front of the empress. She likes to watch to ensure her punishments are carried out."

The healer busied himself, inventorying his stock, pretending he had not heard Rochan's true but unkind words about their leader.

The princess's face fell.

"Boy," he said to Ansh, for his servant was not allowed to have a name, so he only used it in private. "Go to the head scribe and give him this missive." He pulled an envelope with his seal out of his pocket and handed it to Ansh.

Ansh snatched it. "At once, My Prince."

"Meet me back in my rooms!" Rochan called after the boy as he ran, excited at this little mission of his.

Then Rochan turned to the healer. "He will be a scribe, taught his letters. He is to remain here until well enough to learn."

"If the empress—"

"Asks? You tell her I chose him as my personal scribe. One who is mute is a perfect scribe for confidential purposes. She will think nothing of it. Refer her to me if she even notices." Such things were beneath her, which was how Rochan got a tiny fraction of satisfaction for helping his mother's victims.

Rochan turned around to see the princess standing quietly, her face pale and her brow adorably furrowed. Good. She was starting to understand this sphere more clearly now.

"Come." He led her past the servants' quarters toward the bowels under the arena where the fighters were housed. He should not be bringing her there with such brutal men, but as he saw upon her arrival, she could handle herself. There was something he needed to show her for her to truly comprehend the sphere.

"The empress banishes criminals to the Isle of the Gods. It has a very misleading name. There are creatures there, as well as in the mines that connect to this isle, the Royal Isle. These…creatures are used sometimes in fights for entertainment in the arena."

He heard the inhuman sounds before they turned the corner. The creatures were in their cells, their attention drawn to the visitors.

The princess stopped in her tracks. "What is that? What the…what is *that?*" She blurted out pointing to each cell.

"Have you had enough reality for today, Princess?"

She met his gaze and nodded. Good. She was shocked into realizing the truth about Lyft.

9
A NAGA

Xandra had underestimated the prince. He was more than what he seemed, and she doubted the empress knew that her docile, soft son had a spine and power buried inside. The empress was disappointed she had a son, and that unloved child used her indifference as a shield. If he decided to strike, she would never expect it. Xandra began to wonder if she had come to the sphere in the beginning of a coup. As soon as she had been left alone in her guest suite, she had lit a fire in the grate, sat comfortably down, and tried to firebrand—to read of the flames if something would happen. Nothing came to her. As she had feared, due to books professing it, she could not firebrand on Lyft. Her once curse no longer felt like one.

If only she could read the flames to know how to proceed.

Such were her thoughts as she waited in the library, looking through books, hoping the prince would come. She would demand he take her to see her family.

She settled in the window seat with a book about this world's serpent-like dragons, their nagas, making comparisons to Fyr's draca.

After studying a detailed rendering of the creatures he had shown her yesterday, the images haunting her dreams last night, she knew tonight she might not sleep any better. They were terrifying sounding but seeing them in person was something she'd never forget.

The vanaras were not the worst of the imprisoned creatures. Kind of ape, kind of human, reminding her of the evolution concept her mother had taught her when Xandra had gone through her first other-spheres obsession—her Earth phase. Still, to see a concept alive on another sphere was jarring. The one imprisoned had a broad flat nose, protruding mouth, and beady deep-set eyes. Its feet looked like hands, and it crouched on the ground, swaying slightly. It looked as if it would be tall if it stood upright and strong with those long arms. Its body was covered in fur.

What thoroughly disturbed her, though, was the weretiger. It looked like a huge man with bulging muscles covered in orange fur with black stripes. Its back was hunched under massive corded muscles, and it did not have much of a neck. The shoulders rose almost immediately and tapered up to the head which was set down lower and more forward than a human's. The face almost made Xandra scream when she had beheld it. It was a tiger's face with a shorter snout, a wider mouth, and its feline eyes seemed a bit too intelligent. Its fingers tapered into claws. It growled, then paced its cage, watching her like she was prey.

Rochan explained they were the worst to fight. Fighters could become one if bitten or be torn to shreds if they lost. Even the books she perused today said only one legendary hero escaped either fate for being so nimble and quick.

The thought gave her chills.

While, searching for another book, something caught her eye. Rochan was in the courtyard with another man. From his plain clothing, Xandra surmised it was a servant. Both of them moved strangely, undulating in a practiced yet graceful set of moves. There was something beautiful in the way he moved, with an underlying strength and such graceful control. Another indicator he was much more than the empress knew—or perhaps let him be.

"Enjoying the view?"

Xandra whipped her head around to see the empress, arms folded under her chest in a closed off stance. Her face was not amused. As tiny as she was, she had a formidable presence.

Stifling her embarrassment at being caught ogling, she met the empress's steely gaze. "What kind of dance are they doing out there? It's interesting."

The empress frowned. "It's not a dance. It is exercise. Strengthens the core and helps balance when fighting. Not that he will ever fight, but combat training is one indulgence we allow to protect himself, to protect his wife."

Xandra's brow wrinkled. A future wife who would win him in some contest? Why did her stomach feel sour at the thought?

"It sounds like you have chosen his bride already. Will he have a say in it?"

"The games are his say. Otherwise, I would choose for him." Then she smiled and laughed. "I forgot. Your new philosophy in Fyr is to marry for *love*." The empress had not forgotten at all but viewed love as a weakness and insulted Xandra's people.

"I feel bad for those who cannot marry for love. Did you marry for love?" Xandra dug for information. She suspected the empress might have married the woman she loved if her aide was in fact her consort.

"I was forced into marriage with a tyrant. He did not live long." She turned her back on Xandra. She picked up one of the many books Xandra had been reading. "Come. Since you've been reading about nagas, let's go see them."

"Really?" Excitement shot through her. But why was the empress being kind? She had already seen the limitations of allowances she gave her own son. There had to be a reason.

Then it hit her. A distraction. "I'd like to see my family first if I could. Perhaps then, we could speak of their release being worked into the treaty."

"In such a rush to return home, a place you aren't wanted?"

Low blow but Xandra was now understanding this woman's game. "I never said I was unwanted. The people do not want me to rule. My family cannot do without me. The same goes for my uncle and cousin. My uncle has many children and a wife who just gave birth. If anything happens to him, his newborn daughter, Maggie, will never know him." She tried to ply the cold empress into feeling something for a baby girl at least.

"He should not have come then. It is his fault for putting his king before his daughter."

"Do you not expect the same of your people? You come first, no?"

The empress sniffed and walked on, Xandra rushing to keep up despite having a longer stride. She was surprised when the empress led her out into the courtyard.

A pebbled path crunched under her boots, the smell of pink flowered trees sweetening the air. The shockingly vibrant colors of pink flowers, rich green grass, and brilliant blue sky consumed her attention. Fyr was a beautiful planet but colorless in comparison to nature's hues on Lyft.

The only thing to pull her eyes away from the scenery was when the prince's profile came into view. The tension was out of his shoulders, and he moved with ease and rhythm. His thick black lashes splayed onto his high cheekbones. She'd never found anyone attractive before, but she could not yank her eyes away from him. It had to be the picturesque scenery, that was all. He was handsome, though…

The empress's barking voice cut through the spell that had enveloped Xandra. "Rochan!"

The prince immediately went rigid. His eyes snapped open. He stood straight, bowing; his gaze narrowed, hesitant. What would the prince be like if his mother—or the idea of her—never loomed over him? He would be strong, but not overbearingly so. Serious still, but he'd smile more. How she wanted to see him smile—just to see what it looked like. He had broad, full lips, and she imagined his teeth would match to give a wide smile.

"Come. We will show the princess the nagas."

"As you wish." Prince Rochan's jaw clenched. Why?

The empress walked away, and the prince followed. He snuck a peek at Xandra over his shoulder and nodded as if trying to tell her something. She hustled to fall in line next to him, giving him an imploring look. He shook his head slightly in warning. Xandra was lost but knew better than to press him.

Outside the palace, it felt like she was leaving a prison, with its numerous fences and walls the walkway cut through, guards opening each gate as the empress marched forward. Lots of greenery was planted to try to hide the eyesores of fencing and walls with spikes atop. It was clear there had been a problem of keeping people out.

The walkway outside the last fence opened onto a terrace. Wind gently kissed her skin as they entered the open. The sky was wondrously blue, and puffy white clouds dotted it. Peering over the side of the terrace's wall, she saw the jagged rocky terrain of the mountain the palace was nestled up in, the bottom was stories down, the tops of trees not too far below.

Rochan supplied. "Wildcats down below. The city is raised in the mountains. The cats seem to breed faster than hunters can keep them in check. It is why cougar meat will be often on the menu."

"We do not have wildcats. Does their meat taste good?"

"As with all meat, it depends on how you season it," Rochan said. "The cooks have catered to please you thus far. Lyftian food uses a lot more spices."

She nodded. "I appreciate that, but I would like to try your food."

"We get the best cuts, Princess. The Isle of the Gods gets the gristle, but the fat and protein are good for them," the empress cut in, not turning around. "What the prince has failed to tell you, due to his ignorance, is spice means heat. We like our food not only spiced but spicy."

Xandra caught on to another tactic of the empress. Any time her son showed any ounce of power—even just telling Xandra about wildlife and food—she had to insert her power so he would not forget who was in charge. Or perhaps, to show Xandra.

The smell of the ocean permeated her senses, and she heard waves. The empress went to the eastern edge, leaning on a wall. Ahead, there was a metal gate with a stone archway over it and beyond it was a bridge that was long and made of stone. On either side of the gate, two warriors in armor stood behind massive crossbows-like devices.

"What are those for?" Xandra asked Rochan.

"You do not know?"

"I would not ask if I knew, would I?" She cocked her brow at him.

A little grin toyed on his lips, but the empress turned slightly to take them in. The grin vanished as quickly as it came.

Xandra was sorry for it.

"I like your pluck, Princess," the empress said. "Come. The naga."

Excited to see the land's serpents to compare them with her world's draca, she hastened to the empress's side. She had no idea what a serpent looked like but had read they were draca without wings. "Where?"

As they looked at the Isle of the Gods, squiggles in the sky grew into shapes. Long scaly creatures swam through the sky. Magic, wind magic, obviously, kept them afloat without wings, but her initial sentiment was right. They had draca-like faces, with sharp teeth, but they lacked limbs, and were long thin, corded beasts.

One flew by closer, screeching out, and Xandra could not speak to or understand its thoughts as she could with draca, but the sentiment, the emotions came through: a curious greeting. That was when she noticed the tiny limbs folded against its body. Not used for hunting, but perhaps just landing and taking flight. The long body made her think it might coil around its prey.

"They are beautiful, majestic."

"What are Fyr's naga like?" The prince asked behind them.

The empress huffed a breath out her nose. "You—"

Xandra, tired of her nastiness to her own child, cut in with, "We call them draca—Oh, sorry, Empress. Go ahead."

The empress glared at her with dark beady eyes, empty of emotion. "No, do go on. I am curious as well."

"The draca are not as long, but they are hulking beasts with strong, long limbs and claws to capture prey and light them on fire to consume them. They have huge wings, like a bird's that lift their great masses off the ground."

"They need wings to fly?" The empress sniffed unimpressed.

Xandra's opinion of the woman had been so high that every moment on the sphere, she lowered in her estimation. Like her sister Tourmaline, who had turned on her, it reeked of insecurity and a need to feel good about herself. "We do not have wind magic, Your Imperial Majesty, but can yours breathe fire? I imagine our creatures are simply gifted in our spheres, respectively."

The empress said nothing.

Xandra stared off at the Isle of the Gods. There was a massive forest, no buildings. "What's on the Isle of the Gods?"

"Lessers," the empress said.

Xandra looked at Rochan, but his head was down, staring at the ground. Xandra learned a lot by watching the unwanted son with his mother. The lessers were likely "rebels" who were mostly men. It made sense. Brute strength could overpower women, so anyone who did not fall in line must be put somewhere they could not overthrow the empire. It made sense, and yet, the mood the empress gave her was making her uneasy about the cost of such power. Her parents had warned her to observe this.

Looking down at the coast of the other island, she saw a much lower bridge, then a massive gate before the stairs with spike-covered wires to keep them in. Scanning back up, she saw movement in the trees. Then she took in the faraway details: ropes and boards strung between trees, some roofs jutting out between branches.

"People live in the trees?"

The empress's eyes were cold, and her expression spoke of distaste. "Like the savages they are, these exiled creatures are contained by the naga and the wild cats…among other creatures. Mostly men, but occasionally, there are children offered at the gates for a better life, so some females are surviving out there."

Xandra's stomach soured. Perhaps this form of matriarchy was not worth the suffering of so many. Observing Rochan, it felt far from worth it. Part of Xandra wanted to free him from this woman. But it was not her place to do so. She had to focus on her uncle and cousin.

"Your Imperial Majesty, I was wondering—"

A naga came flying by them, forcing Xandra to dive out of the way. Its tail whipped around as it slithered through the sky. The empress ducked. It roared and turned around coming down toward them.

Xandra asked the empress, "Cannot you control these things?"

The woman's lips pressed firmly down. Oh, god of fire and goddess of light, the empress could not and yet brought Xandra here, why? To intimidate her? In hopes the naga would devour her?

Xandra stood up valiantly, throwing up a fire shield and unsheathing her sword. *Stop!* She mentally commanded, hoping they spoke the same language of thought as her sphere's draca.

Nope. No such luck. The naga came flying back toward them. The empress pressed herself against the wall, glaring at Rochan. "Do something, *boy*!"

Rochan glared at the empress as if he would not intervene on her behalf, but then he turned and stepped between Xandra and the approaching naga. He muttered something aloud in a language Xandra had never heard before.

The naga stopped in midair just a foot from him, its tail whipping in the wind. Its snout was shorter than a draca's, but its teeth were similar—many dangerous little daggers. It had sets of three larger fangs on the top and bottom for tearing through flesh. Above the deadly mouth was a piggish nose with large nostrils. Fleshy skin hung from its chin and atop its head like a fleshy mop of skin-hair and beard—almost like a chanticleer. Its pointed tongue matched its golden eyes as they darted to her then Rochan as if trying to figure out the situation.

Intrigue. She could sense its mood but could not hear the words that it and Rochan were mentally exchanging. Rochan touched its snout gently. The naga closed its eyes as if that was a pleasing sensation. This naga's color from afar had seemed a bluish green, but up close it was blue with a shimmering sheen to the scales as it moved.

The naga retreated, Xandra watching the interesting colors undulating blue dusted with gold.

"Beautiful," she breathed.

Rochan turned around, a small smile playing on his lips. "Perhaps, but he wanted to eat you, Princess."

"Rochan," the empress barked. "You are no longer needed. You're dismissed."

"He just saved our lives!" Xandra protested. Instead of thanking Prince Rochan, the empress seemed angry, but why?

The prince was already storming away. Looking at the bitter empress and the naga swirling in the distance, it clicked. The empress could not speak to serpents, but her son could. Simple petty jealousy or resentment for him being better— maybe both.

Xandra and the empress stared at one another for a moment. "I'm not about to stay out here without his protection."

She stormed inside, but the prince was already down the hallway, ready to turn the corner. From his angry stance, she knew if she called out, he would not stop.

Hoping this amount of her magic could be conjured on this sphere, she conjured fire all around her and transported directly in front of him: on Fyr, it was called dragon's trapdoor.

Rochan stopped, surprised. He was inches from colliding into her. He did not back up, but stood, staring down at her. His expression was guarded, but his eyes wide.

Xandra spoke first. "She cannot speak to nagas."

"No. Do not speak of it though." Then he cocked his head. "How did you do that? Disappear and reappear?"

"Dragon's trapdoor?"

"We call it windwalking. I am not allowed to learn it. My…" He stopped himself. "I am told my heritage should allow me to do so."

Xandra understood what he had wanted to say. He had to have a father, and that father must be the one who spoke to nagas, the one who could windwalk if the empress could not. She wondered whom his father was or if he were the one the empress said had not lived long.

When the prince did not say more, she tempted him with an offer hoping to barter for her family's freedom later. "I could teach you."

He shook his head. "Not with the empress around."

The empress's return inside cut off any plans to do so. Walking inside the normal way confirmed the empress lacked the windwalking power too. What kept this prince from overpowering such a weak mother? It was clear there was no love or respect between them. What was stopping him?

10
A CONSEQUENCE

Rochan left Xandra alone with the empress after his dismissal.

Now was the time for her to ask. "Empress, I am thankful for the tour and hospitality, but I would like to see my uncle and cousin to confirm they are all right."

"Is my word not good enough?" She raised her brows.

"You know as well as I that no one in their right mind would negotiate without checking."

The empress stared at her and said nothing. Xandra realized too late that even suggestions that were not the empress's own offended her. How did a woman make it through each day if upset by anyone voicing a request?

"You are an opinionated girl." Yep, they must bow their every opinion to hers. That meant she was spoiled at getting her way all the time. Dealing with the empress would be very much like…dealing with Tourmaline. Xandra just had to make the empress think things were her idea and that she had control to sway her.

"I am. But perhaps you are right. We can negotiate the treaty, but I will not sign until I see them, and their release is secured in writing."

"Practical," the empress mused, leading the way back to her throne room.

When they turned a corner, a woman held a little boy's wrist who was struggling to get away. The woman full out backhanded the boy. Had she not held his wrist, the child would be sprawled onto the ground. Xandra gasped as the poor boy's head whipped around from the impact.

The empress smirked at her. "Are bad children not punished on Fyr?"

"They do, but not with that much vigor. What has the child done?" Xandra asked the woman since her simplistic sari did not speak nobility, lacking the rich details Xandra had seen on the empress consort's clothing, but a more common woman.

The woman looked at Xandra confused but then bowed to the empress.

"Answer the Fyrian princess, Meera."

Xandra noticed she had not been called "Lady."

"Your Imperial Majesty, I apologize. The boy spoke back at me. Told me I could sweep the floors of my rooms myself."

The empress examined her. "Is he your child?"

"No, Majesty. An orphan I was burdened with by relation, my sister's child."

"Do you wish to continue caring for him?"

"No, he is a troublesome little beast, and his behavior has rubbed off on my little girls."

"Guard!" The empress shouted. One materialized off the wall nearby. Xandra hadn't even noticed him. "Take this boy down to the dungeons. Have them cut out his tongue so he can no longer talk back ever again. Then send him to the servants' quarters. He can spend the rest of his life sweeping floors."

The boy and his aunt went wide-eyed. He clung to his aunt in desperation as the guard moved to seize him.

Regret and fear flittered across the woman's face briefly before she reigned in her emotions. "Please, Majesty. My sister would not have wanted that for her child. Perhaps he could live with his other aunt on his father's side. She might discipline better than me."

"He talked back. A boy who does not know his place, who does not know his betters, is a boy who does not belong in our world. He deserves death or banishment to the Isle of the Gods. I am being merciful. He will have food, shelter, and his life spared. More importantly, you will be spared this burden."

Xandra thought for a moment the empress was trying to teach the woman a lesson, that she should not wish for a child to be gone unless she was ready to go through with it, but the woman had been terrified. Was showing emotion a bad thing on Lyft?

"But—"

"Take the boy!" The empress's shrill shout echoed in the corridor. She was not making an example. This would really happen—just like what the prince had done in trying to help the other boy after by making him a scribe.

Xandra's skin crawled.

The boy was pulled off his aunt and thrown over the guard's shoulder.

The woman sank to her knees crying, "Please—"

The empress sneered. "Perhaps you will learn to curb your complaints in the future as well, Meera. And stop the hysterics before you are punished as well."

Then she walked on as if all this was nothing, an everyday occurrence.

Xandra had been in shock throughout the exchange, but as the boy's shrieks and cries reverberated off the walls, his tear-stained face and arms reaching for help, reaching for his aunt, who bawled her eyes out in regret, made something snap in Xandra.

Her eyes stung with rage and pain at the injustice of it. "No!"

She should not have said anything but could not help herself because the boy was about her little brother Matthew's age, seven. Her vivid imagination put Matthew in the boy's place and her stomach went sour as she envisioned his tongue being cut out, his face being slapped so hard. How she missed her family, despite how loud and overbearing they were. Fyr was warm and had love. Lyft felt cold and cruel. Forget its pleasing architecture and vibrant colors. Xandra now saw how right her father had been about how violence sparked women's control over men in this sphere. It made it no less right than some worlds that did the same to women. For once she saw how the balance of genders was so important; it contributed to Fyr's success and peace. Her parents were perfection.

The empress turned severely as if to attack her for protesting.

"He is just a boy, and his life will be ruined without his tongue. He will learn nothing from this but pain."

There was no empathy, only cold, dark eyes in a blank face. "He has learned to never talk back. This is the way of Lyft. It is how he will learn his place and lesson. An unruly boy if not checked becomes a monster."

Fury and desperation overwhelmed Xandra. She had to save this child. She thought of the boy whom the prince made his scribe. "He will not be able to talk back because he will not be able to speak at all!"

"Precisely."

"You cannot do this. I could take the boy as my charge, my servant. I will take him back to Fyr with me if you want him gone. I will teach him not to speak out of turn. There are ways to teach rather than punish."

The boy cried, reaching for Xandra now, which broke her heart. The guard stopped, and she could see a glimmer of hope in his eyes. He did not want to punish the boy.

"Yes, please," the aunt begged. "Please, Your Imperial Majesty. Let her take him with his tongue, for my sister's memory."

Through a feigned attitude that she was annoyed by the woman, Xandra saw a glimmer of panic in the empress's gaze before it was schooled into a cutting glare. "Your sister would care little for a son. Begone Meera, or I'll have you sent to the dungeons as well."

The woman got up and ran away crying loudly.

The little boy screamed out, knowing he was abandoned.

The empress looked at Xandra as if she ate a sour lemon. "And you, *Princess*, shall join the boy in the dungeons for your insolence. How dare you challenge *my* word in front of *my* subject? It's too bad I cannot cut your tongue out. Or could I? Sending you back maimed surely will teach your father not to tread where he is unwanted."

Xandra blinked back the tears that had formed upon hearing the child scream. She braced her shoulders and sneered at the empress with her best attempt to mimic her mother when she spoke to spoiled, whining nobles. "I promise that my parents will launch a war if anything happens to me or my family. We, in Fyr, love severely with everything in our being. Family is everything. I warn you of this just this once. This is no insubordination but truth. You harm me or my imprisoned family, and the rest of them will come with dragons, ones that could tear yours in half and torch you to the ground. You do not know who you are dealing with."

"And neither do you, *child*. Arrest her." The empress gave Xandra a creepy grin.

"For what? You are throwing me in prison for pointing out the obvious? You're cutting his tongue out for misspeaking? He is a little boy! How does he learn from his mistakes if you permanently maim him? It will get you the opposite. He will hate you and so will others. I imagine there are many who want you dead if this is how you operate."

"How dare you." The empress seethed. She raised her hand up as if to backhand Xandra.

Xandra leaned in toward her hand, daring her.

The empress shook with rage but did not swing.

The child stopped screaming, the soldier bouncing him in comfort as he came down off the trauma. He did not know he was far from safe, poor lamb. And Xandra was powerless to save him.

Regret reverberated through her. Thomas, her parents, and Rochan, all had warned her this matriarchal utopia came at a great price. She hadn't wanted to believe it. The empress, although not having a great first impression, had given her a tour that portrayed the place in such a grand light. For a moment, the wool had been pulled over her eyes and Xandra had been fooled into thinking it a paradise. The prince had enlightened her. Had he not, this moment would've.

Xandra was proudly her parents' daughter. Injustice was unacceptable in her sphere. There was no going back. It was not in her nature. She would stand up for those who could not do it for themselves. She would always do what is right. "Your Imperial Majesty, I worshipped you. The idea of a matriarchy was inspiring, and I longed to see it. But my mother and father warned me. I defended you, wanting to believe you were good, a just ruler. But…look at you. All I see is an inhumane killer who hates men, little boys, her own son, simply for their gender. How is that any better than patriarchy?"

"Well, you are a fool for first thinking you can rule without violence and yes, I *hate* them. Every. Single. Man. All of them on this sphere would be dead if we did not need them for breeding!"

Her comment was so grotesquely honest, Xandra could not respond except to shake her head. She did not fight the guards that led her from the room, down the hall, toward the dungeons. She could not believe such a person full of so much hate existed.

Then it hit Xandra. She had majorly messed up. Xandra had come to rescue her family and failed, now on her way to being locked up and stuck in Lyft forever or until her death—and her cousin's and uncle's? Oh no. What would her parents do if the three of them did not return? How long would they wait without word to start an inter-sphere war?

As soon as she entered the poorly lit and damp dungeon area, she saw Uncle Cobalt, weary and filthy, his bright eyes eager. Thomas was up, his face in the bars smiling. "I knew you would come for us, Xandra!"

His eager expression made her stomach plummet. Guilt made her face flush. Her ever-perceptive uncle's face fell, and he plopped back on the dirt ground in defeat.

When they pushed her roughly into the cell next to them, yanking the chain and pouch from her neck that held the charged stone for her return trip to Fyr, Thomas groaned. She could not watch the transformation of his face, from hope to despair, so she stared at the ground.

The cell door locked without an ominous clank. Why could she not hold her tongue? Tongue. What a stupid thought. That poor child was losing his right now, and she failed to stop it.

"What happened?" Uncle Cobalt asked softly.

"I got upset about a servant boy who was going to get his tongue cut out for talking back to his aunt. He was Matthew's age."

Uncle Cobalt sighed. "It's not your fault, and this is not Thomas's either. She is unconscionable. You did right and stuck to the principles every Fyrian would. Both of you."

"Stop trying to protect me, father," Thomas growled. "I messed up. You told me as much. Xandra was our only ticket out of here. She messed up, just like me. And now we will die."

"I told you I was angry when I said that. I took it right back. The empress is to blame. And now our king will need to send soldiers for us. He'll raze Lyft to the ground. He thought…it matters not."

"What, Uncle? What does my father think?"

Her uncle sighed and met her gaze, his eyes saddened. "You already know your and Thomas's futures do not exist on Fyr. He thought sending me would ensure Thomas's safety. According to his and Mary's visions, I returned to Fyr." He said no more, but Xandra and Thomas's gaze met in full understanding that the two of them might not make it back.

"No." Xandra said. "I can get us out of this. I will figure it out."

"How?" Thomas asked, his tone impatient. "She is difficult, unpredictable."

Xandra took a deep breath in before whispering, "She is insane. I'm not exaggerating. She has lost her mind, likely long ago. I was fooled by the empress at first but figured her out—too late. Thomas, I apologize for not listening to you about her being a crazy man-hater. If I had, I could be pretending to agree with her, win her over, but I let the prince convince me…" Then something stuck a chord in her. Rochan. They had become friends, had a connection. He was amiable. How did someone so good come from such a horrid mother? Regardless, that goodness in him matched hers. He was the key. "The prince. He will help us." Surely, after such a fast connection he would not abandon her.

"He's powerless," Thomas fire back. "We're doomed."

"No." Uncle Cobalt said firmly. "Xandra, you remind me of your father when he was your age, well, he was a tad older. Facing certain death, believing your mother was dead, he was ready to fight till his last breath. This is not a physical war with the empress. It's a mental one. If the prince comes to visit you, do what you can to get his help."

Thomas was still defeated. "What can he possibly do,?"

"Anyone can do anything if they believe in themselves. I fear the prince needs help seeing that. If he can wrestle an ounce of power or favor with the empress or their people, he could garner our release."

"Yes, Uncle," Xandra said. "He has more powers than he lets on. The empress could not talk to the nagas—their serpent-like dragons—but he controlled them. He mentioned thinking he inherited their version of transporting—windwalking—and I offered to teach him. So, if I can get out of—"

The door burst open and slammed into the wall, metal reverberating off stone. No one had opened it, but it was enough to shock them into silence as wind blasted past them. Air magic.

Rochan entered with guards scurrying after him with all sorts of pleas about the empress. He gave Xandra a glare. Had she imagined the instant connection between them, a friendship forged simply from their few moments together? Would he help her? His face was stoic, his mouth tight, eyes bold and full of fury, but who was it directed toward? Her? His mother?

"Silence!" Rochan shouted at the guards. They were as taken aback as Xandra. This was out of character for the gentle boy she had met. "Get out."

They hesitated. "I do not have the keys to the cell, and you are stationed right outside the door. What can I possibly do? I merely crave a word with the Sapphirians, and then we are moving *her* as by the empress's own law of prisoner gender separation. You knew it was illegal to even put her in here. I will speak to them, move her myself, and I will deal with the empress's displeasure."

Move her?

The guards reluctantly withdrew, closing the door he had blasted open with his powers. He certainly was powerful.

"Why?" Rochan demanded.

She stood up, coming to the bars in earnest. "How could I not? There was a little boy. Your mother ordered his tongue cut out for talking back to his aunt, and that boy you helped who had the same fate, the one you made a scribe… I thought of him. I am sorry. You tried to warn me, tried to show me the truth. I knew what I was doing, my eyes were open. I could not let it go. I was raised better than that."

"Raised better? To insult your superiors? I do not understand your sphere if you think what you did would result in anything positive. The boy will still lose his tongue. Your family is still in prison, and now you are stuck here with them. *Why*, Princess?"

"Because where we come from, we believe in doing what is *right*, not what is easiest, not what is safest." Thomas berated from his cell.

Rochan's eyes darted to her cousin.

Xandra needed to draw his attention away from Thomas. "He is right. I could not let the boy lose his tongue without pointing out she was in the wrong. On Fyr, we fight for those who cannot fight for themselves, as a duty."

"But you're in prison." He shook his head, disappointed. "You cannot go against her. She is too strong."

"No one is above right and wrong," Xandra challenged, staring deep into his eyes, not blinking, not wavering. "Not even an empress."

They were silent. The prince's chest rose and fell, exposing his anxiety, energy, whatever he felt. She did not know for certain, not knowing him well.

"The princess is right," her uncle said quietly. "The empress may be everything here, but if anything happens to one of us, she will see the wrath of Fyr. My king, her father, is just and kind, but if his loved ones are harmed… He is the *Draca*, and our version of nagas that protect us royals will do his bidding, and our family can bring them here. He will tear the universe into pieces for his daughter, for me, for my son. I do not wish to see this. You must talk sense into her."

"Sense? That is not possible. You are under a misconception if you think I can do anything."

"You can speak to the draca—I mean, the serpents. The empress cannot. If you are not keeping the nagas peaceful, who is?" Xandra challenged him. "I saw it, Prince Rochan."

"In our world, in Water, and in Lyft before your mother took over, your emperors or empresses controlled the serpents. Rightful leaders control them.

They were chosen because they spoke to them." Thomas tried next, always using his rational thinking and endless pool of knowledge.

"Be quiet." Rochan's hands gripped the bars of Xandra's cell, his knuckles turning white. The pressure was too much for him.

She touched his hand gently, and his gaze darted to hers. He was torn, afraid. So afraid. Those eyes, those rich brown eyes, bore into hers. There was anger but there was something else. If she pushed, tried to be appealing, she had a feeling he could not deny her.

Quietly, Xandra asked, "Why did you come? Just to chastise me?"

"No." He pushed back off the bars. "Women aren't put in the dungeon by the empress's own law. They get locked in a prisoner room with a bed and washing chamber. I came to move you."

"But my uncle and cousin—"

"Go, Xandra," her uncle cut in. "Go. Figure out a way back to Fyr." His eyes bore into hers. He did not mean she should abandon them. He meant to find help, find a way for them to escape.

Xandra nodded to her uncle.

Rochan gazed at her from her boots, traversing her body, up to her face. "I'm turning my back for ten seconds before I call for the guards. I have a feeling a princess like you is 'equipped' in case I cannot protect her family." As promised, he turned his back.

Ten seconds. She had a dagger sheathed in both boots. She squatted down and removed the covered dagger from her left boot because she was likely to go for her right first. She slipped it to Thomas through the bars, and whispered, "Not allowed to search women, touch them, aside from cuffing and prodding along into the cell."

Her uncle took it from Thomas and slipped it into his boot. He gave her a nod, his blue eyes full of so many varying emotions, but she saw pride, love, and worry.

She kissed her cousin's hand through the bar and then her uncle's. "I will not leave you. I will find a way."

"Work on the prince," her uncle whispered as he leaned through the bars to kiss her forehead. "He needs a push is all."

"He likes you," Thomas whispered. "Use it to your advantage."

The first thing Xandra wanted to do was protest, but she would be stupid to rule out flirting. She had seen Tourmaline do it enough to copy it if she needed. There were many ways to fight, and manipulation came in handy. She would feel terrible using him, but this was life and death—for all three of them. Plus, although he seemed weak and soft, he came immediately to get her out of prison.

She had to be honest with herself. The moment the prince grabbed her after her arrival, there seemed to be some kind of connection between them. A magic connection or simply intrigue? Never having liked a boy before, she was not sure where the draw came from, that weirdly anxious but exciting feeling that pulled her toward him.

She told her family, "I *will* return."

"I know," her uncle said. He believed in her. Just as he always believed in her father. She could do this. She would. Or she would die trying. Perhaps that was why her future disappeared from the flames. She did not like putting her life in the hands of this powerless prince, but he was the only hope she had.

11

A PROPOSAL

Rochan walked briskly, ignoring the plethora of questions she had. He led her and the soldiers upstairs to the next level. It was a well-lit corridor with doors on each side, like an inn on Fyr, but these doors had a lock on the outside.

The guards opened the first door and prodded her in. Rochan followed and shut the door behind him.

"But my uncle and cousin, please. You must do something!" Xandra cried out as the door locked behind them.

"Enough." Rochan sliced his hand through the air. "You have caused enough trouble. And I will be in more for moving you. If you would please just listen instead of being so stubbornly headstrong, I can explain."

Xandra gave him an incredulous look, wanting to rebuke his comment, but plopped onto the bed. It would only prove him right if she protested. And she had not seen him assert himself this directly to anyone. Xandra felt slightly intimidated. but she'd listen and then give him a piece of her mind. After that, a long hot bath was on her list.

"I want you to enter the Empress Games," Rochan blurted out.

"Huh?" She shot up to a rigid sitting position as she processed the comment. "The games to *marry* you?"

He looked away. She could not read his face, determine his mood. Shame? Embarrassment? She had to take the lead with this conversation because he would not. The idea of weaker men who would let her do whatever she wanted had been palatable when she first arrived, but she liked Rochan. He was kind, and she'd be a liar if she did not admit he was attractive. Shockingly dark glossy hair, rich brown eyes under a strong brow, golden skin, with those sharp high cheekbones was all that was manly and appealing. But she wanted him to be stronger, free to make choices, speak his mind. That's what made her parents work so well: being partners. No one led the other.

And she was thinking way too much about being his partner. The awkward silence stretched out between them. He was not about to break it, let alone look at her, so she had to. "Why?"

His eyes darted to her face, her lips. Was he proposing this because he liked her? Or was he negotiating with her? She could not use him if he truly liked her. And yet, she wanted him to like her. Why? Did she like him? Ugh. She did not get along with her twin, but Tourmaline would help her figure out the feelings in her head that Xandra always had trouble understanding and labeling. She barely knew this boy—more of a man—but she wanted to help him.

Impulse struck, so she went for it. "Do you like me, Rochan?" She stood up, anxious for his response. Part of her wanted him to say yes and not just to ease her conscience if he would help free her family.

He would not look at her. "Men are not allowed to admit anything like that, not allowed to feel that way about women unless the women ask the men."

"I just asked you."

Rochan stared at the ground.

Frustrated, she transported with her fire right in front of him, making him jump and finally meet her gaze. "Close your eyes," she ordered.

"Why?"

"Close them." When he finally did after an annoyed eye roll, she continued. "Pretend you are on Fyr, free of here and your future is open. It is your own choice. You can say whatever you want without punishment—except threatening or hurting the royal family—my dad is a bit over protective…"

His lips quirked at her joke. She wondered what a genuine, full smile would look like on his face. She stared at him for a moment, her gaze lingering more than she wanted on the planes of his face, his chiseled jaw, so strong yet beautifully elegant. His black lashes were longer than hers and made him all the gentler. He was perfection: strength and softness. Realizing she was ogling him, she spoke again. "Now answer the question. Why do you want me to enter a competition to win your hand?"

"I…do not know." He breathed out. "I thought, if you could win or at least disrupt it enough, I could be free from this fate. I would help your cousin and uncle escape and if things went badly, and I am forced to marry another or my mother tries to kill me, maybe you could give me refuge on Fyr."

She was about to tell him her future did not exist there, but something he said clicked and her heart nervously picked up its pace. "Another?"

He opened his eyes. "Huh?"

"You said, 'marry another.' What if I do win, and your mother allows us to marry?"

"Doubtful." He laughed, his eyes dancing across everything in the room but her face.

She scowled. Getting answers from him was torture.

Then his nervous smile fell as he dared to peer at her and register her expression. "I mean my mother allowing it, not your abilities to win."

"What would you do though?"

He examined her, his brow adorably wrinkling. Cultural differences set aside, if he were interested, would he not simply hint to his feelings?

"Ugh. Rochan, on Fyr women do not do the prodding."

"Prodding?"

Xandra wanted to smack Rochan and kiss him simultaneously. This kind of boy would not need flirting and the falsities of court. He would love honest words. "Would you marry me if I won?"

His confusion gave way to understanding. "I can imagine a million worse fates than being shackled to you." Rochan smiled broadly, finally understanding what she had wanted to know. It was an awful compliment, but the meaning behind it and that smile were staggering. He liked her. She was starting to think the same about her own feelings.

Xandra leaned into him. He was taken aback, but after a moment, wrapped his arms around her. She felt his heart thudding madly in his chest. He was warm, safe. She looked up, knowing what might ensue, wanting it to happen. A curiosity within her swirling urges and her impulsive nature wanted more.

Her eyes met his, so dark and warm, but he hesitated. She tugged his neck to make their lips meet and closed her eyes. Then she wrapped her other arm around his back.

He cringed in her arms and gently pushed her away.

Xandra's stomach dropped. Her face burned with embarrassment, his rejection slicing through her heart.

Instantly, his eyes widened, and he gripped her shoulders. "Sorry. Sorry. Oh, Alexandra, please. I ruined that. I'm sorry. It's um…my back."

She felt like throwing up, and her head spun. "Back?"

He backed away and took up her hand. "It's injured. Please. May I kiss you properly? It was the best feeling of my life before you grabbed my back."

"I barely touched your back!" Why would her gentle touch hurt him so badly, enough to make him jerk away from her?

He was flustered about her question. "Seriously?"

She had to acknowledge kissing was more important than talking about his back. The moment was slipping away. "Kiss me but then explain after."

"So demanding," he breathed upon her lips with a grin and kissed her. She withheld the urge to wrap him up in her arms and squeeze him. His lips were soft and full, and they gently pressed hers. Too soon, she pulled away to see a small smile on those soft lips that made her heart flop and butterflies wreak havoc in her belly.

Her first kiss. Glorious. Oh, how she liked him.

They awkwardly stood there. He shifted his weight, shyly rubbing the back of his neck. Like her, he probably did not know what to do or say next.

She collected herself. "Your back?"

"Do not worry about it." His jaw clenched. He stared at the ceiling. His defensive stance. He did not want to tell her.

"I am already worried about it. What happened? The truth. We will be honest with each other if I'm to enter these games."

His gaze landed on hers, his brows raised in surprise by her mentioning entering them. Then he sighed. "I was punished by my mother for trying to protect your kin."

"And what was that punishment?"

"Five lashes of a whip. I've had worse. At least it was not her. She flogs until blood is drawn, so it was not as painful when the soldiers do it."

Xandra felt sick. Rochan was being abused mentally and physically, and he did not even realize it was not okay. He was downplaying it, making excuses that it was not bad. Her heart panged for him. She took up his hand. "Your mother is a monster. You do not deserve any of that. I will free you from her, Rochan. One way or another."

"So, you'll enter the games?"

"I want to." Xandra nodded, feeling oddly as if they had entered an engagement to get married instead. "No matter what, I'll overthrow her, or I leave here with my family and you."

Rochan kissed her forehead. "Thank you, Princess. I'm afraid to stay any longer. Can I come see you tomorrow?"

Xandra nodded, giddy at the thought of seeing him again. What happened to her warrior spine? The suppressed prince made it all mushy. She had to focus if she was to win these games.

When Rochan left, the guard locked the door. She let her fire magic zing around her to remind herself she was not technically imprisoned. She transported closer to him moments ago, so she could move in and out of this room, unlike the dungeons. If she just knew where Rochan's rooms were, she could pay him a visit unobserved, teach him windwalking so he could come to hers. The empress would be none the wiser.

Rochan had not commented on her ability to use fire in the room. He had moved her purposely. He knew her magic would work in these rooms. He was clever as well.

She must keep her ability to transport within her new prison a secret from the empress. She could not step out of line again. Rochan would be punished and that would break her heart.

12
BRIDES

Rochan was nervous. It was round one of these ludicrous games to auction him off.

He was to meet the contestants for the first time. To make it worse, his mothers insisted on being there, holding it in the empress's rarely used entertainment room, an intimidating room. One would watch him with loathing and the other with curiosity. He hoped Amma could control the empress. He prayed the empress would not react too harshly to Xandra's late entry. Xandra. *Xandra.* He would dare to call her that only in his mind; it made him feel closer to her. He had played their uninterrupted kiss over and over in his head last night, futilely trying to find answers in the ever-changing wind. He desperately wanted Xandra to win, to prevent a terrible future with someone horrible, but as the night and visions wore on, he wanted her to win so they had to marry. He was falling hard and fast for the Fyrian princess, and part of him did not want to hold back. He hoped she felt the same, and by kissing him, he believed she did, but his intense feelings made him question it. He wanted to feel everything—love, lust, companionship—everything he had been deprived of or told was wrong. It was a thirst he could not quench when it felt so addictively right and was suddenly possible.

He was not stupid. He knew Xandra's second and equally strong appeal and hold she had over him: freedom. Whether they ran away to Fyr or fought for Lyft, she represented his freedom. He hadn't realized his entire life all he needed was a moment, and reason to spark the fires of rebellion he had repressed for survival. He smiled to himself: fire. That was what she was: the spark metaphorically and literally.

The first contestant came out in a red dress. He had to at least pay attention and try to hide his disinterest. She was short and slender with pale skin. Some would say her oval face and dainty features were lovely, but Rochan had lost his ability to be unbiased. Her dark hair was missing the brown and red streaks that reminded him of fire, all brightness and darkness together. The girl's dark eyes did not pierce his soul like those steel-gray ones did.

He looked at his mothers. Amma was steadfast, keeping her expression blank, but lips upturned in a polite grin. The empress failed to hide her feelings and scowled slightly. She was not a fan, likely because the girl was elegant and not strong in appearance. He'd try to keep this girl in the games to spite her. Maybe, just maybe, the empress would dislike her more than Xandra.

The next girl was thick-waisted, brawny, and tall—a strong warrior, without much grace. She was tan and her face was plain but not wholly unattractive. The empress smiled. One of her favorites. He would find a way to get rid of her then. Anything to rankle the woman who beat her own child and found pleasure of cutting tongues out of little boys. He hadn't realized it was not normal until he saw Xandra's appalled and sympathetic expression when she found out he was beaten. The honest emotion on her face made her transparent. He could read her so well, just like he could the only people who loved him: Amma and Dev.

Then the girl plaguing his thoughts came out from behind the screen the girls were huddled behind and walked into the middle of the room. She wore a form-fitting purple dress. Rochan had no idea how Xandra had gotten it. He was too busy watching her slight curves move through the flowing fabric to note Amma's or the empress's expressions. He could not look away. Xandra had hidden her figure in loose fitting boyish clothes, and he felt almost betrayed at this discovery that she had breasts and hips. Neither were supple, but they spoke of grace and femininity. It made him feel things he had always been told were sinful, evil, dangerous. *Natural. Perfect.* That was how their kiss had felt. He was having normal feelings about a beautiful woman—and she was definitely a woman, one with subtle curves and lithe muscles. Strength and beauty—he did not know how one existed in such harmony with the other.

"What is this?" The empress cut through his severely distracted thoughts. He turned to look at her. She stood, glaring daggers at poor Xandra.

How could he look away for even a moment? He turned back, not wanting the empress to see his face because he could not hide how he felt.

Xandra did not flinch or cower. "I entered the contest, and my questionnaire scored high. If I become the next empress in waiting, I can free my family." It pierced him deeply to hear her say that, as if that was her only motive after such a wonderful kiss, after he admitted he liked her, liked the idea of marrying or running away to Fyr with her. He had opened up to her too much, too quickly, and now she acted as if it was a political move.

The empress shouted. "You cannot!"

He feared what his mother's anger would mean for Xandra. Amma met his gaze and winked. The dress. That had been Amma's doing. She always saw into his heart and now was helping him. He was grateful but worried about her and Xandra, the only two women who mattered to him.

"The questionnaire never expressed a rule that contestants had to be Lyftian," Xandra said, putting a hand on her hip. The action accentuated her curves.

Rochan was torn, looking between the empress and Xandra. The empress smirked. "But an heir to the throne of another sphere cannot rule here."

"I am no heir. My people insisted I must be left out of the line of succession. You planted the seed in my head, Empress, when you said, 'Why go back to where you are not wanted?'" Xandra crossed her arms and raised her brows. The motion made her chest look bigger. Her stormy eyes were more vibrant due to her confident expression.

He blinked to clear his mind of where her charms were leading it. Had his mother truly said that to Xandra? He would not put it past her. Did Xandra dare to fight back?

Ignoring Xandra's barb, the empress grabbed up the forms and read them over, talking to Amma in quiet tones. A bit louder Amma said, "She scored a one hundred percent on his questions. They are very compatible. I do not think you can kick her out."

How had Xandra scored a one hundred percent? He had wanted to coach her and give her the right answers, but the empress had him and Dev on naga duty to keep them in line after the incident the other day. Then the cutoff happened, leaving Xandra mere hours to complete the form. Had Udaya helped her when she procured a dress? Or had Xandra scored that on her own? If she had, she was the one for him. He found himself wishing and needing to know if it was her real score.

"It matters not. She'll never score well on a Lyftian intelligence test, and she looks hardly able to wield weapons in combat." The empress sat with a cocksure grin and waved to continue this awkward fashion show of women who would fight over him for the sphere.

Xandra was gone, and more girls who he hardly paid attention to came through one-by-one. He was worried. How could he discreetly tutor Xandra about Lyft and she retain the information in such a short span of time? How was she with combat? Her figure looked soft, supple in some areas but athletic in others. If she was agile, she might do well. He had to help her or come up with some backup plan. He would not lose her, and he would not marry another.

Not after seeing her in that dress. Not after that kiss.

He just hoped that the empress did not have plans to eliminate her from the games…or worse.

As soon as the empress entered the throne room to deal with her council who were in discord, Rochan made a move toward her quarters. The whispers the servants brought him were about their dislike of the Fyrians being kept prisoners and the threat the princess had apparently given the empress in front of others: her father would come with dragons.

What a woman.

Focus. He knocked on the door to the empress's quarters. A guard opened the door from within. He stepped aside once he noted who it was. They never did that when the empress was in the room, a much needed hint for him as a child to know whom he'd face when he entered his mothers' quarters.

"Amma." He rushed in.

She jumped off the couch as the guard closed the door. "Rochan, my sweet boy." She pulled him in for a tight hug. When she let go, she ran her hand through his hair, and touched his cheek, her eyes soaking him up. Love, pure maternal love, he only was able to get in these moments of stolen time away from the empress.

"Amma, thank you."

"For what?"

"The dress. For helping the princess with the questionnaire. For appeasing the empress when it comes to my right to choose my wife in these ridiculous games."

"Ishan," Amma commanded.

The guard turned to her. "Yes, Your Imperial Consort?"

"Make sure no one overhears us."

He nodded and headed outside to call off the other guards and watch outside.

Once the door was closed, Rochan laughed dryly. "Ishan?" He was astounded. "You gave him a name?"

Amma gave him a stern look. "No. He chose his name. Apparently from a book he somehow got ahold of and mysteriously could read. How did he learn how to read, I wonder?" Udaya smiled widely. When she did, he saw himself in her because she looked so much like Dev. On another sphere, Dev would be allowed to act like his father. On Lyft, he was a servant, a means to an end.

"No comment."

"Be careful, my boy."

"I always am."

Udaya gazed at him as if she knew his every thought, then sat down, and patted the cushion next to her.

He sat.

"Rochan, I can tell, and if I can see it between you two, your mother will catch on. She'll react. You must hide your heart."

"Amma, what?"

Udaya sighed and patted his hand. "You only have eyes for her. She only has eyes for you. I sent her the form to enter the games. Well, a seamstress too—that is all. She ended up with a perfect score without my help. A sign from the gods of wind, and maybe those of fire, that she is the one for you. I risked it because I want you to be happy."

Rochan's heart thudded in his chest upon hearing the words. Was it true? Xandra suited him in interests and beliefs? He trusted Amma in everything.

"Be careful, my prince. Take things slowly, hide everything, and you must ensure the Sapphirians' freedom foremost. We do not need the Draca coming for us."

"The Draca?"

Udaya sighed heavily. "Princess Alexandra is named after her father, King Alexander Sapphirian. He inherited a sphere full of turmoil. Your grandmother took advantage of the situation when the king had been cursed to sever all ties to other spheres. Your mother sent people for intelligence, so we'd know the situation. The fact she has his name shows her importance. He did not give his name to his first born or, from the sound of it, the first few children. He chose this child, marked her as a favorite. The Fyrians of late love hard and will fight hard to keep it. We stand no chance if anything happens to the princess."

Rochan cringed at the very thought.

Udaya gave him a sad smile. "Yes, you must do all you can to protect the princess. I will do all I can to protect you."

Rochan looked away, ashamed he could not spare Amma the shame of the abuse the empress put them both through. He hoped her battle was only mental and not physical as well, like his was.

"Amma—"

"This is the rest of your life. Trust me, do whatever it takes to be happy. Think of no one but yourself." Her eyes stared into his. "I once gave this advice to your mother. I gave her a way out. I was foolish, in love, overprotective. I did not think she'd kill him. I thought she would keep him at bay with it, the weapon, until she was ready to do her duty." Udaya sobbed, covering her mouth.

Rochan had heard the rumors, the tales of his mother's murderous wedding night. When she was forced to marry an unkind man and took over her own destiny through murder.

Although knowing his Amma was complicit in the crime broke his heart, he could not blame her for anything. "So, Dev stepped in because she needed a serpent whisperer child?"

"You know this already. The version I told you as a boy is the truth. Nakano and I wanted the closest thing to our own child we could create. She had to bear you as evidence you were the heir. Dev did his duty for us to have you." She touched his cheek then stood up and walked to the window. "I do not know how much longer I can hold sway over her. When a relationship becomes predictably monotonous, it's hard. When it crumbles even more from the hatred inside someone that cannot be removed, a hatred that runs deeper than love… What do we do, Rochan?"

"I do not know."

"I have had only one thought every single day since you were born: do what I must to keep you alive. That's all."

Rochan could not help himself. He crossed over and pulled his Amma into his arms to give her a crushingly long hug that made her laugh, although halfheartedly.

Ishan—apparently—entered. "She comes and is angry."

"Go out the servant's entrance my sweet boy. Now."

Rochan knew better than to get on the wrong side of the empress. It would mean pain for his Amma, something he could not deal with, and the empress used too often to keep him in line. *"Obey, or Amma will pay the price."*

As he reached the safety of his room, he crashed onto his bed worried about how much he wanted the princess versus what having her might cost Dev and Udaya.

He had a sinking feeling that they all would die if he did not tread carefully.

13
A TEST

Xandra was too tempting, sprawled across Rochan's bed on her stomach, studying his books. He kept his hands and lips to himself because time was of the essence. He could not waste their precious time and regret it later when she lost the games and he… No, he would not think about having to marry another girl. He wanted Xandra. The problem was how could he choose between her and Lyft? He said he'd escape with her if it meant their deaths, but the thought of leaving Dev, Amma, and his people under the Empress's hateful reign filled him with guilt. It was a coward's way out, running away.

Rochan was not a coward.

"Well, how am I doing?" She asked, those gray eyes met his and made his spine tingle and his stomach drop with nerves.

"Your general knowledge is superb. But…" He scooted off the bed and crossed over to his bookshelf. "Your current affairs are lacking." He handed her a book that bound together the most important news articles over the last two decades.

Xandra frowned.

Rochan grinned at her adorable pout. "It's not an insult. How would you hear any news in Fyr after my mother stopped sending any ambassadors?"

"I need a break. My brain hurts."

"We cannot waste time."

"Then let's use it wisely."

At first, Rochan thought she was alluding to kissing, but her tone was not coy. Then he felt ridiculous for thinking it. His mind went to what the empress had said of men and their blinding lust, suddenly feeling unclean, unworthy of Xandra. He pushed the thought away. Everything about Xandra was pure, wonderful, beautiful. If she felt the same urges as him, it had to be natural and good—far from vile. It showed him one of the many lies the empress had told him. Women felt the same as men. There was nothing wrong with wanting to kiss, to hold, to touch someone if it came from love. It was becoming clear he did, in fact, love her, but it was much too soon to admit such things aloud.

Instead of bursting out with his feelings, he touched her head gently, the cool metal of her circlet a reminder of her power. He stopped his hand on her shoulder although his mind wanted his hand to travel down her body. "What do you have in mind?"

She smiled, sitting up, taking his hand off her shoulder and holding it in hers. "If I teach you how I transport, we might be able to figure out if you can windwalk."

He was up and off the bed, pulling her up with too much exuberance. Xandra teetered into his arms, looking up at him. "Deal." She pushed up on her toes.

An invitation. He kissed her but pulled away before he got lost in those lips.

"Sorry." She shook her head. "Focus. Okay, to transport, I imagine where I want to be. You must have a clear picture of it, but maps can work too. The more precise, the better. So, I'm thinking about the roof directly above us. Then I let my magic curl out around me and—" fire came out of her and instinctually Rochan pulled away. "It will not hurt you, Rochan. I can control that. It let it build until I encircle all of me, then you."

Rochan tried not to panic as a weird tingling sensation covered him head to toe. Flames engulfed him, but with no heat. "Then I give a little push with my magic, all while thinking of where I'm headed."

When the fire snaked up to his face, he closed his eyes. He felt breathless, weightless, and a subtle squeezing pressure.

Her hands touched his face, along with the cool breeze of evening air.

"Open your eyes, Rochan."

He did and they were indeed on the roof. He could not subdue his smile.

"Now, I did it slowly so you could see," she said. "It used to take me longer, but once I learned, it came in a split second."

His brow furrowed. "No matter the distance?"

"No matter the distance. When we have idle time, I'll tell you the story of how my father transported repeatedly to all his forts to bring his soldiers to defend the palace during the war, but really it was my mum who tamed the draca that turned the tides."

"I would love to hear about it all one day, but first I want to windwalk."

He tried releasing his power slowly, but it was strong. It pushed Xandra back a little. She stepped away to let him try again. He was able to keep his wind magic close, but its power had always been "too strong" according to the empress. He closed his eyes, imagining his room below and tried to let the magic encircle him. He accidentally made a wind tunnel that started to lift him off the ground, so he pulled the magic back in.

He hated failing. Even more so in front of a girl he desperately wanted to impress.

He tried a couple more times to the same effect, his confidence dwindling lower with each. He shook his head. "Maybe I cannot." He was embarrassed to show his weakness.

"Maybe you are trying too hard. I can tell you're getting frustrated."

"That is not helpful," he told her exasperated.

"Relax. You push out your magic very forcefully. Why?"

Rochan had to think about why he had little control over its power. "How much were you allowed to practice your magic and when did it start?"

Her face scrunched up in confusion at his change in topic rather than answering her question. "Five, and I had to practice nonstop because the maturity of a five-year-old and fire is not a god combo. Two of my brothers started fires way too many times, and my sister, my twin, she lit our tutor's clothes on fire because she has a temper."

"Twin? Oh, my gods, there's another one of you out there?" He was not sure if the idea was tantalizing or terrifying.

She rolled her eyes and crossed her arms. "Not identical, polar opposites in disposition and looks. She looks like my mum, and I look like my dad—but swap the eye color. Wasting time." She gave him a pert look.

"I was not allowed to use my powers—not in front of the empress. She gets mad when I do, and as you have seen, she inflicts harsh punishments." He could not meet Xandra's gaze in case she realized servant boys were not the only ones the empress enjoyed torturing.

Xandra's eyes met his as she shook her head.

"Do not do that." He snapped.

"What?" Her shock made those gray eyes framed in those thick black lashes even more captivating. He imagined surprising her in a much better way to gain a similar expression.

"Pity me."

Xandra came over to him and took up his hands. "I do not. I was shaking my head at how foolish I had been. I come from a sphere that fights for equality between women and men. My parents have made so many strides, I've been told and have seen for myself, but I want to be a warrior, a fighter. I was allowed to train, but the court frowns upon marriageable women wearing pants, not wanting to be pleasing and pretty, for dabbling in swordplay. You can see how this sphere intrigued me, why I had studied it so earnestly."

Rochan fastened a flyaway strand of hair behind her ear. "You do fit in well here, except for…" He ran his fingers down her neck to her collarbone, not daring to go farther when his lower palm brushed against the fabric over the start of the flesh of her breast. He dared to leave it there since she did not object. He cleared his throat, for it had gotten tight from so many conflicting emotions. "…your heart. It is full of empathy, not a trait of a warrior here."

She nodded, taking his hand off her chest and squeezing it. "I idolized your mother. But I learned I had only idolized the idea of a woman in power, even though my father had warned me that he worried how she maintained a matriarchy. He guessed violence."

"He is a smart man." Rochan said.

"He is." She sighed. "And he was the one who taught me how to control my fire when I had been scared of it. I'm going to do for you what he did for me. Close your eyes."

Rochan obeyed. Her arms curled around him, hugging him to her.

"Calm yourself down. Do not try, do not think, just feel. Let your power seep out. Do not push. Let it curl around you and me in a protective way, not combative, not defensive."

Rochan took three deep breaths, calming himself. He thought of protecting Xandra. He could not do something stupid like blast her off the rooftop. He let his magic seep out of him. like he did when practicing wind exercises. He imagined the graceful moves, and as he always did when performing the exercise, he let the wind envelop him and held himself in a cocoon of his own power. Then he pictured himself below, at the foot of his bed and felt that strange squeezing sensation before he opened his eyes…inside his bedroom!

Xandra appeared in front of him in a ball of fire. "Well done!" She pulled him into a hug, laughing with excitement.

He beamed as she praised how long it took her and how fast he got it. When she started to pull away, he tensed and held onto her, wanting to feel her warmth against his body. He touched her cheeks.

Xandra did not object, those eyes probing into his. "How did you do it? What did you think about? Because, whatever it was, use that every time."

"Wind exercises. I do them in the courtyard to center myself, connect my mind and body to my power. They help with the balance needed for fighting and health, and it helps me use up pent up magic without the empress noticing the strength I hide."

"I saw you doing them. It's beautiful to watch. Will you teach me?"

If only he could. He was afraid she'd be taken away from him without ever seeing her again, back to Fyr with her treaty if the empress would even let her live. The idea of losing her forever chilled him to the bone.

"Your smile," she said, frowning. "I rarely see it, but it transforms you."

Deeply moved and unable to tell her she was the one who made him smile, he chose action. Rochan leaned down and kissed her gently, an innocent kiss just to feel their connection. "If you win, if you stay, you and I will teach each other many things."

"Or if you must flee with me, the same." She kissed him gently.

He could not admit to her he was not going to leave his people behind. He did not like lying to her, but hopefully, she would never know. He was desperate for her to win his hand, which meant they needed her to win the games.

"Time to study."

"No, you windwalk us up to the roof first and back for practice. Then, I will study."

She made good on that promise. After she left to go to bed, he practiced windwalking until he was exhausted. He had to, for it would be the only way he could sleep.

Still, he tossed and turned.

Rochan was beyond frazzled. He tried to hide it, but could not, his hands shaking. Ansh brought him chamomile tea to calm him. It made him a tad drowsy as did the quiz. They were well into the third round of questions. A woman of his mother's cabinet who had superb enunciation was hosting the trivia round, a Lady Diamond-Serpentine. She asked each girl questions off cards picked at random. Xandra held her own so far. Her knowledge of history, political policies, culture, and geography were outstanding, and she was safe in second place, far from being cut.

Most of the girls who made it through to this round varied in looks. He had cut three girls from the "decorum" round—which was really a beauty contest— but did not dare cut the empress's favorites. He suspected the favorites' high scores on the form were not true. Typical of her. He'd find out soon enough after getting to know some of them,

Feeling bad about rejecting anyone, he chose objectively. He cut girls who lacked imperial decorum. He cut a girl who was clumsy and had no elegance, another who looked as if she never walked in heels before, and a third who had no female curves and a top lip hairier than his own. He felt oddly inferior with his lack of dense facial hair.

In this round, the empress's warrior-type women were struggling with their knowledge the most, followed by the girls who—if Rochan could be unbiased— were deemed beauties. Not everyone can have it all, but he hoped Xandra was one of the exceptions. Girls were cut after three wrong answers and/or the lowest points at the end of each round. Xandra only had one wrong answer so far, but the dwindling group of girls worried him. He had agreed to this, putting brains above all else, making this an aggressive round.

Xandra's incorrect answer about an actress in a contemporary Lyftian play, in the first round, peaked his anxiety. After that, it ebbed away as she got every answer right. It had made the empress's initial smile from round one shift to a grim line in the second, and a frown after the third.

Not good.

As the fourth and final round began, a tired Rochan dared to hope. There were five girls left. As second, by a big sum over the other three girls behind the two leaders, she just had to not get two more wrong.

The empress had intermittently watched him, but he kept his face stoic and eyes trained on whoever was being quizzed. He did not dare share a secret glance to Xandra and hoped she was focused enough not to as well. He had to act aloof, disinterested, because if the empress found out he had a preference, she would eliminate it. She wanted nothing but his misery.

The empress stood and walked over to Lady Diamond-Serpentine who was asking the questions. She shuffled the question cards while she spoke. "As this is an important round, I'll ask the questions…at random. Thinking on your toes is a good test of a strong empress."

There were murmurs among the ladies who were watching, mostly curious at the exciting new development. Lady Diamond-Serpentine was tolerated by the empress but not beloved. First, she was attracted to men over women; adding on her husband's "Diamond" name in front of her own was a cutting move toward the ruler's views. Why the empress included her in the government was a mystery, but the lady and her husband were extraordinarily smart and clever. His mother needed this pair.

Rochan peered back at Udaya. Her eyes were wide, her mouth frowning. Not good at all.

"Who was referred to as the Emerald Emperor? Let's see, Sashani."

Of course, the elegant beauty the empress favored for her looks got an easy question, one Xandra would know. This was not going to pan out well. The empress would ask her the hardest one. She was going to lose. The empress would make sure of it.

"Emperor Kabir Emerald the third."

"Very good," the empress purred, a smile actually crossing her face.

"What year was the Treaty of the Spheres signed? Since this involves your sphere as well, Princess Alexandra, you can answer it."

Rochan's heart hammered in his chest. They had not studied this.

Xandra appeared calm, her face devoid of any emotion. "1895," she said without hesitation.

Rochan let out a relieved breath. The reforming of the treaty likely mentioned reinstating the 1895 draft or perhaps she knew.

The empress's mouth went tight. "Can you name the exact date?"

"What?" Xandra asked shocked to have a follow up question.

The crowd of ladies murmured, the tone shocked at the unfairness of the empress's behavior. Rochan's stomach turned sour. Would the woman stop at nothing to get rid of Xandra? To make him miserable? In doing this, would the empress lose the favor of the court, the people? What might happen to him and Udaya if she was usurped?

"Exact date?" She smiled smugly at Xandra, like a spider who caught a fly in her web.

"Your Imperial Majesty," Lady Diamond-Serpentine spoke, "that is not what the card says. The ladies of the court made these questions." There was more murmuring. The lady spoke it on purpose so all would know the empress was cheating the games. The fact she did so proved she was someone to side with if things went astray.

He could not trust her. He could trust no one but Xandra, Dev, and…no, he could not fully trust Udaya either. She loved a monster.

The empress glared at Lady Diamond-Serpentine.

The lady withstood her glare with raised brows and crossed arms.

His mother commanded, "I make up the rules to this game."

"It's not fair!" someone dared to call out in the small crowd.

The empress whirled around, her eyes like daggers, her fists clenched as she fruitlessly looked for the dissenter. The murmuring was rising. Amma stood up, put her hands out for quiet, but they were not listening. If it continued, Rochan could envision them rioting. Amma went up to the empress and whispered to her. The empress's face lost its anger, and she scanned the unhappy crowd.

Amma turned and raised her voice. "Silence. To be fair, the Princess can opt to answer a follow up question for more points—as will every girl this round. We will come back to Sashani in a moment."

"Princess?" Amma asked, taking the cards from the empress.

"I would like to answer."

Was she crazy? Rochan did not even remember the exact date.

"October 12th."

Rochan was not sure if that was correct—he knew the month was—until the Empress's face distorted into an enraged grimace. Then she stormed out of the room, the guards opening and closing the doors with her departure.

During her dramatic exit, Udaya said quietly, "That puts the princess in the lead."

Loud murmurs of discord erupted. Udaya spun around and demanded silence.

They finally settled down into whispers.

Udaya cleared her throat. "I will be asking the questions and ensuring the fairness of the round. The prince deserves to gain the hand of the *worthiest* candidate, not one hand-picked by the empress."

Rochan was torn. Udaya would pay for that later, although he was grateful that the empress could not get rid of Xandra unfairly. Udaya asked Sashani a follow up question, that she got wrong. Then the other girls had their turn for questions and follow up questions.

The next question that Udaya asked Xandra—sticking to the order that was now established involved fashion. "What designer created the Empress's wedding dress for both her weddings?"

Rochan swore under his breath. He had not told her any fashion questions, and Lyftian society was passionate about it. Xandra in her boots and pants, most likely was not a fashion expert. How stupid of him. This was an easy question but not for Xandra.

Xandra stared at her clasped hands. "I do not know."

Guilt washed over Rochan. He should've taught her these things about Lyft instead of learning to windwalk. Sashani got hers wrong in the last two rounds. She was out and that pleased Rochan. One of the empress's favorites. It felt like a minor victory, a barb thrown at her.

With the four girls left, Xandra was clinging to second place. In first place was a muscular warrior, Lin. But she got a literature question wrong, one he was unsure Xandra would've known.

It was the last question, the determiner whether Xandra would be cut or possibly pull into first place. Rochan's pulse was skyrocketing. His life, his future, everything he wanted could slip from his grasp.

"What is considered the oldest martial art in all of the spheres?"

Lin cracked a smile, thinking Xandra would not know.

They had not studied much with fighting styles because she had insisted she was fine with that and wanted hands-on training not all the theory and terms behind it.

Xandra's eyes met his, and the twinkle in them gave him relief. She knew. "Kalaripayattu."

All the tension, doubt, and anxiety left Rochan immediately. The follow-up question did not matter. They were not ones to kick anyone out, just point boosters or dockers as Udaya had decided as soon as the empress changed the rules.

"Would you like the follow up? You are now only ten points behind Lin. Getting this right would allow you to win this round but getting it wrong would solidify second place."

Knowing her personality, Xandra would've gone for it no matter what, but at this point she had nothing to lose. She smiled and said she'd take it.

"Where and when was this style of fighting invented?"

That was a double question. He knew Udaya was making it hard because all of this would be reported to the empress, and she had to make it look like she was giving Xandra a hard time to please his mother—or to avoid a terrible punishment.

Xandra was beaming at Rochan now. She knew! "The Earth sphere, on a continent called Asia, in a country called India. It was the 4th century."

An answer that precise made every woman in the room erupt in whispers and gasps. And since the follow up questions had been fabricated in the moment, not on the cards, the empress had destroyed any chance of denying the win by proclaiming Xandra somehow cheated.

Udaya announced her as the winner. She smiled and bowed her head at Udaya politely.

He was beyond proud of her. He knew she was clever, but not this intelligent and well-studied. She would make a great empress. Even his mother could not deny that, if Xandra won every round. The court would revolt if she did not. Xandra had the personality, the beauty, and the brains. The question was, did she have the brawn?

There were only four girls left: Xandra, Lin, another warrior type, Balan, and a lithe girl with large eyes, Ahana. That meant two rounds of combat and a date outing between them to win. Xandra needed to practice to keep her head attached to her body. Two other lives depended upon her keeping hers.

And his future happiness.

14
LOVE

Rochan hurried to his mothers' quarters before his courage failed him. He needed the empress to know she could not tamper with his games, but he needed to be careful not to anger her and bait her into cheating. She could do something to make Xandra lose, or worse. He feared for Xandra's life. The empress was not of sound mind, had no conscience or care for consequences. Her impulses would not be deterred or regretted, even if they started a war of the spheres.

She had killed her husband on her wedding night. The former empress, his grandmother, mysteriously died, and it had not been investigated. No one would challenge the empress.

It was time someone did.

He stopped at the double doors and took a deep breath, staring at the ornately carved pair of nagas on the door. The words in the language of ancients ran across the top in an arc above them: the one who speaks to nagas speaks for all.

But the empress did not. Udaya could somewhat, but the nagas listened to him, Rochan. He inherited the gift from Dev, which was one of the reasons the empress chose him to father her son. Dev was extraordinarily powerful, but his concern for his sister's welfare kept him in line. Otherwise, the empress ignored his existence. She must've despised giving her body over to a man to create her child. She blamed him for Rochan's gender. Blamed Rochan for destroying her womb in his difficult birth despite him not having a say in it.

His mother should have married Dev, given him a semblance of power and honor for fathering her child. He spoke to the naga. And these rooms should become Rochan's, according to the saying on the door. He should be speaking for all—for *men* and women, his people. The empress should've just been a placeholder for him to reign. She could control nothing.

He wondered what would happen if he, Dev, Udaya, and others who could master the talent just stopped controlling the naga. Many would die, but the people would revolt against a weak empress who had no ordained power.

No. No. He did not want blood on his hands. There had to be another way.

He opened the door a crack but stopped when no guard opened it fully for him. His mothers were alone, unguarded.

He froze. He should leave because they might be having an *alone* moment.

Their voices made his feet unable to move.

Udaya said in a soft tone, "My love, you must not push back against the boy. He is of that age and if he is to be in power alongside his wife, he needs to have some kind of say."

"If he chooses wisely, he will need not rule." The empress's voice was gentle. He rarely heard it that soft. Memories of hearing her sing to him and use that tone of voice came back to him. When he was six years old, he had been sick with the speckled fever. They had been told he might die. That was one of the only moments he recalled the empress acting like his mother. Her only legacy, her future rule—despite her hate of his gender—had been on the line. She had cared about that. The sentiment left not long after, and her hate grew stronger than her obsession with carrying on her bloodline. As soon as he started leaving boyhood for manhood—pure hate.

Udaya propelled him out of his memories back to the present. "I meant how you treat me, my love. You listen to me and let me have my way to a point. Does he not deserve that?"

The empress laughed. "Because you manipulate me, little minx, with that beauty and promises of love."

He heard a kiss. He really should leave. It was such a private moment, but his feet would not budge.

"My love, please do not hurt my boy. I love him like he is my own."

The empress sighed. "Once he has a wife, he is no threat to me."

"He is no threat now. If you were only a tad kinder, he could love you. If you stopped those horrible beatings—"

"Udaya, I am his mother. I must do what he deserves for disappointing me."

Udaya sighed. "I do not understand how you love me but have no room for anyone else."

"Because you fill up my heart, little minx. I have no room for anyone else. Do you remember that day in the gardens under the cherry blossoms?"

"Which time?"

The empress laughed. "The first time."

"When you kissed me and told me you loved me? How could I ever forget?"

"What else did I tell you?"

"That you would do what was necessary for us to be together."

"And I have."

"I did not expect you to go so far. The katar was to threaten him, take control of the situation, not kill him. And then your mother too?"

The empress huffed. "I told you. I did not poison her. The attempt was on me. I was lucky I did not drink the tea."

"I'm not sure I ever believed that, Nakano. And now the state of Lyft where the prince does not have power, men punished for what? You've never told me what made you hate them so very much."

"You know what I wonder time and time again? Why you defend them." Her voice lost its loving tone.

There was slight movement inside which almost made Rochan flee, but he had to know. Why did she hate him, her own flesh and blood?

The empress huffed out a breath. "I was not happy with you stopping me in the games. I could've gotten rid of the Fyrian princess. Sent her on her way home with her stupid family. Now, I have to keep them imprisoned as leverage over her to keep her in line. If forced, I'll hold their lives over her head. She cannot win." Her tone was softer again, the topic shifting away from men and hate.

"Why? Nakano, you heard how the court noticed your bias. They were not happy, and we must keep them content. My love, I want Rochan to be happy. If this princess wins every round, she will be the best suited for him. It also means she would make a great empress and wife to him." That pleading voice usually got the empress to comply.

But not when it was about him. "Why do you defend him? Why do you defend any man?"

"Because I love some of them. Not like that, Nakano, so get that adorable pout off your face. I love Rochan, and I love Dev. There are many types of love, and you are missing out on that. The love of a family."

"I only need you, Udaya. That is all I want."

Rochan swallowed hard. He felt sick to his stomach. To hear the empress speak such tender things, to show she was capable of love, felt like a knife to his gut. He had thought she was completely incapable, but she truly cared for Udaya. It made sense, or why else would Udaya have married her? But it stung to know she could love no one else, that she did not love the child she bore. He felt like a waste of space. Worthless. A disgrace.

"Is the door open?" the empress suddenly asked.

Oh, no. There was nowhere to hide and if he ran, she would see him. He'd be thoroughly punished. He panicked.

The air around him tickled his flesh and then it enveloped him, pressing hard against him, squeezing. He closed his eyes as he heard footsteps approaching the door.

When he opened them, he was in his room, scaring his servant half to death.

He had just windwalked. It felt great to escape her, to leave her ignorant of his powers. He imagined her searching the hall and coming up with nothing.

Rochan would show the empress he was worthy of love, that she was missing out due to her lack of pride in him. He would pay her back for all she had done to him.

Tonight, he would rebel.

Tonight, Rochan would act for his people, no matter the cost.

First, he would spar with Dev while his mothers were too busy to eavesdrop. He was the only person Rochan could fully trust.

Rochan had a plan. And a reason to act.

Rochan waited for the empress to throw a fit. It happened the last time Xandra had gotten through the "decorum" round. Predictably, the wind picked up so strong that it shook the palace windows. He looked outside and saw the cyclone coming. She was out of control.

It was perfect. Not for the people who might be killed from her hissy fit, but it gave him an opportunity to prevent something much worse.

Immediately, he windwalked to Dev's rooms. His father nodded to confirm he had been successful. Perfect. He went to take up Dev's hand to windwalk him to collect Xandra.

"No need." Dev cracked a grin. "Where do you think you inherited that power from as well as controlling the naga? I'm just too smart to get caught using it."

Rochan smiled despite how nervous he was about this large act of defiance.

"I can do this myself. There's no need for you to risk this," Dev told him. He gripped the back of Rochan's neck and squeezed it in a loving gesture. Dev had said the same when they sparred earlier. Dev had told him the council had already secretly asked him and Udaya to do something about the prisoners. Dev was waiting for Rochan to act. He—as always—sought to teach and protect Rochan.

Rochan sighed at the idea of backing down and letting Dev do it for him. He could not let everyone do things for him. He had to prove himself to the council but more so himself. "No, the council needs to know I am strong and willing to put things right. I will need them."

Dev nodded. "I am proud of you, Rochan. I never got to be what I wish I could have to you, a real father, but I did what I could. Know that I am proud of you, and that I love you."

Rochan's heart sang, especially after hearing his mother felt the opposite. But as Dev hugged him and then touched his cheek as if to memorize Rochan's face, his worry increased. It was as if Dev was saying these things before he could not, as if he were saying goodbye. The man could see the future. What were they walking into?

"You *are* my father. I love you too, Dev."

Dev smiled.

"But, what did you foresee? Will something—"

His smile fell. "No time, Rochan. Let's go get your girl. Let us put everything right with Fyr that we can tonight."

They windwalked into her room, making Xandra jump a little despite expecting them during the storm.

Rochan drank in the sight of her. "Ready?"

She nodded stoically; her hair was braided back away from her face, revealing adorable little ears he hadn't seen before. She did not wear her circlet for once. It made her look more attainable, approachable—just a regular girl.

"On the count of three," Dev commanded.

Rochan took a deep breath and windwalked at three, envisioning right outside the entrance to the dungeon. The rock inside was made of alumina bricks which prevented magic use, blocking some elemental powers—including fire and air. This was as close as they could get using powers.

The guard was startled and went to withdraw his sword. Dev pulled his scarf over his mouth and nose, then deftly threw a small pouch at his face, hitting the guard square in the nose before it bounced to the ground. The man blinked twice. His powdery white nose twitched. Sleeping powder. Rochan pulled his collar over his nose and mouth, and he lunged down and retrieved the now unconscious guard's keys as Dev gently lowered the man to the ground. He threw them ahead to Xandra who had appeared behind the guard at the door. She unlocked the door as Rochan joined her, his blade drawn, hoping he did not need to harm the soldiers within. In the prison, the Sapphirians were up, wide-eyed in surprise, clutching the bars. Rochan blocked the swinging blade of a guard who then dropped it to the ground, his hands up. "Sorry, Your Imperial Highness."

Rochan stopped in shock. The man should not call him that. He should not drop his weapon in the prince's audience. And he should not be going down on his knees now as if Rochan was asking him for fealty.

Xandra was already by the cells her hands shaking as she tried key after key. Dev had dragged the outer guard inside and shut the dungeon's door, locking it from the inside.

"Pick up your blade, man," Rochan ordered. "Get up."

"Your Highness?" he questioned as he followed orders.

"You cannot be seen as assisting me. It will be your death."

Dev held out a pouch between his fingers. "Sleeping draught."

The soldier nodded. Dev threw it and they covered their faces as the powder made impact. Rochan caught the soldier as he fell and placed him down gently. He would find this man once everything was finished, since he had been instantly loyal to him.

The Sapphirians were out of the cell. He grabbed Xandra's hand, giving her the two necklace pouches Dev had procured. "I will meet you in the travel room."

Xandra's brow wrinkled. "What are you—"

"You're wasting time," Dev growled. "I will meet you right outside it. Go."

With a torn expression, she unlocked the door, and the Sapphirians filed out vanishing as balls of fire as soon as they made it past the dungeon's magic-suppressing power.

"You were supposed to go with her, Rochan."

Dev squatted down to the guard, looking for something on his belt.

"I will, with you."

Dev looked up to Rochan, his rich brown eyes full of concern. He stood, shackles in his hands. He hooked them to the chain on the wall as he spoke. "You must go. I knew what I was doing, Rochan, the consequences. It will be for nothing if you get caught."

Rochan did not understand until it literally clicked. The shackles, around Dev's wrist.

"What are you doing?" Rochan grabbed his hand to stop him clicking the other one.

"Someone will pay for the empress losing the Sapphirians. You wish it to be these men? You? Udaya? Your princess? I see how much you love the girl. I want your happiness and your freedom more than anything. Trust in her. She is your freedom. She is your future."

Rochan shook his head, feeling very much like he was choosing his father's doom to attain his future.

"Rochan, you must go. I need you to do it, for Udaya. You must free my sister from the empress too. Free everyone. Rochan, go now. Do not think. If you do not listen to me, I shall never forgive you in this life or the next."

His words shocked Rochan so much, his grip on Dev slipped which allowed the man, his father, to click the other shackle in place.

"You and the princess were never here. I did it all. I was saving Lyft from the wrath of Fyr."

"Father," Rochan said in merely a whisper.

Commotion down the hall told him he had seconds to get out alive. Torn, Rochan gave one last glance to Dev and slipped into the hallway, leaving the door open.

"Son," Rochan heard whispered on the breeze as he vanished to the traveling room. The word was full of love and pride. Rochan wanted to break down and cry, but the Sapphirians were not safe yet.

But they would be.

For Dev.

15
A FEEDING

In the travel room, Uncle Cobalt pressed the stone pouch into Xandra's hand. "You and Thomas go back. Your father would never forgive me for leaving you behind."

"Absolutely not. You go. My aunt needs you. She is beside herself, bedridden with fright." Xandra laid the truth on thick. She needed him to go.

It worked. Her uncle's throat bobbed as she pressed the pouch into his hand.

"Maggie needs her dad, Uncle Cobalt. And you know my future is not on Fyr. I will be fine. My father will understand."

"No, he won't. Mary—"

"Fine, if he doesn't, my mother will talk sense into him. She is the one who wrote the commands to let me have a stone to get here."

Her uncle sighed torn, and she knew she had won until…

"Then I stay," Thomas said boldly. "It was my mistake that landed us in trouble, my mistake that got you sent here to save us. Xandra, my future disappears."

"No, Thomas. You are wasting time. We will get caught. Uncle, tell him he must go. He will die, and I have a chance. I'm halfway through these games. I could conquer Lyft."

Rochan rushed into the room. "We have a minute, seconds maybe. They are upon the prison now and Dev sacrificed himself to be the scapegoat. It cannot be for nothing. Xandra, we must go."

Rochan used her nickname without an honorific. That would be engagement on Fyr, just like her parents had slipped up. Her eyes darted to him, but back to her family. She had to get them to leave.

"Xandra, you are my best friend," Thomas choked out, his eyes glistening.

"And you are mine." Xandra hugged him and kissed his cheek. "My future is here. It matters not. I am not leaving the prince." She gave Thomas a pointed look.

Rochan laced his fingers in hers, a loving gesture, but she knew it was also practical to pull her away.

Thomas gave her that knowing look and smirked. "I wish you a long future. Promise I will see you again one day."

"Ha," Xandra tried to make light of it. "Course. Your future is elsewhere too. Perhaps you come back here? Or end up on Water?"

Uncle Cobalt urged Thomas toward the center of the room.

Thomas grinned and nodded.

Rochan pulled her into the hallway, and they watched as her uncle and cousin stuck a finger and thumb into the pouch to grasp the charged stones. They looked up at her with clashing expressions, her uncle concerned, her cousin with understanding.

Flames flew up and surrounded them. When they dissipated her family was gone.

They heard something down the hall.

Rochan, still holding her hand, fingers entwined, windwalked them. She opened her eyes to see the inside of her room. He kissed her but pulled away quickly.

"I want to go back for Dev but know I cannot. Please. Help me, Xandra. We cannot let his sacrifice be in vain. Get yourself into bed. Pretend to sleep. I must do the same. That way, he is punished so all four of us can live. I want to be here with you, but we must not get caught."

Her family was safe, but Rochan was not. She understood the sacrifice the father made for his son, the brother made for his sister. Rochan had grown strength from her feelings for him, but how would he react to Dev's imprisonment? It would make or break him.

Despite not seeing a glimpse of the future, her mind clicked. Dev was a talented future reader of the winds on this sphere, a place where air held power. He would not risk his life unless…

She kissed Rochan. Her lips shaking. She could not tell him and destroy the thread of the future Dev had just created.

Xandra pulled away, hurrying to her dresser and yanking out a nightgown. When she turned, Rochan was still there. She threw it on the bed, his eyes following it. Then she unbraided her hair, giving him a look. "You will also get us killed if you stay here to watch me undress, Prince Rochan."

He blushed, but his eyes were full of want at the thought. This was a dangerous game to play. She approached him, touching his warm cheeks, and kissed him again. When he tried to make more of it, she pulled away whispering on his lips, "go."

The wind swirled around her, and he was gone. She hurried into her nightgown, placing her clothes onto the chair the servant would remove and wash the next morning, then knocked off the light, hurrying into bed.

Xandra lay there restlessly, recalling and processing what they had just done, when there was pounding at the door. Her servant stumbled from his mattress in the adjoining room, then fumbled around, grabbing her clothes and stashing them into the laundry bin. Finally, he opened the door. He had waited up for her but feigned a slow answering of the door as if they had been asleep.

Then the door opened, the hallway light spilling onto her and the bed. The empress stood in a vibrant red robe glaring at her. Her servant instantly blended into the wall. Xandra squinted as if the light bothered her, and she pretended to be groggy.

The empress growled. "Where has she been?"

"Your Imperial Majesty?" asked the servant, his eyes cast to the floor.

"She has been out of her rooms."

"No, Your Imperial—"

"You have!" The empress entered the room flying at Xandra, using her wind magic to glide across the room at an alarming speed.

Wide-eyed, Xandra threw up a fire shield to protect herself as she sat up in bed.

The empress backed off with a hiss, putting out a flame that had gotten the sleeve of her robe. "How dare you attack me?"

"Attack you?" Xandra screeched. "You literally flew into my room to attack me. I am in bed! All I did was defend myself. Your whole retinue saw it." There were at least four or five soldiers outside the door.

"And if I tell them *you* attacked me, they will agree because their lives depend on that truth."

That truth? She called her lies the truth. What leader does such a thing? Creates lies and forces everyone to see them as the truth? An utterly deranged one. How does one deal with someone who suffers from madness, who has their own warped sense of reality?

"You cannot attack me. I am a princess. I keep warning you. If you harm me, my uncle, or cousin, my father will retaliate. All he needs is one word, and he will send draca to wipe out your naga. Do your serpents spit fire? The books suggest nothing of the sort. As we just saw, your wind magic made my flames burst higher. Air feeds the flame. The draca will wipe out any animal or human who uses wind magic." She made sure she used present tense to assert she believed her relatives were still imprisoned.

"A few weretigers upon your father's precious army, and they are dead or as good as dead. What if your father got bitten? Dracas or not, we could wipe out the humans. I never wanted another sphere, but the idea seems appealing now." The empress sneered.

Xandra knew the empress was bluffing but thinking of her father coming and turning into that beast Rochan had shown her gave her the chills. She tried not to show her concern.

The empress continued. "Perhaps your cousin and uncle will give your father that word, and we will be ready with our beasts to slaughter your father? He would have to bring multiple draca, no? Your brothers and cousins no doubt, who would be left to rule Fyr after we are through with them?"

She was trying to get Xandra to slip up. That was what this carefully planned bluff and challenge came from.

Feigning her ignorance, Xandra gave the empress a look as if she were crazy.

The empress did not like that, likely doubly because her bluff was not working and more likely she was used to that look from dissenters because she had lost her mind somewhere along the line from hate, trauma, or a massive power trip—perhaps all of them.

Xandra pushed on. "My family? How can they give him a word from your dungeon cells—where they should not be in the first place. I do not understand—"

"Do not pretend you did not have a hand in this."

Xandra continued to look at her like she was mad, thankful her twin Tourmaline had been obsessed with acting out plays for amusement when they were little, insisted upon teaching her courtly falsities before they had grown apart. "A hand in what?"

The empress stared her down.

"You're scaring me. I want to see my cousin and uncle right now." Xandra scrambled out of bed. "Did you kill them?" She let out the terror and anxiety she had about this place, thinking about the weretigers, Rochan's beatings, the punished servant boys, what might happen to Dev—letting all her fears spread across her face. Her eyes pooled with tears, and blinked until one spilled out, as her lips shook.

"Absolutely not. You'll see, tomorrow. There will be a trial. You must be in attendance."

Xandra continued the façade. She wiped her eyes and begged. "For what, Your Imperial Majesty? I beg you. Do no harm to a Sapphirian. It will not end well. You'd feel the same if you sent ambassadors to another sphere, and they were put on trial. Please, see reason."

"See reason? How dare you call me anything but reasonable." Then she turned, pushed her soldiers out of her way harshly with her wind magic, and slammed the door closed behind her. The locked clicked into place.

Xandra sighed and climbed back into bed, hoping Rochan would not brunt the punishment she only escaped because had she admitted it, she would be executed for treason.

Despite her worry, she slept soundly. The exhaustion from the escape effort, constantly thinking it could be the end if caught, saying goodbye to her family, maybe forever—it all was overwhelming.

Her servant boy woke her early. Considering their night escapades, she had gotten less sleep than normal—as did he. She dressed, let the servant pull her hair back into knots around her circlet, a combination of her own style and that of Lyft's. The servant was a young boy whose name she did not know, and now she felt bad after he helped her with such gentle kindness and covered for her last night.

"What is your name?"

He stopped working her hair, frozen. "I do not have one."

She whirled around, making him let go of the tress of hair that had been in his hands. He was wide-eyed, with pale blue eyes in pale skin. She was sure he was assigned to her because he was a Fyrian descendant. It had been a message from the empress she had understood on day one: Xandra was no better than her servant because she did not belong.

"Your parents did not give you one?"

He stared at the floor. "I did not know them."

"They came from Fyr, my land?"

"I think so, Princess. I was raised among the servants."

"Do you have magic?"

He shrugged. Her parents had said criminals who had tried to take her father's crown had been stripped of power and sent to other spheres to have a new life. She hoped her father did not realize the horrible life the children had of the people he'd sent to this sphere. Criminal or not, this sphere was vicious and unfair toward men. No matter what the parents had done, these children were innocent. Xandra was not sure what occurred when two people of stripped magic had a child. Maybe he could tap into his powers if she tried to teach him.

"Give yourself a name."

"In the servants' quarters, the man who raised me called me 'Finn.' He had a parent from Fyr and another from Water. He said Finn means 'fair' for how pale I am, and a 'fishy' name reminded him of his childhood on Water." The boy grinned.

"Please finish my hair, Finn. Thank you."

The boy obeyed but she hoped with a good feeling in his heart. If she stayed, this would be her personal servant. Or perhaps she would make him her ward and teach him magic if possible. Combat. It was staggering—what she could do for all the young boys if they could be freed from servitude… She almost laughed aloud. Her mother's charity acts—the orphanages and schools—Xandra and her siblings were forced to "volunteer" at as kids which had annoyed them. She understood now. It was to teach them about the unfortunate people out there who needed their help. Well, her mother would love how her message got through to Xandra. If only she could tell her.

If everything worked out, Xandra could make a difference. In the name of her mother's kind heart, she would exude one, make both her parents proud.

This determination waned when she found herself seated in an arena rather than a courtroom, guarded, and forced to watch Dev, the man who had helped her family escape, be tied to a pillar as if on an altar. She turned and her eyes met Rochan's who was in the empress's box above her to the right about two rows higher. He was staring right at her. The emotions in his gaze versus his stoic face and stance worried her.

This *was* an altar.

The empress put her hands up and then sliced through the air. The entire arena quieted. She spoke, using some kind of aid—the air around them perhaps—because it felt like she was speaking in Xandra's ear. "Dev Starsapphire has been accused of treason in the highest degree."

Starsapphire. Goddess of Light and God of Fire! He and Udaya were the sapphire stone family. Not any sapphire family. Xandra had read Lyft's history and reviewed it for the quiz round of the games. The original settlers of Lyft were from a place on Earth called India. Being a large family of their version of sorcerers, they poured their magic into The Star of India and transported to Lyft. The large family married and lost names, some died, but here were two of them left. Another reason for the empress to strengthen her reign through marriage to a Starsapphire and to make her son one.

It was good though, if there was a shift in power from mother to son, Rochan could play upon his heritage as a rightful descendant of the first queen of Lyft. He must know this but was too modest, too afraid of the empress from years of oppression and abuse. More than ever, Xandra wanted to free him, not only from this woman but to free his mind instead so he'd realize his worth.

The empress's voice cut through the gasping and chattering crowd. "The Sapphirian prisoners who were sent to tempt us into a treaty in a false aim to take over our sphere with their draca and fire army have been freed and returned to Fyr."

Another murmur rippled through the arena, but Xandra thought if they agreed with the lies about Fyrians, they would react instantly. Confusion was the vibe around the massive room, and the people around Xandra all looked at her. "A lie," she said aloud. "My father only cares for our lives and for peace." She knew she was going too far, but if it could move the empress's anger onto her, it might spare Rochan, his father, his aunt. If she could create doubt, rumors would flourish. "He will come for me if she tries to hurt me. Otherwise, my father is a peaceful man. If Dev actually did this, he prevented a war. Unfortunately, I'm still stuck here."

The women around her whispered. The few men around them held their tongues, but a couple stared at her, their eyes intense as if beholding hope, if she dared to believe it. If court life here was much like Fyr's, the spread of gossip would be like fed flame.

"Normally, we put citizens on trial, but Dev has confessed to his crime. He has tried to purposely thwart his empress, acknowledges his crime, and so he shall die."

No trial? Xandra was sure that must be wrong, even on Lyft. From the murmurs all around that drown out what the empress continued to say, Xandra was right that things were off. The murmurs turned to some shouts of protest from both women and men.

"SILENCE!" the empress boomed.

The room went quiet, but the tension was palpable.

Then the empress raised her hands in the air, doors opened, and she did some weird chant. Rochan was watching her, confusion across his face. Two other men on her sides were chanting what she was saying in unison. It meant she needed help. Rochan looked back and forth, to Xandra, then to Dev.

Dev looked at Rochan, then closed his eyes. Then Dev screamed out "The Starsapphire never dies. We will rule again!" his power booming his voice over everyone else's.

The arena went silent.

Then Dev screamed out something in a language Xandra could not understand. People gasped or cried out. She had not realized she had grasped and squeezed the guard's arm who was next to her. She looked to her hands, then up to his face, and his eyes tentatively met hers before she let go.

The guard whispered, "He asked for a merciful death. The naga will not torture him as the empress has requested. *He* is the one who speaks to the naga."

"And so does the prince, but not her," Xandra whispered back.

He did not respond.

"I know you cannot agree with me, but it is the truth."

He squeezed her wrist, daring to touch her subtly behind the swell of her dress so no one might see unless nearby.

A naga came flying in through the opening, and consumed Dev in two bites. It made everyone scream in horror and Xandra faltered when the bottom part of his body fell to the ground with the top of him gone, blood and innards everywhere. The guard bolstered her as she bit back a retch as the naga finished its second bite and flew out.

The chanting from the two men at the empress's side ceased.

"Merciful death?" Xandra could not help but speak about the horror she had just witnessed.

A woman next to her lunged over and grabbed her shoulder. She whispered in Xandra's ear, "It would have been worse with the poor abilities of those naga whisperers ordering it. Dev knew what his death would cause. He had foreseen it, chose it. We are all a pawn in this game, are we not, Princess?" She slipped something in her hand. Xandra stared down at a pebble, not sure what it meant. She looked back to the woman, but she was gone. With the outraged and upset crowd, the only way she could've vanished so quickly was windwalking.

Clutching the pebble, she looked back to the empress's box, but Rochan was not looking at her. The empress and Udaya were gone. He simply stood there, frozen in shock, alone.

"I cannot go to him," she said more to herself than the guard. "Someone needs to." She met the guard's gaze. "Please?"

He gruffly yanked her arm. "Fight me," he breathed out as a whisper.

Xandra started thrashing in his grip and pushing back, shouting out raving nonsense about how it was not a trial but was an execution, how the Fyrians were not a threat and wanted peace, how she never saw such injustices on her sphere. The guard covered her mouth and dragged her out of the mayhem. She let him, not knowing if she took it too far or helped carefully to flame the rage against the empress. Once in the hallway, he saw another soldier. "Get some men to help you. The Princess of Fyr has commanded you to get the prince out of there and safely in his quarters. The empress and empress consort abandoned him. I'll see her safely back to her rooms."

The soldier ran off.

The guard dragged her along. "Come, Princess. Let us go through the motions of being seen walking you to your room for witnesses, and then you can do whatever magic you have done so far under my watch to see the prince. No one but me, your servant, and the night guard of your room knows. It needs to stay that way or we—"

"I just saw. You die, horrifically, and so would my young servant. I place the trust you have in me in you. We are a team."

He nodded, but she noticed a tiny smile on his lips where the visor broke to show his mouth.

When Xandra was locked into her quarters, she was instructed to wait for three taps on the door before seeing Rochan. She paced, upset, worried about Rochan. Xandra tried to be strong, not to puke, to cry after witnessing a human being eaten by a giant flying serpent. She had heard stories before. In Fyr, they still had draca patrolling and devouring the worst of criminals, but they had been people who had committed multiple crimes way worse than Dev's.

Two bites.

She cringed.

Finally, the three knocks came.

She transported in earnest, not caring if it were a trap. She had to see Rochan. What he was going through…she could never conceptualize it. If Xandra's mother or father died so horrifically, she might crumble into uselessness or light all of her sphere on fire.

Neither reaction from Rochan would bode well for him becoming the rightful ruler of Lyft.

But he needed to be.

16
A PLAN

In Rochan's room, a little boy stood in front of her. Not Rochan. The boy peered at the ground and bowed but quickly fell onto his bottom and scooted away when he saw the fireball in her hand. Xandra pulled her magic back in.

"Sorry." She leaned over and extended her hand to the boy.

He stared at her hand and then her face, cocking his head in curious confusion.

"Ansh, is it? I'm helping you up since I made you fall down," she explained, looking around for Rochan.

The boy hesitated before placing his hand in hers and allowed her to pull him to standing. "Now you can help me back. Where is the prince?"

"On the roof, Your Highness." He pointed up as if she needed directions. Then he pointed to the balcony door. She did not bother using it but transported there. Rochan was standing in the whipping wind. It was so powerful she almost fell. She threw up a wall of fire to block the wind, the heat triggering Rochan's attention and intensifying her fire before she reeled it back in. He turned and his agonized face fell into one of lost sorrow.

Her heart ached for him.

The wind stopped instantly. Had it all been his magic?

"My anger." He told her quietly, looking down. "I'm having a hissy fit like *her*."

"No, you're not. You are nothing like her. I do not see anger. I see pain."

He nodded. Then as if something snapped in him, he came to her and embraced her tightly in his arms, kissing her hard with more passion than he had ever dared before—rough and carnal. Xandra's stomach did a somersault, but then a warm feeling pooled within, her lips matching his. They kissed madly for a moment.

But then he started to shake in her arms. She pulled her lips away. His face was screwed up in mental agony. Unable to bear seeing him like that, she held him tightly, guiding his head down onto her shoulder.

Rochan shook more violently, the pain wanting out, but he was suppressing it.

"We are alone. Just you and me. Let it out. I am here for you, always."

Rochan broke down into sobs, holding her way too tightly, but she did not stop him. He was holding onto her as if his life depended on it. Perhaps, within that moment, it did. Not knowing what to do, she whispered things she thought would help like letting it all out was good and that she would take him away from this awful place.

At that last comment, he stopped crying and went rigid backing away. "No." He wiped his tears away and glared at her.

Xandra would rather see him cry than have his anger directed toward her. What had she said that was so wrong?

"I cannot leave, not now. Amma."

"I'll take her too. My father transported a dragon once, and an army. I must be strong enough to take you both."

Rochan shook his head. "I need to stop her."

Then it clicked. "Your mother?"

"She's no mother of mine. I might have her blood in my veins, but she just killed my father, my other blood, the blood much dearer to me than hers. She did it to break me. It backfired."

"What are you saying, Rochan?"

"Xandra, I'm going to take over Lyft. If that means killing the empress, so be it."

Making up her mind instantly, she knew her future was here and with Rochan. "I will help you. You are a Starsapphire. I should've known that, but—"

"The empress does not like to be outshined. It is rarely spoken of, although well known. Wait, no. You cannot stay." He shook his head. "I need to know you are alive and safe on Fyr. Otherwise, I…" His eyes searched hers. "She took one person I love away, and she'll take another. Amma is safe because the empress loves her too much, needs her too much, so you'll be next. I'm sure she senses I love you. She's not stupid, and I have a hard time hiding my feelings."

Two things simultaneously went through her head. Death and— "You love me?"

His mouth quirked despite his serious gaze. "Focus, Xandra."

Then the first thought overtook her. She did not have a future on Fyr. She thought it would mean she would strike out her own path on another sphere, this sphere. But what if she died here? Doubt crept upon her as it had when she was momentarily in that jail cell.

She blew out a heavy breath. "Ever since I was a little girl, I saw my future vanish on Fyr. It means I am destined to be here."

"Or die here." It pained him to utter the words, his emotions transparent in his eyes.

"Or die here," she affirmed. "I'm not leaving the man I love to die alone."

He yanked her in against him and kissed her. This was passionate like before but not with grief, anger, or pain laced through it, but with adoration and desire.

She transported them into his room still kissing him. She pushed him back toward the bed not sure where this fire in her belly came from, this need to have him close to prove her feelings through her lips.

They crashed onto the bed, breaking their lip-lock. Rochan smiled, his hands cradling her face as he gazed at her with admiration, his grief and anger momentarily at bay. "I love you, my fire princess. If we must die, we die together."

The idea of death put a damper on her joy at hearing him say how he felt. It would not do. "Or we win together and forge a new world, one of equality, one where we sic the serpents onto the weretigers and roam the sphere freely."

"You were made to be an empress," he said breathlessly, simply drinking in the sight of her.

"Raised by royalty." She shrugged. But he was not giving himself enough credit. She needed him to believe in himself. She snuggled up into his side as they lay on his bed. "Rochan, despite the empress's new edicts, you are the rightful heir to be emperor. If my gods brought me here, yours made you male for a reason." Xandra kissed him again.

After a few moments, Rochan pulled away. "As much as I would love to kiss you all night, we might just die if we do not do something productive, like plan." Then he smirked. "I am all for the kissing, but it is a moot pursuit if we die because we were distracted by it."

She shrugged. "I am an impulsive girl. I like to just figure it out as I go."

Rochan examined her, that playful smirk lingering on his lips. It suited him oh-so-well. That wide smile she had longed for made her feel love, but that smirk made her feel so many things, but what she loved most about it was how it hinted to his hidden strength and power.

He pushed them up to sitting, and they leaned against the intricately carved headboard. "That will come in handy because it serves you well—sometimes. A plan would be the best course, and your impulsiveness can be our weapon if the plan goes awry."

She'd rather kiss than plan and showed him by huffing. "I will win your hand. Is that not the plan?"

"We must make that happen. Do not be overconfident, Princess. The empress will turn the tide if you keep winning every round."

"She will cheat?"

"Do you think she would not after all you have seen?"

Xandra again felt guilty about how naïve she had been on her arrival. She had been warned. But now, she had just witnessed what happened to men's defiance. Dev was killed for helping them save her uncle and cousin. The man who gave her a son, a man she must've had intimate relations with was as expendable, as if he weren't even human.

Rochan was safe—for now—because he needed to marry and beget a daughter. Would he be killed after that? Even more puzzling was why Xandra was still alive and out of prison. Was the empress deep down afraid to punish a princess—more so than her male relatives? That was the only answer. She would've let Uncle Cobalt and Thomas rot forever in a cell or kill them had Dev not acted.

Rochan's hand touched her face, bringing her back to reality. His gaze was puzzled. "Xandra?"

She shook her head, tears filling her eyes.

"Tell me." The way his voice pleaded…she could never deny him anything.

She blew out a shaky breath. "Do not judge me, please. The reason I passed the intelligence trivia round was because I knew everything we had in books about Lyft. I knew my future ended. My cousin Thomas, you met, he has a similar situation. Where he feared it meant a young death, I persistently felt I was meant to be elsewhere, that my young life would cease on Fyr because I found a new life on another sphere. There is Water and the magicless Earth, but something drew me to Lyft. Anyway, after my people rejected me as being in the line for succession—despite the fact it would be unlikely with all my older siblings and their offspring—I became quite obsessed with the idea of a matriarchy. I come from a sphere where men ruled, and women were nothing. The reverse of here. But my parents changed that. Change is slow. It takes generations, so when I was born with the wrong eyes—"

"Wrong eyes? I do not understand. They are beautiful, like a stormy sky, so full of energy, power, and beauty."

Xandra kissed him, unable to stop herself. Never had anyone but her parents appreciated her eyes. Rochan gave her tender kisses back, but now she was the one shaking and bubbling. She pulled away sobbing, covering the very things they spoke of.

Rochan pulled her hands away from her face. "Xandra, please. Do not cry."

She took a deep breath. "Fyr was such a patriarchal place because genetically the eye color of a father was dominant, passed down. Even if a man strayed away from his wife and had a child with another if the eyes matched, they had to proclaim the baby as their own. Likewise, if they did not match, they denied them. I have an uncle like that, that my father accepted as a sibling. Anyway, had I not been born with a twin sister who had Sapphirian eyes, had I not had fire power…my mother would have been accused of adultery. Because a true Sapphirian has the eyes of the draca. Without that, I do not belong.

"I idolized your mother because of the anger I harbored against my own sphere—how they rejected me and demanded my removal from succession. Thomas warned me about here and my father was suspicious about how your mother overtook the sphere. I was stupid to think one gender ruling over another was a good thing. I just saw equality forming on Fyr that I was not a part of. But now, I see it is much worse to see someone you love feeling helpless, being beaten down mentally and physically. I am sorry."

He cradled her face and, oh, how she loved his palms upon her, holding her together, giving her strength. He was powerful and tender, both at once. "Do not be sorry. Fight for that equality. Lyft was once equal. Whoever could speak to the naga was the one who ruled. That changed back and forth, but the empress murdered her husband on their wedding night who had been the most talented and wealthiest naga speaker at the time. As you witnessed, she has no control over them. She was not trying to kill you that day with the nagas. She made me come along to protect you, but her anger came from me not being discreet enough to make her look good in front of you. She wanted you to believe she was the one commanding them. Not me, never me."

Xandra nodded, digesting what Dev had done and what Rochan could do. He should be the emperor. Her mind spun off to think of what that might be like if she stayed. "I feel like I belong here, but not with her in charge."

"Agreed." He sank back onto the mattress, pulling her neck gently until she was lying down on the bed next to him again. They gazed at each other for a moment. "I want you, my fire princess. My life was as bad as you can imagine and have seen. Then you appeared in flames—a light in my life. I'd do anything for you."

He kissed her forehead.

"I am doing that for you too." She met his gaze, their faces close together. "You are right. Let's plan. You know her best. If I lose a combat round—"

"Ugh, I do not want to think about you fighting."

Xandra pushed his shoulder back onto the bed on impulse and threw a leg over him so that she was sitting on his stomach. "I do like a good fight, and I am well trained. I am not who you should worry—"

His shot up to sitting, his lips cutting her off, but she could not complain. Too soon he pulled away. "How in our short time together have you made me feel this way?"

Xandra grinned. "Likewise."

Then he dampened her mood. "My princess, we need to stop these kisses and admittances so we can plan. I want to share so much more, but my love—" he kissed her lips. "We need to survive."

With reluctance, she drew away from him. Their feelings were a distraction. She knew this but was loath to admit. She had to focus. Once things were over, she could do whatever she wanted with Rochan, steal as many kisses as possible, marry him, and be an empress. Out of all of the possibilities, one stood out: Rochan.

No matter what happened, Xandra would never leave him.

Life or death. Together.

17
AMMA

Rochan woke up the next morning feeling much different. He was not filled with dread, and he was not stricken with grief as he assumed he would be. He was filled with a fiery hope backed by a plan, and a few backup plans. It was time to discreetly put them into action without getting caught by the empress.

His first stop was to comfort Amma. He might've lost his father—who he had been forced to not show affection for—but she lost her brother, the person she loved most outside of Rochan and the empress. Amma must feel conflicted. The woman she loved killed her brother. The fact the empress went that far made Rochan worry about his own life. If he married and had an heir and a spare, would she kill him? The thought gave him more drive. He would save himself, his people. With Xandra by his side, he could do anything.

As he went to knock on Amma and the empress's door, he heard something shattering in the room. Hand on the knob, he was about to burst in to save Amma from the empress's wrath, but the guard outside touched his arm as if to tell him to stand down. His eyes met the servant's. He dared to look him in the eye. Good. This man, Ishan if he remembered correctly, could be persuaded to help him.

That's when he heard the angry shrill voice screaming was actually Amma. "My own brother, Nakano! My family!"

"What did you expect me to do? Kill the boy? The princess? Someone had to suffer for the escape of the prisoners. He helped set the Sapphirians free. Confessed it. I cannot prove it, but that girl and Rochan must have been involved!"

"Why do you insist our son is always up to no good? When has he ever disobeyed me? And this princess was guarded inside her room. Why do you believe everyone is up to something and out to get you?"

"Because they are!"

"Paranoid. You are ridiculous! You worry about the wrong things. My brother prevented a king from coming with dragons. The princess even admitted her father can transport an army with fire-breathing draca. You have to let the princess go in the end of all this. Otherwise, we will all die."

He heard a slap and instinct made Rochan grab the knob, ready to storm in and spare Amma any further pain.

Ishan yanked Rochan away from the door, wide-eyed, shaking his head.

The empress spoke in low, bitter tones. "You do not tell *me* what to do. You were once my lowly advisor. I heard your advice. I am done with the topic. If you persist to whine about Dev's death, I will be done with you. There are many beautiful, younger, and more malleable women to replace you."

The empress was coming toward the door, so Rochan quickly knocked. The empress yanked it open, a scowl on her face. "What are you doing here?"

"I wanted to see how Amma was doing."

The scowl turned into a full-fledged glower. "I thought you would be spending time with the *princess*."

Rochan kept his face stoically blank, but his stomach flopped. Had she found out Xandra was in his quarters? "What do you mean?" He hedged, being sure to look confused.

"I see the way you look at that girl. The way she looks at you. She will not be empress. I will not allow it. Best get that idea out of your head. You cannot possibly even know her, since I have made sure you two are never alone, so your regard is surface value. Typical of your kind. *Men*," she spoke the last word with disgust, her face screwing up as if she ate something bitter. Her hatred was so deep, her behavior toward her own son so abysmal, a long-held suspicion clicked in his mind as a fact: she was truly insane. He hadn't seen it before, being so used to her behavior and no one questioning it. Until Xandra entered his world and opened his eyes.

If he could prove it in front of people, beyond a doubt, push her too far and break her, he might be able to get her deposed as unfit to rule. There were rumors already, what he needed was for her to publicly react beyond what a strict dictator might do, prove her completely nonsensical and unhinged.

He knew exactly where to start.

"Your silence is telling. If you cared about the princess more than an object to ogle, you would profess it."

Oh, how Rochan wanted to protest, to explain to her that he knew more about love than she ever would. He did not rise to her bait, letting her think what she would in her warped mind. He was too smart to play into the empress's hand.

Then she walked off, leaving her quarters, shaking her head.

Amma was on the couch, her head in her hands. She looked up. Her eyes were red-rimmed and fresh tears ran down her cheeks. She wiped them away and stood, her mouth opening to speak but like him, she had no idea what to possibly say.

Rochan embraced her. She clung onto him fiercely, burying her sobs into his shoulder. He sure hoped the empress was not coming back to see this level of affection. These mother-son moments with Udaya were rare and always secret.

Then he let the worry go. Forget the empress. He would not live in fear of her. He said soothing words to Amma—how sorry he was for involving Dev, for his defiance, for the loss of her brother—until she pulled away.

Her face was full of the regrets he felt. She touched his cheek. "Stop. None of this is your fault."

"You do not deserve to suffer."

"Neither do you, Rochan."

"I'm not going to anymore."

Amma stared at him wordlessly for a moment and then walked toward the closet. She was busying herself. Rochan was dying to know what she was thinking. If Amma would go against the empress, usurping her would be so easy, but he could not risk it if Amma chose to protect the empress as she was often inclined to do. Did Amma love him enough to defy her wife?

"I heard the empress talk to you about the princess. You did not argue. I had thought it was real regard, which is why I've done all I could to help the girl. I want nothing more to see you happy, Rochan. She is a great match in rank, raised to understand how to rule, intelligent, and resilient. I had thought you wanted a future with her. If it is only your eyes that are intrigued, I can get her out of the games, get her home safely."

Rochan felt awkward talking to his mother about Xandra, his mind drifting to what parts of him were intrigued by the beautiful Fyrian. He was thankful Amma was not looking at him as she swept up what looked like a shattered vase. It was one the empress had gifted her. Perhaps she might be as through with the empress's rule as he was. To break something that had once been so sentimental spoke volumes.

"I…it is more that her looks, Amma. It is love. I did not want the empress to know."

Her head whipped around. "How? Nakano has kept you apart, the princess locked up and watched over."

"She can use something called 'dragon's trapdoor.' She can reappear wherever she wants using fire magic. She has been, um, coming to my rooms ever since I got her out of the prison."

She gasped. "Like a windwalker." The empress did a good job of wiping out their magic in fear they would appear in her room and kill her while she slept. There were a few still alive, but hard to know since all hid it—just like he had to.

"Dev could…" Amma did not speak the thought. She knew about Dev's power and was now looking at Rochan in unspoken realization. Why Dev did not simply windwalk out of the arena and hide, bide his time on the Isle of the Gods, confounded Rochan.

"Udaya, the princess, she has taught me how—"

"If your servants tell Nakano—"

"They won't."

Amma stood, her eyes worried. "Have you been smuggling them books again?"

He did not answer because he had been caught doing it—and whipped—when he was a little boy. He did not want to admit he had never stopped educating the men deprived of it due to his mother's hate.

She lowered her voice. "Are they yours? Loyal?"

"To a fault, like Ishan." Taking a chance, hoping Amma would love him enough to protect him he uttered, "I have plans."

She walked to her desk and opened a drawer. "Do not tell me, Rochan. The less I know, the better. Like I do not know you were there with Dev freeing the Sapphirians." She pressed down in the back of the drawer, and it popped open. "Please do not go up against her, Rochan. With her temper, she might kill me to hurt you or kill you to hurt me."

"By temper you mean she lost her mind years ago, and it is getting perpetually worse."

Amma pressed her lips together, refraining to agree or disagree. Then she withdrew two small pouches from the back of the drawer. "Dev did more than steal back those stones for the Sapphirians to escape. He procured these long ago."

She handed the pouches to Rochan who gazed at them in confusion.

"Carnelian. Charged for a round trip to Fyr. After that first beating—I do not think you remember—when you were two—"

"What?" Rochan remembered the whip being used when he was a small boy, and the first caning, but he did not know the empress's abuse started when he was just a baby.

She sat down on the couch again.

He stuffed the pouches into his pocket too upset to sit down with her.

"You would not stop crying, particularly around Nakano. From the day you were born and she was disappointed in your gender, you sensed that. You did not like her nor she you, so she tried to instill fear and "discipline" you. The first time," her voice vibrated with emotion. "I got a beating for interfering. That's when Dev procured these stones. They were for me to escape and take you away to another sphere. He only could get ones for Fyr."

"You never took me."

"I was afraid. We do not get news from Fyr often. The latest news that I received at the time was an ill king and a young fire prince who was cursed and grappling to keep control of his kingdom and then there was a war. I could not take you to an unstable war zone. The water sphere was worse and still is. A civil war started by squabbling siblings. Dev asked me to go often, but I became complacent and despite who she was and who she has become, part of me cannot leave Nakano." Udaya's face screwed up in pain, and emotion vibrated through her voice, "I love her, Rochan. When you give your heart fully to someone, you will understand. You can never get it back. Even if you despise what they do and what they have become. I hope you never have to face that."

Rochan could not understand the sentiment. He could never love someone who would harm his child. The thought of a child brought him back to Xandra. His heart thudded, picking up its pace. If he had a child one day—with her—he could not imagine anything more beautiful, more worthy of affection and protection.

Then he suddenly understood the power of love. He could see why Udaya was weak and powerless.

Rochan would do anything for Xandra. *Anything.*

"I do not want you to usurp Nakano. Rochan, I want you to escape her. Take the stones and the princess and go to Fyr."

He shook his head. If she could not free herself, he'd do it. "I am not leaving you here. The princess's stone. If we get ahold of that, we will have three."

She shook her head sadly, futilely withholding her sob. "After Dev got the two stones back for the Sapphirians, the empress locked the third up somewhere. She is not taking any chances."

He would not use the stone. It was not just Amma and Xandra he wanted to save. "I cannot go, Amma. Our people."

She looked at her hands. "I have raised too good of a man. I knew you would say that." Then she looked up at him, pride shining in her eyes as she blinked her tears away. "I will help you. Tell me nothing, but I will divert her attention, make excuses, protect you as much as I can."

Rochan nodded. "Thank you, Amma."

"Now go. The empress is speaking to her council who are angry with her about Dev, the Sapphirians being held prisoner then escaping, and the fear Fyr will still come for retribution. Your mother will be looking for an outlet for her anger. Steer clear of her."

Rochan started for the door.

"Be careful, my beautiful boy."

He nodded, not turning around. He wanted to tell her he loved her too, for that was what she was imparting, but could not. He knew exactly who would brunt the outlet of the empress's anger. He had to free Udaya. He had to free himself.

He knew exactly where to start: the servants' quarters. Revolts start with the oppressed but are best fed by the majority.

Dev had taught him that. As he walked through the halls toward the servants wing, something in Rochan's mind shifted. Just like Udaya was doing, Dev choose death rather than escape. He did not want Rochan to pay the price, but it also was a stroke against the empress. Her killing one of the few remaining Starsapphires would not go well with the people. It was like attempting to wipe out historical legends.

Rochan must see this rebellion through.

Dev's sacrifice would not be in vain.

18
A BATTLE

Four girls had made it through to the final rounds. Two were very strong, broad shouldered, one of them tall and the other stockier—Lin and Balan—while Xandra and the Ahana were thinner and likely light-footed. Of course, the empress, split them up into pairs of whom she thought would be weak versus strong in hopes to get her warrior women together in the final round. She valued brawn over brains. Xandra knew the best warriors needed both. She refused to lose. Rochan needed her to win. She needed to stay here with him. Love had to give her an edge on top of skill and intellect. None of these girls cared as much as she did. Sure, they had the drive to be in power, to possess Rochan, but she was the only one who cared for him, wanted him for who he was, not what he represented.

They allowed Ahana and her to stretch and warm up in one room, the other opponents in another. Ahana did not speak. She had large eyes that made her beautiful, but at the moment, they looked frightened. Her hands shook.

"Take a deep breath and grip your urumi steadily. Your nerves are showing. She will take advantage of that. Move fast. Lin is tall and strong. You have my body type, so you are fast and sinewy?" Xandra might do better with the lighter metal whip that was used by many quick fighters, but she was more confident wielding a sword. In this case, two lightweight swords. Her goal was to score points, not injure her opponent.

"Like I would tell you, *foreigner.*" The girl's lips curled in disgust. "I am not stupid. You would use it against me in the final round."

Xandra sighed. Sometimes, she truly disliked when people acted like her twin sister Tourmaline. It was either fakeness, jealousy, or plain cattiness. "Look, trying to help you, but fine, have it your way."

They were silent. Ahana stretched her arms and legs, jumping up and down.

Xandra had quickly gotten a grasp on how to use the swords Rochan helped her select, talwars. They were lightweight with a disc hilt she could use to slam on a girl's head in a bind. She chose to wield two instead of a shield that would slow her down and not prove much against Balan's heavy looking sword—the name escaping her but the detail of slashing off animal heads for sacrifice stuck with her from Lyftian history books. It was used for intimidation, but the move would be in vain if it made Balan slower. Xandra was confident that two slashing swords would be the key to the battle, being her forte since she could not block such strong swings, like those her brothers would relentlessly bash her with in training.

She had learned to move quick, be agile, clever, and slashes added up. The bonus? Using the weapon type the empress's paternal ancestors had brought to Lyft with them would infuriate her even more, like using the empress's own insecurites against her. If she won. Xandra needed to do that first to strike the empress's pride.

Ahana glanced over. "Why would you help me?"

The bait was taken.

Xandra shrugged. "I am not fighting you. None of us are stupid, or we would not have made it through the trivia round. I do not have to glean info from your fighting style if we make it to the final round. I am allowed to watch you and Lin since you are going first, just like you will watch ours for the same. I could glean all the information I need off watching you."

Her eyes narrowed. "What do you want then?"

"To help you, and maybe you help me back."

"And if we end up facing each other in the last round?"

"Do you want to be empress, or do you want Prince Rochan?"

"They are the same thing. My parents want me to win. I have to. A lot rides on it."

"I want the prince for who he is, not to rule over this sphere."

Ahana stared at Xandra for a long time. "Perhaps, when we both win, we can have a conversation about what might happen if either of us wins that makes us both happy."

Xandra was not sure if that meant Ahana became empress and Rochan got to leave with Xandra for Fyr, and the empress dead, but that was where her imagination took her. This was no empress supporter.

"What's your last name?"

"Why?"

"I want you to tell me Lin's and Balan's too. It is only fair. You know mine is Sapphirian. You know my stone magic. The empress purposely has kept the contestants' surnames hidden from all, except for mine. An unfair advantage, no?"

Ahana gave her a nervous smile. "I am one of many families of Quartz, Lin an Agate, and Balan is Epidote."

Xandra nodded. "In other circumstances, I think we might have had a chance of being friends."

"If one of us loses, maybe we can," she countered. Her grin relaxed, despite the battle ahead of her.

"Like that is going to happen," Xandra scoffed. "You have this."

Ahana smiled. "So do you, friend." Then she turned away, toward the door and jumped up and down to get her adrenaline pumping.

The girl was kind. She did not deserve to be pummeled by Lin. "Be fast, light of foot, and swing high. She is a bull, and you are a fox. Be cunning, outsmart her."

Rochan had told her animals were important in Lyft and finding your animal nature was the key to learn to become a great warrior. He spoke of these things, the teachings from Dev that might help her win, during their stolen nights in his rooms. She had not felt akin to an animal yet, unable to find her nature but simply would have to fight.

Ahana nodded. Jumping up and down. "Only fair to keep this even. Balan is a wolf. I do not know what you are."

A draca. No, using her fire powers would be a last resort. If Xandra could save that for the final round, she would. She would fight as much as needed so the winner of this match would not know the full extent of her abilities. "A naga, but I am hoping I do not have to unleash her."

Ahana's mouth dropped, and she looked away, stretching and focusing. She said no more, and Xandra distanced herself from the girl to let her get in the right mindset for a battle. Perhaps it was wrong to be so bold as to proclaim she felt akin to the naga, but there was no other equivalent to the raw power of a dragon that the girl could grasp. Ahana never witnessed the draca going in for the kill.

Xandra stretched and practiced with the new weapons. The fact they were lighter and there were two of them felt empowering. She would be better with two as long as she remembered one was used for attack and the other as a shield to block a blade or staff.

The doors opened and the sound of a massive crowd made Xandra nervous. She crept up to the door guarded by a soldier so no one within might intervene, even though today it was just Xandra.

She said nothing to Ahana as she walked hesitantly toward the doors. She did not want to break the girl's concentration.

Ahana met Lin in the middle of the arena, the official announcing their names and explaining the rules—not that ambitious girls vying for a prince and sphere would listen to them. The moment the two opponents bowed toward each other, Xandra took in the smug look of one and the insecurity of the other.

Ahana would lose.

Wanting to turn away, she forced herself to watch every one of Lin's moves. She noted some of Ahana's, but it was clear that three-quarters of the points were going to Lin from the start. Uncle Cobalt's lessons in swordplay came back to her. The sparring with her brothers. Remembering the basics and her brothers' tricks helped her mentally prepare, but most of all how Aschen would dissect every wrong move would prepare her.

She watched the girls, how they interacted, how Lin and Ahana defended and fought back at each other's attacks. Lin relied on her air magic to push more force into her blows but slowly exhausted herself—a telltale bull of a fighter as Xandra had pegged her only after training with them in the arena for a couple sessions. Ahana was unpredictable and sly. Lin's many swings only landed when she could guess by happenstance which way Ahana would go.

A horn blasted. The battle was cut off, and Lin announced the winner. The crowd went wild. Ahana's face fell. She slunk away out the other side of the arena to hide in the shadows and watch in shame. Xandra felt bad for her, for how this sphere put such a strong emphasis on honoring one's family and what disappointment and censure Ahana would face… *Focus on your battle, Xandra.* She jumped up and down to get her heart pumping, her leg muscles warm again.

The exercise gave her a rush of confidence. Fight a wolf? She was a draca, a naga. Simple. Easy. Only she had to hide that until the final round—or if she started losing. She closed her eyes and contemplated, trying to feel and use the fire inside her as Rochan let the wind magic help him do wind exercises, how he found inner reflection through his magic.

If she had no powers, no magic, what animal fighter could she pretend to be? *A cat. A wildcat.* Although they did not live on Fyr, she had read about how Earth had massive cats bigger than man who hunted. Seeing the weretiger's form, she would be that but full of stealth and less brawn. And she felt like a tiger the moment she was instructed to enter the arena. She did not hear the crowd. It was just a hum in her ears as her heartbeat took over all sound. That and her breathing. She searched for him, Rochan, and found him in the empress box, a mother on each side. She did not look at either of them but made eye contact with him as she performed her obligatory bow to the empress box. From this far away and her helmet on, the empress would not know Xandra was bowing to Rochan instead.

Then a leather armored official went over the rules: nothing intentional over the shoulders, nothing intended to main or kill. Points were given for hits to the armor in the chest and abdomen region as well as points given to blocking or deflecting such blows.

Balan scowled at Xandra with an overly confident look on her face. Good.

Xandra had been worried about Lyftian helmets. They protected the head and nose well, but the side and mouth flaps were only chain mail. But now she realized the power of being able to read an opponent's face through it. And enacted the power to intimidate. Xandra made her first move to disarm Balan before the signal to start by smiling broadly and saying in the sweetest tone she could muster, "Good luck."

Balan lost her scowl, bemused at Xandra's tone.

They bowed to each other and then the official made a hand motion. Xandra was taught by her dad and Uncle Cobalt, who both had been through real warfare, by her brother Aschen who could best them in sparring. She was one of the best fighters of Fyr, but she was also taught by her mother who used her quick-thinking cleverness to outwit her opponents and by the steadfast Thomas, his patience. He was not a strong warrior, but he compensated through observation. Both Mum and Thomas would warn her to let her opponent show off their moves first.

Like the promised wolf, Balan pounced for Xandra's jugular, pretty much literally going for her shoulder. Xandra simply leaped backward and put up one sword to stop it. Then the wolf tried the same move, but Xandra was ready. The blow glanced off her other sword.

Balan's eyes went wide. She did not know what to do when Xandra would give nothing away? She next thrust toward Xandra's abdomen with both swords. Easily deflected. Was she testing Xandra or was this the best the girl could do?

Xandra threw out a sword to feint her. As Balan glanced it away, she struck hard across her chest and abdomen, spinning away before Balan could retaliate. God and goddess of Fyr, her mother had been right about those awful dance classes to teach grace for swordplay.

Balan growled, fury in her eyes for letting Xandra gain the first points. Xandra stood her ground, ducked down and slashed two swords across the girl's armor as Balan tumbled down into the sand.

Balan scrambled up, her eyes wild. She realized Xandra was no scrawny pup she had thought she'd deal with. Everyone always underestimated Xandra and that rose up the fury of three dracas combined. Why did they think she was helpless?

Xandra turned and decided to fight back, thinking about the weaknesses they all saw in her that were lies. Thin. *Thwack.* Gray-eyed. *Cling.* Outcast. *Thwack.* Removed from succession. *Bam.*

Balan was on the ground, scrambling backward on all fours, all feet and elbows like a crab. Xandra followed her, thinking things were too easy but equally scared of how zoned out she was during her attack, giving way to her fiery temper that helped her fight. Yet her body moved with the grace her mother had enforced. She was a tiger. A lone wolf was no match for her.

Balan had dropped a sword, so Xandra had the advantage. At the same time, the girl could not be this bad of a fighter. Perhaps, she wanted Xandra to think that? How far would she go to pretend to be weak, how many points lost, before the wolf attacked?

Xandra closed in, keeping Balan on the ground, working for points. She battered Balan's sword away repeatedly while her other sword gently struck the girl's armor over and over and over. Point after point. Finally, the girl finally landed a blow to Xandra's armor.

Then Balan blasted Xandra with wind magic. Fire could end this, but she refused to use it yet. She would not transport either. Instead, she embraced the wind and did a backflip away from Balan, landing on her feet.

Xandra had ignored the crowd prior, but they went wild at this new development. She figured they'd be booing her by now. She obviously was winning by a lot. One, maybe two strikes hit her armor for the ten or twenty she had given Balan.

The girl came flying at her next, quickly, using wind magic. Xandra dove onto the sand floor, flat on her stomach. She rolled over, sheathed her swords, and did a kip-up to her feet. Balan had almost hit the dirt hard but righted herself using the air around her. So Lyftians liked to use it to keep themselves standing and ready? Good to know.

Xandra withdrew her swords as Balan charged. Simultaneously, Xandra swung both her swords, the two-lighter-sword research paying off. They were blades that worked better with the wind, slicing through the air, and yet, a fire wielding princess held her own. Glance and hit, duck, and hit. She was in the zone. Her wrists twirling the swords in tandem, striking, then alternating. Balan squinted. Her body straining, unable to keep up with the pace, the wolf was gone. Fear filled her eyes.

A horn blew.

Xandra stopped.

Balan did not. After a howl of loss, she ran at Xandra, blade pointed toward the vulnerable area at her neck where the chain mail flaps could not protect.

Balan went for the kill.

Xandra almost froze seeing the rage on her opponent's face and the blade coming for her throat. Time seemed to slow down. Or her mind was spinning quickly. Xandra leaned to the left, dropping her swords. She grabbed the girl's forearm, and pushed it in two directions, one toward her, the other shoving hard away to get the blade away from her throat. A resounding crack and a shriek of pain reverberated around the arena due to the silence after the horn.

They tumbled to the ground, Xandra's helmet tumbling off.

She pressed up onto her hands and knees, grabbing a discarded sword.

Then the crowd started booing and chanting, "Cheat, cheat, cheat, cheat."

Xandra stood, dusting herself off. She was shaken but did not let anyone see it. She pointed her sword at Balan's throat, who was crying and moaning, cradling her arm.

Confusion swirled in Xandra's head, the adrenaline falling, leaving her exhausted. Who were they calling a cheat? Surely, not Xandra who acted only to save her own life? The girl had been trying to kill her.

But this was Lyft…

She looked up into the empress's box. Rochan and his mother, Udaya, were standing, her hand on his shoulder. The empress's seat was empty.

A man walked out with a shackles and chains.

Xandra's heart leaped to her throat. *Think*. Be Thomas, use your mind. Remember your studies.

Then she took a deep breath. An attack after the bell or breaking the rules of combat on Lyft called for imprisonment. They were not there for Xandra.

They took Balan away in chains and she screamed. The pain of her broken arm made Xandra feel guilty despite the girl going for blood.

She raced over and gripped the girl's broken arm, and poured in her fire healing magic, fusing the bone together. To her credit the girl did not scream. Instead, she yanked away and then Balan's eyes went wide in realization. Xandra squeezed her hand and put her finger to her lips. She hoped the girl would forgive her and keep the healing power a secret.

Why? Why did she heal her or help? Why did she expose that power to someone she did not know she could trust? She had been able to see the goodness in Ahana, but not Balan.

Xandra looked up into the empress's box again for Rochan. It was shadowy, his face indiscernible. She would see him later. For now, she was quickly announced the winner and unceremoniously rushed to the infirmary. She needed a moment to catch her breath and did not want to tell them she could heal herself.

She had to get out of there quickly. She had to make sure Balan would not say a word.

Would Xandra's kind heart get her killed?

19
MAGIC

Rochan rushed toward the infirmary, looking for Xandra, not letting himself windwalk lest he get caught. Everyone knew he had been in the arena. To appear somewhere a two-minute walk through the palace a moment later would be a dead giveaway. Worse if he beat the injured fighters there.

When he arrived, he knew he should not be there, that checking on Xandra would show the other girls he had marked her as his preferred choice, but he could not help it. He needed to make sure she was okay. Sure, the other girls would resent Xandra—more than they already did since she was a foreigner on their sphere, trying to steal what they wanted most: a kingdom. He would have to check on all the girls to balance it out. Even if he loved Xandra, if she did not win, he might have to marry…

No, he'd rather leave Lyft forever than to be with anyone but Xandra. He knew what that meant too. He was in love and weak because of it. He could not let the empress know. He had thought his people mattered more, but he was torn between protecting his people and Xandra. She had to stay, to be in his life.

He entered. The healers and patients looked at him oddly. "I came to check on the contestants." Then he glanced around the room looking for Xandra. "I hope none of you were hurt badly. This is my least favorite round. To see anyone get hurt over trying to win the Empress Games has made me conflicted. We need a strong empress, but I would hate to see any of you get seriously injured in proving it."

Xandra was not there. One girl smiled at him, the pretty-eyed Ahana, and the burly one Balan smirked at him as if his comment was silly. He could not end up with her. She would beat him into submission, like his mother. No, he could not afford to think such thoughts. He would defend himself in that situation. Xandra cracked something in him, made him feel all sorts of things. With her around, his restraint was useless, his feelings quick to the surface—including his anger. He would fight. He would not be pushed back down into his obedient box ever again.

He grabbed the closest head healer's arm gently. "There are only three girls here. Where is the fourth?"

The healer looked at him grasping her arm as if his touch sullied her. How could he ever gain respect in this sphere after his mother had made these women hate him simply based off his gender? He dared to tighten his grip when she did not answer and narrowed his eyes. Her light eyes locked on his. Under her cap, he noticed the lighter hair. She was not fully Lyftian, perhaps Fyrian as well. After a moment of challenge, she looked down and bobbed her head in reference. "One of the girls had not been badly injured at all. The Fyrian nobility needs no healing."

Rochan let go of the woman's arm. "Are you sure she was not injured?"

"The princess said she needed no healing, refused care."

Balan spoke up. "Your Highness?"

He clenched his jaw, trying not to think about how the girl swung swords at *his* Xandra and then after the horn went off tried to kill her. He glared at her. "Are you looking for redemption, *cheater?*"

The girl flinched. Then she shook her head. "I would like to tell you something."

He leaned down, annoyed about extending his ear toward her in case she might attack him.

"I think I nicked her forearm on the underside. That is all."

He moved to pull away, but she grabbed his collar. "She broke my arm in half after my unwarranted and illegal attack. Then healed it. I think…she gave me compassion. Tell her 'Thank you' and 'I'm sorry.' That is, if you are going to see her."

"I will," he said.

"Prince?" Her eyes were desperate.

He put his ear to her lips. "The empress commanded me to wound or disqualify her but 'not kill.'"

Rochan pulled away. How could he protect this girl and Xandra and thwart his mother without outwardly doing so?

He looked to the healer. "Pack up what you think the Fyrian princess needs. I'll take it to her personally."

The woman's eyes opened wide.

"After I check on the other ladies, here, of course." He gave the healers a winsome smile as he made eye contact with them all. All but the light-skinned woman blushed and looked away.

She bowed her head and started putting together materials.

Rochan needed to be more careful. He was stuck making small talk and checking on each girl. The others—after Balan—tried to do something to prolong his stay with them, from acting in pain to flirting. He was lucky to get out of there. Wasting enough time, with the little bundle in hand he left the infirmary. Finding the halls empty, he windwalked directly outside of Xandra's room. The last thing he wanted to do was to startle her after a battle like that.

The guard at the door jumped and then immediately got out his key to unlock the door to allow Rochan's entry.

Rochan knocked despite her likely being alerted by the loud lock unclicking.

"Who is it?" Xandra's voice called out, muffled by the door.

"Rochan," he answered.

"Come in."

The guard opened the door.

"Potted plant down the hall. Do not get caught." He tipped off the guard with bribery of a book he'd hidden previously for when he needed to buy the guard's silence and for him to disappear for a moment. A smile tugged at the man's mouth, and he bowed before leaving the door.

Rochan hurried in, closing the door behind him, turning to see the girl he had been longing for. He needed firsthand assurance that she was okay.

Xandra was fresh out of the shower, in silky pajamas and robe wrapped around her, her wet hair wrapped up in a bun atop her head, making her look more Lyftian than he ever thought she could. She was sitting on the padded bench by the foot of the bed examining a cut by her elbow.

"You refused the healers' care?"

Her gray eyes met his and a pleasing chill went down his spine. "I'm fine."

"Balan said you were hurt. I was so worried. Xandra, it took everything not to react, not to launch myself into the arena—"

"Rochan." She was up, gripping his shoulders. "Hold it together. I do not need a hero to save me from these girls. Stop underestimating me like everyone else has been." She let go, pushing him away, frustrated.

Rochan captured her hand in his and pulled her back toward him to stop her from moving away. He kissed her palm. "You misunderstand me. I know you can hold your own. I have seen it round after round. I am no hero either, but the thought of you hurt broke me to pieces. I care too much, Xandra."

She gasped breathily as he pulled her closer, but she peered down at the floor. "I can heal myself. Fire has healing qualities if you can learn the art of it. I was just trying to clean it out properly first."

That made him remember the bundle in his hands. He let go of her. "Yes, Balan mentioned what you did for her. I got this for you in case. Here."

"Thanks." She sat back down. "I should not have healed her."

"I disagree."

"Rochan, she could tell the empress and—"

"She won't. The empress pushed her to take it too far. Balan says she is sorry, and she thanks you. I think you have an ally in her and if not, at least no longer an enemy." He sighed. "Let me help you, please?" He tried to subdue his feelings and focused on cleaning her cut. Then he watched her heal it with her fire, her face grimacing.

"It hurts?"

"Yes, but a small price to pay for it to be gone." She removed her hand and smiled. "Look, no scar."

Rochan stared at that dazzling smile, wanting to make her look that exact way every day. But her smile fell too soon as she cocked her head, perplexed at his expression. Rochan needed to speak but the words were hard to form when he felt so many things that mixed with his hopes and fears. "I thought…Xandra I do not know what I would do if something happened to you." He left the "too" unsaid. Dev was gone. He only had Udaya and Xandra left. The empress would not hesitate to hurt them so she could control him.

Her confusion left, and her hands grabbed his. "Same, Rochan. That is why we have each other's backs. But listen, we cannot get distracted. That could be what puts us in danger more than anything else."

He stared at those gray eyes, those pert little lips that lit him up each kiss, "How can I not be distracted?"

He could swear she moved toward him, but he also moved toward her, so they met in the middle—arms around each other and lips crashing. He needed Xandra's lips and touch like he needed air to breathe, wind for power. It was a weakness, but one he would easily embrace.

The kissing intensified and before he knew it, they were stumbling onto her bed. Fantasies flooded his mind, and he wanted to enact every single one of them. For the first time, he did not chide himself for his thoughts. After all, these thoughts, these impulses, were natural—Xandra was feeling them too.

Xandra pulled away. "This is distracting us, Rochan. I have to win this fight, win you. You are supposed to be getting the backup plan in place, an escape."

"I already have, but you are right about distractions. I should not come here so often or you to my rooms. We could get caught." He fished into his pocket and pulled out a pouch on a string.

"A stone to Fyr?"

"Yes, and I have mine." He unbuttoned his collar to show her the string.

Her hands touched his neck under his collar making pleasant chills shoot across his skin. She ran them up to his cheeks and held him gently as she kissed him. "You should go. I may have won, but I am exhausted. I should rest."

Rochan kissed her back and got up, leaving the pouch for her. "Goodnight, Princess."

He windwalked into his own quarters feeling more than smitten. Xandra was a light in his dark life, darker now by the absence of Dev.

He could not wait to see her again and keep that flame in his life, in his rebellion, alight.

Oh, how he burned for Xandra, for the freedom for the entire sphere. It was all connected.

Xandra was everything.

20
DATES

Rochan was nervous. This round of the games were dates, and he had to pick them, trying to cater each outing for the specific girl. As if he knew them well, or at all, after such a short time. He did know Xandra thoroughly. He was over this charade. He knew the bride he wanted.

There were three girls left with Balan in a women's prison and disqualified, but he was not allowed to cut any of the three even after this round. Ahana was supposed to be cut, but her points overall were tied with Lin's. He was sure the empress was happy to not have the odds be fifty-fifty with Xandra in the mix.

The dates were to be chaperoned and scored for how well Udaya thought they suited. He was glad the empress was too busy to bother with his dating life. Udaya would hopefully indulge him when seeing his true feelings.

The first date with Ahana actually went well. He took her to a play and at dinner she held good conversation, laughed at his corny joke and it seemed authentic, and talked about the play and books. There was no praising of his mother, thankfully. She was awfully pretty with those large, dark eyes—no Xandra, who could be?—and maybe she would be someone he could resolve himself to marry if he could never have his first pick. She seemed kind and treated him as an equal. Udaya never had to intervene. He hastily kissed her hand in parting to give his mother something to say to the empress that she was marked as a favorite. It would be dangerous after all to only mark Xandra as a possibility.

The second girl, Lin, he took to the Parinaaz Arena, named after the first queen of Lyft. Back then, almost a thousand years ago, Queen Starsapphire had it built for her love of arts and plays would take place there. If alive today, what would she think about what his mother had turned it into? It now hosted warrior games, where professional fighters entertained by battling until first wound, but at least these public ones did not end in death like the private ones in the palace. Women fought too, whereas the empress's deadly games were only fought by men because in her head they were expendable.

The evening started off well. Lin was excited for the match. Once the three of them were seated with snacks in the empress's box, he tried to start a conversation. She prattled on about the fighters and her fighting abilities.

"I do enjoy a nice sparring match myself," Rochan said as he watched the entertainers clear the arena to allow the first match to begin.

"They are entertaining," Lin said.

Rochan laughed lightly. "I meant sparring myself. I prefer katanas." He had learned them to please the empress when he was younger, but she was not touched by the gesture. The fact he helped Xandra adapt her two-sword sparring to fit the style of the empress's male ancestors instead of female was sweet revenge. She looked livid during the games. The fact Xandra was a quick learner, already highly skilled and trained, and how she could mix Fyr's and Lyft's styles was unsettling and unpredictable to her opponents.

Lin's smile fell from her face instantly. "You fighting? Good joke."

Rochan was shocked at her attitude, so much so he could not speak at first from the insult. He wished he was with Xandra today instead.

Udaya cut in, "Rochan is an excellent swordsman. I do not know who can best him. He was taught all forms of fighting and weapon use."

Rochan's heart panged because it had been Dev who had taught him that. His gaze met Amma's. She gave him a sad smile.

Lin's eyes were wide in disbelief, a snarl of incredulity upon her lips. "Ho, this I would like to see. I can say for sure you cannot best me. Men cannot fight."

Rage flashed through Udaya's eyes. He subtly squeezed her arm for her not to react.

"Men can, I assure you. Biologically, most of us are stronger."

"Stronger in muscle but not wit. Any intelligent warrior can outwit brawn."

"I agree, but both combined are the greatest force, do not you think?"

She frowned. "You think men are equal to women?" Lin asked, blinking rapidly as if trying to understand the concept.

"I believe all human beings are regardless of gender, heritage, or powers."

"Power is everything. Gender is everything." Her voice was stern as if she was trying to assert power over him.

"Explain to me why, then, the Empress Guard are all male?"

"If we marry, you will not be allowed to fight."

"Well, that was a random change in topic. Do you always do that when someone disagrees with you?" He had not meant to be unpleasant, but he would not marry a woman who would dictate to him as his mother did. He would marry to be free of his mother, find a partner in things. All he could think of was Xandra as he narrowed his eyes at Lin. He would flee to Fyr with her rather than marry this younger version of his mother in attitude.

"How dare you," Lin went rigid, her eyes narrowing.

"Always thought it would be fun to spar with my wife," he pretended to muse, enjoying making her angry and cutting her off.

"Whatever the empress allows you to get away with, no husband of mine will wield a weapon."

"Afraid?" He met her gaze.

She stared him down, but Rochan did not waver. A thrill went down his spine at the thought of defying this girl, this symbol of someone just like the empress. It was just like defying his mother, only there would be no whipping afterward. She could not lay a hand on him, not yet. After marriage…that would be a different story, which was why he would never marry Lin or anyone like that. Ahana was the opposite, too soft and genteel, and they both would be under his mother's rule. He needed someone strong who would treat him as her equal. Xandra was the one, not just because of how he felt about her, but because she was seemingly genteel and soft but underneath, she was fire and strength, a force to be reckoned with. She sure would push back against the empress.

"You will not speak like that when we are married. You will be seen, not heard. You will not engage in any combat. You will not—"

"That is too many 'nots' for my liking." He could not help but grin despite her threats because needling her was too much fun.

"—interrupt me." She glared at him, her fists curling up in her lap.

"You are either overly confident or under the false presumption that my choice does not matter. I assure you it does, more than you think. You also underestimate the abilities of your competitors. I am the empress's son. What makes you think I would condescend to choose a wife who will command my every move?"

"Because—"

"You only see what I present publicly. You have no idea how my parents are or what my life is like behind closed doors." It was a lie—well, not with Udaya and Dev who acted more like guardians should—but Lin did not know that. Rochan knew the empress kept her abuse of him secret and so did he because they both would appear weak to others—her unable to manage her temper or her child without resorting to violence and him because he was too scared to fight back.

"I see." Lin made a face and turned her attention to the fight.

"Do you?" He challenged, trying to put her in her place.

"*When* I win, aside from a female heir and you continuing your public act of submission, we will stay out of each other's way."

A sarcastic 'How romantic,' wanted to slip out but Rochan bit back the retort. Not from fear of her but fear of her winning. He should accept such an alliance, if she won. It was the most she would give. Lin was worse because she wanted to be *the* empress, whereas Ahana just wanted to be *an* empress.

They wordlessly watched the battle, and he cut the night short after the match by grabbing food from a street vendor and depositing her back to her home, no kind farewells between them and anger and resentment written across her face.

Last, finally, he got the much-awaited date with Xandra. He had thought he had been nervous before, but he was beyond frazzled. He had to impress her, hide his feelings in front of others to make sure Udaya could report nothing out of the ordinary to the empress—not that she would but if others observed and she left it out, the empress would react against her or them all. His entire future might depend on this date. *No pressure.*

As he knocked on her door, he fidgeted. Udaya raised her brows at him.

"Do not," he warned in a threatening whisper.

This made her smile. "I said nothing."

He scowled, but as soon as the door opened and he saw Xandra standing in front of him, it slipped into a grin as he took her in. She had on a lehenga choli of a vibrant purple hue with silver floral foil print on it that made her gray eyes appear purple. The top showed off her flat stomach, athletic arms, and just a tad of the top of her breasts. She wore bangles and dangly earrings, her hair up, much of it around her circlet, just the bejeweled front showing.

His smile dropped in the realization of what she was wearing but more for how much he liked it on her. She looked like a bride. His mind was spinning into how much he wanted her to be.

"You look…" he shook his head unable to finish the thought aloud. Bride would be too much, beautiful might give away all his feelings to Udaya upfront. He was not sure what she would tell the empress.

Udaya spoke since he was still incapable of uttering a word. "Well, that is an interesting choice of dress, I must say."

Her eyes went wide. "Finn, my servant procured it. He said it was not just for brides but special occasions too. Do I need to change?"

Udaya pressed her lips down in thought.

It was a bold move of a servant to procure such a gown. It definitely would send a signal to everyone, perhaps start rumors that they were to marry. Rochan found the bold move something he was excited about, anticipating the empress's angry reaction. "No. The servant was right. Royalty before empresses wore it often. It is a dress for a Lyftian princess if the title still existed."

Udaya gave him a questioning look, then gazed at Xandra. "You should know that many will see it as princess attire, but many might speculate it means a marriage."

"So, a rumor? Gossip?" Xandra asked. "I am used to that. They are scathing on Fyr. We call them gossip rags, but they do make nobles' crimes known which puts them in check and on their best behavior. My uncle was apparently an infamous cad, until he found out my aunt was sweet on him. And I am an outcast, according to the papers, because my eye color is my mother's not my father's."

Udaya gave a tight smile. "That sounds ridiculous, so you must explain it to me on our outing. Shall we go, Princess?"

Outside the front steps of the palace, a gaja awaited as their means of travel. Udaya must have done it—a tad of rebellion from her against the empress. Only the former deserving royalty, the "real" ruling princes and kings, were bestowed with such a travel method. Prior, Rochan was limited to the lords' way of travel via a carried cart—not this massively amazing animal from the gods.

He watched Xandra's face as she took in the large gray animal, her mouth falling open into an adorable O shape.

"My mother—she grew up on Earth—told me about these. Elephants. I have never seen one before. That carriage type box atop it, are we riding in that? Is it safe?"

"A howdah? Yes, it is safe. We are safer up there than any other conveyance, on this packed street, and you will get the best view." Rochan wanted to thank Udaya then and there for such distinction and a way to impress the girl he wanted most.

Several more questions raced out of her mouth that he lost track of, smitten by her enticing excitement. The number of days he could surprise her with new things in his world and see that intoxicating surprised expression was more than appealing. He was drunk on her.

"Safe, yes, and like an elephant, but from my understanding, these are larger than Earth's and have more tusks and other minor differences." He could not remember how many Earth's elephants had, but he doubted their tusks split into two on each side to protect their front and sides from nagas and other creatures.

Udaya smiled and took over explaining their white coloring was lighter than elephants, explained how they would get up onto the platform ahead where the animal with kneel so they could climb up.

Once they were up, Udaya took the back row and allowed Xandra and him to sit together in the front one. Xandra clung onto his arm as the animal stood and swayed as it walked. She looked terrified, and it amused him to see the proud warrior princess dependent for once. He longed to kiss her to distract her but could not, not in front of Udaya or the people around the city who were peering up into the imperial decorated howdah.

On his previous dates, they had walked or ridden in his chariot, but he wanted to give Xandra distinction but also so she could see best from the high vantage point. He used it as an excuse to take her out earlier than he had the others, while the sun was up, to make the day last as long as he dared.

"What are we doing today, Prince Rochan?" Xandra asked.

"I thought you might like to sight see, a tour of our imperial city. Then some shopping and food."

"Shopping?" Her brow wrinkled.

"Not that you seem like a girl who loves shopping," he rushed out, hoping not to offend her, "or maybe you do? I just thought…you do not need servants to procure your clothes but choose them yourself."

Xandra still seemed a bit at a loss and met his gaze. He leaned in and whispered so Udaya could not hear. "I wanted to make the day last. Plus, you will need clothes if you are staying." They had confessed their feelings, made plans, but he could not bring that up in front of Udaya.

He pulled away from Xandra and pointed out a historical statue of the Queen Parinaaz Starsapphire. She took it in but grabbed his hand subtlety under the edge of her skirt that rested on the seat. Rochan weaved his fingers through hers and she squeezed. This was all they could have in public, hidden away atop the gaja, or the empress might find out. If she learned he loved Xandra, she would not hesitate to kill her. The empress already took his father from him, Xandra would be next. Nothing, in all of Lyft, scared him more than that.

He enjoyed sightseeing and greedily basking in Xandra's smiles as she took in the new world around her. It really was too cute to see her excitement as she discussed the differences in architecture on Fyr. She said her world felt "boxy" with buildings made of right angles and stones piled onto each other with visible mortar, mostly of whites and grays. She gushed over the domes, arches, windows, and colors. She made them stop to take in a temple, its tampered layers, with a story of the gods painted across each floor, like a book she longed to read. He watched her, unable to speak a word. How unaffected she was, so real and raw in her taking in his world.

Udaya spoke for him, answering her questions, telling her about the history behind the building—things he knew but he could not utter a word as he watched her gray eyes going wide, her mind a sponge.

Udaya cut the sightseeing and insisted it was time to go shopping. The sun's position told him he had not realized how much time had gone by, lost in watching a beautiful girl be happy. Xandra proved to actually like shopping because the different styles excited her. She proclaimed to have hated it back on Fyr where she said the clothes were more constricting, not as vibrant or as soft. She picked the brightest colors, but by far his favorites were blue and purple, her gray eyes turning those colors when she wore them.

Then he surprised her by taking her to Universe, a restaurant with special cuisine he hoped to impress her with and to steal more of her smiles. There was nothing he enjoyed more than seeing her happy.

Udaya sat at her own table close by, affording them a little privacy she had not given to him with the other girls; she was watching them closely though. What might she tell the empress? He was trying hard not to show his preference, but Udaya knew him better than anyone. Was she seeing through him?

His worries vanished with that perfect smile and those sparkling gray eyes.

"The menu pleases you, Princess?" Rochan asked.

"Yes, food from all the spheres and to know I can eat Fyrian dishes when I please is a comfort. But I smile because you thought to take me here. My father took my mother to such a place, I have been told, to woo her."

Rochan smiled. "I am glad to hear it worked in his favor. Perhaps I might be so lucky."

"Perhaps," she allowed.

"He sounds like a smart man."

"He is. I adore my father. He is the very best man I know." She tilted her head. "You kind of remind me of him in ways. Your moral code, your honesty, your inner strength, and your seriousness."

Rochan frowned. "Seriousness."

"Both brooding over large issues. I think it comes with the territory of ruling."

He did not like that description.

She sensed that. "Not to say my father did not have fun or is not playful; he just went through a lot to get Fyr to its Golden Age. That takes a toll on a person. Then they went and had too many kids which must be exhausting."

Kids crossed Rochan's mind now. Even when Lin had mentioned heirs, he did not really think about it. He would marry. He would become a father. These were things he was not ready for. How could he be a good father if he never truly was raised by one? Dev and Udaya snuck some parental care and affection in here or there when they dared, but all he knew was an abusive mother who was filled with hate and was losing her mind—if it was not already gone.

He pushed the idea away. One thing at a time. One round of these games at a time. He turned the conversation to lighter things, asking about her siblings, Fyr, and her mother. She did most of the talking since there were so many siblings and apparently another one on the way. He did not mind. It allowed him just to watch her animated way of speaking, the tilting of her head in thought elongating her neck, the way those kissable lips moved, and her adorable formal accent. He loved everything about her.

The evening came to an end much too early. He left her by her room in the palace, kissing her hand and then walking with Udaya back to his rooms, where she grilled him about all the girls and his marked preferences. He kept his feelings about Xandra downplayed and upped the ones for Ahana, so Udaya did not have to tempt the empress to act against Xandra. Deep down she must know, but Udaya would not speculate upon what he had not said aloud.

He waited a painful five minutes, locked his door, then windwalked into Xandra's room. She had waited for him. He claimed the kisses from her lips he had longed for all day, trying to get her to let him stay in her room that night but she would not allow it. He was glad she had more sense than him when they were swept away in their feelings.

It was one of the best days he ever had. If only he could have days like this one for the rest of his life.

21
A PEBBLE

There was a knock at her door early the next morning. Xandra had just woken up and wrapped herself in her robe. Expecting it to be her breakfast, she was surprised when she opened the door to Rochan. He opened his palm. There was one pebble on it. He had received it too. Xandra had not thought about the pebble that someone had slipped into her palm during Dev's execution. The trauma and then Rochan and her date…she was getting too distracted.

Rochan went on, "I figured it out. When the sun dial casts its shadow to one, that was when Dev…" he cleared his throat. "That was when Dev and I would do our wind exercises. These are the very stones that created the pathways, but they all lead to the large sun dial in the center of the courtyard. I think someone wants us there at that time. I think they tried you, but you never met them. So now they tried me."

"What if it is a trap?"

"How so? I simply will go and see who is there. I have a ready excuse because it was in my daily routine. You need to find a reason to be out there but not with me. I cannot let the empress see any partiality toward you."

"Are you not risking that right now?"

"No." He handed her an envelope. "Udaya is having a luncheon at three with the last contestants. I am off to hand one to Lin now." He rolled his eyes. "I'll be back tonight to talk over how you can beat her. She's formidable."

"I saw the match. I have a strategy against her."

"I have one too," he smiled. "See you in the courtyard later, Princess." He kissed the back of her hand.

Then he was gone too soon.

Her breakfast arrived not long after. Then she bathed and dressed for the day, letting Finn braid her hair, working her circlet in. If she had to leave Lyft without Rochan, she was going to steal this boy to give him a future on Fyr. He was sweet and memorized every little preference of Xandra's immediately, just wanting to please her. She made sure to praise him, even though boys were not used to that kindness on Lyft.

After she was ready, she asked her guard to escort her to the library. If she did not have one of the guards with her, the empress would send another to spy. The guards at Xandra's door were loyal to Rochan and then to her. It did not take much to get them to turn on the empress.

Reading a book outside in the gardens, away from Rochan enough to not raise suspicions, would be a good ruse. The empress already knew she was interested in the wind exercises she had seen the prince and Dev do. She might even suspect she admired the prince, but if she was not with him or talking to him, and had her guard, then the empress could hardly object.

The guard stopped outside the library doors.

"You are not coming in?" Xandra asked.

"I am not permitted, Princess. Most men are not allowed to read, especially those taught to fight such as guards, so I am not allowed to step foot inside the library."

"Preventing education? To keep women in power and the men in ignorance," Xandra muttered in understanding. Then an idea sprung. "What if I command you to enter? You have to do my bidding, no?"

"On what believable pretense?" he mused.

"I am getting a lot of books to go through, and you must carry them."

The man tried not to smile, and he nodded. She entered, him trailing behind her. There were two women in the library who started whispering and staring. They each had a book, but it was clear they were there talking or gossiping rather than reading.

Xandra searched the shelves, finding books about war and fighting techniques. She glanced over her shoulder to see the guard perusing the shelves. "You can read," she whispered.

His eyes went wide when they met hers. His gaze darted to the floor. He kept his voice low, "The prince pays us for secrecy in books."

Xandra checked to see if the ladies were watching but thankfully, they had lost interest and did not see the servant's slipup. "Keep your eyes to the floor when away from my rooms. It is suspicious."

He nodded.

She placed a book on the stack of four he already held and then another and another. She doubted she'd have time to peruse them all this afternoon, but she had to prove it was necessary to bring the guard along.

Xandra moved to another section and grabbed another book. It was a bribery one.

She went out into the garden, her guard trailing, arms laden with books. Rochan was not there yet, and she was glad for it would make it look like an accidental meeting. To the empress, to whom everything was likely reported, knew that Rochan had not done the wind exercises since Dev's death.

Xandra opened one book, then the next, reading the contents and turning to the same fighting style in multiple books, cross-referencing the details and envisioning the moves that would suit her and surmising ones that suited Lin or recalling the traits of her fighting style against Ahana. She took in as much she could to prepare as much as possible. She opened a fifth book and placed it by her left side, her guard behind her about two paces. She tapped the page. "I command you to read through and find a name."

"I cannot. If I am seen—"

"Do not touch it, merely peer down, read two pages, and then do your survey of the courtyard as you should be, and I will turn the page. Do not rush it. I want you to have a name you like. I want to call you one in private, and you will need one later."

"Princess?" His brow wrinkled.

"I am going to win the prince's hand. And when I do everyone without a name will get one."

"The empress will not allow—"

"She will not know…until it is too late. She can demand you not to use it, call you what she wishes, but she can never take it away."

He gave Xandra a small grin.

She turned her attention to studying. If she did anything suspicious, it might draw a spy, and they had to meet up with someone. As promised, Xandra turned the page every now and then for her guard, while also turning all the pages in her books.

At one point, she looked up and saw Rochan exercising. She did not let herself get distracted. She spoke, not looking at her guard. "Someone wants to meet with the prince and me. Would you know whether I could trust them?"

"I hear lots of things," he mumbled so it did not appear he was talking to her. "So likely."

"Rochan—the prince, I mean—believes they will be here at one. I need you to let us know whether to trust them or not."

"One is the safest time. The empress and consort meet with the council. The prince used to always do wind exercises out here at that time. It should work."

Xandra studied more, and finally the guard cleared his throat. "Someone is approaching. It is a spouse of someone on the empress's council, one known as a dissenter. She argued often against the empress's moves against men. She voices for equality. I think you can trust to hear them out, but do not say anything incriminating."

He stopped talking, and a moment later, a shadow cast over her book. She noticed sandals, then looked up to see a middle-aged man with a golden complexion clad in a long navy kurta over white pants. A man. Her mind had expected a woman, someone who had power, sway with the council. "Princess," the man said warmly and dipped his head down in a bow. He opened his palm and in it was one pebble that he dropped into the grass. "I am Lord Hiren Diamond-Serpentine. I am an inquisitive man. I was hoping you could regale me with tales of Fyr. I would like nothing but to walk and speak with you about your homeland. Would you honor this scholar by updating my Fyrian information that is woefully behind?" He offered her his hand. Xandra looked over to Rochan, whose eyes were open and watching. He nodded ever so slightly but made it look like part of the controlled, graceful moves he was making.

She took Lord Hiren's hand, and he helped her up. They went to the path, the guard trailing. "So, you are a lord? Which name is which?"

His hands were clasped behind his back. "I am a lord through marriage. Men of intellect, manners, and lesser brawn are seen as more valuable in the empress's eyes, but the real reason I was elevated was my wife's doing. We have a rare marriage that sprang from love. She is Serpentine, the men's names go first because people tend to ignore them and only say Lord Serpentine."

Xandra nodded. "I understand this sphere's ways." She also recognized he had the surname of a noblewoman high up in the council. Xandra had to tread lightly—was he loyal or a rebel of the current ruler?

"And how do you view them, Princess? Do you agree with them?" His dark brown eyes bore into hers.

Xandra was about to protest, she did not. What if the empress purposely sent someone to set her up and then arrest her for treason? "You wanted to hear about Fyr." She deflected. "The texts you have likely say it was a patriarchal world, male-run. My parents have changed that. My mother—it is a long story—she saved the sphere, became the firebranded—that is reading the future off flames—Bladesung heroine, and our world is getting very close to one of equality in gender and less divides between social classes."

"I am familiar with firebranding and yes, the Bladesung myth—well, not a *myth* now it seems. So, you are a supporter of equality?"

"It works on my sphere. To be honest, the idea of a matriarchy seemed ideal to me. It stemmed from not fully having the freedoms I wanted as a woman on my sphere. I wanted to be a fighter, a soldier, and I was allowed to indulge in my fancies. Yet I was ridiculed and teased, and as a royal forbidden to be a soldier although my brothers and cousins were allowed to become captains—not that they see battle in such a peaceful sphere. I admit, after coming here, I saw that *this* version of matriarchy is not the way. One gender over the other never works well. I think my real problem was being an outcast."

He gave Xandra an inquisitive look, so as they loped the path around the garden, she explained her eye color, the meaning, of being a twin, but still being written out of the line of succession.

He nodded, his dark eyes full of understanding. "I think that is what every man feels here, right now, like an outcast, written out of power, decisions…history."

"I will listen to you, Lord Diamond-Serpentine." She purposely used both his names. "But I cannot agree to anything that might get me in trouble."

"Before I say anything, I trust this does not leave the garden?" He looked over his shoulder at the guard.

"He is trusted." Xandra said.

"Who else is?"

"Why?" She suddenly worried she'd served her guard onto a platter for a trickster.

"I would rather not endanger my wife or self to hand you a pebble. There must be a way to meet more discreetly. A rumor reached me that you visit the prince through some magic. Your version of windwalking. *That* is not in our books, something the empress does not know is possible. We are approaching the prince, and we do not know if he has the gall to fully do what we want, but you will tell him our conversation, yes?"

Xandra nodded.

"May I ask a personal question?"

She nodded.

"Why are you still in these games? Your family is safe. The empress would wish nothing more than to send you home at this point to rid of you."

Xandra gave him a truth unsure how to tell a stranger she and Rochan had feelings for each other. "I came here to save my family, and I entered the games because I have no future on Fyr. It disappears. I cannot firebrand here. I would need something strong, magma, a volcano."

"There are two volcanoes on the Isle of the Gods. Cannot risk you going there, though. It is very dangerous too, but if you win and decide to stay…"

"I am staying…for the prince."

The lord smiled broadly understanding everything in an instant. "Dev would have loved to hear that."

"He knew, I think."

"Of course, he did. The prince takes after him completely. He knew everything about his son." He stopped walking, lowering his voice as they were now almost to Rochan whose servant Ansh had approached her guard. "Back to who can deliver you and the prince pebbles to communicate?"

Ansh whispered to her guard, who leaned down to the boy's level.

The lord smiled. "There is our answer. No one would think it odd for a little boy to have pebbles in his pocket."

"Lord Diamond-Serpentine," Rochan greeted, walking toward them. He looked between the man and Xandra, his eyes full of suspicion and worry. "You and the princess enjoy your walk?"

"Yes, and thanks to her, I have enough information to write my book, updating Fyr's current climate. It is a strong model of equality from what I hear."

Rochan's shoulders relaxed slightly. "Yes, Princess Alexandra, he is quite the historian. I am sure you have given him valuable information."

"Yes, she has. And now, I leave you two to enjoy this nice weather together. I thank you both." He politely dipped his head to them. "Until we meet again, Princess, Prince." Then he left.

"So?" Rochan prompted.

"He did not say anything straightforward. Testing me out, seeing my opinions about equality on Fyr and why I want to stay. It felt very much like a possible revolution happening behind the scenes, but he was careful not to incriminate himself, and I was careful to do the same. He is unsure about you."

"Did you assure him?"

"No. How could I? I was worried he was setting us up, doing this for the empress. Are you ready for this, Rochan? If they plan to usurp her, can you do it, do it yourself?"

He huffed out a breath. "In this scenario, are you by my side?"

"I cannot be your heroine, Rochan. That is a lot of pressure."

He shook his head. "Not my savior, but my partner." He snatched up her hand.

Her guard cleared his throat and walked around in front of them to screen the view of anyone spying out the windows. They were under the cherry blossom trees, obscured. He leaned in and gave her a quick kiss. It was daring. "Win, my princess. That is what I ask, what I need."

"I plan on it."

She had to part ways with him and go back to studying, and Rochan went back inside before the empress would leave her meeting.

About an hour later, she closed the name book, having gone all the way though. "Well?"

She made eye contact with him, and his mouth tugged into a smile. "Harsha. It means happiness. I did not feel it until you arrived. Seeing you and the prince happy together, and you telling me to choose a name. I am so happy."

She smiled back. "I am happy for that too." Then she sighed. "But we have to keep acting our parts so enjoy your happiness, Harsha. Once inside, we go back in the library, and I dump some of these books off, the name one particularly. The others we take to my room."

He nodded smiling and then let it drop back into a stoic gaze of scanning the courtyard.

Udaya was wonderful at tea. She was why Rochan was such a kind soul. Lin, her main competitor, was not at all wonderful. Still, Xandra ignored her barbs and bonded with Udaya and Ahana about the merits and interests of the prince. Lin grew frustrated because she could not enter the conversation much. Xandra's firsthand knowledge of the prince was a bit of a cheat, but it was nice to make Lin worry about her worthiness as the prince's partner. That was the sentiment Udaya was measuring, although Lin did not pick up on it until the end of the luncheon. After the dates and the tea, Xandra was fifty points ahead of Lin. Ahana was now in second, but with no upcoming battle points, no hope to win. If Xandra could gain enough points to stay in first, she would win.

When Xandra returned to her rooms, there was an envelope on her beside table. She took a deep breath, scared of the envelope's contents. Unless going in on this revolution would free Rochan to make his own choice in a bride…a backup plan if she lost the competition.

She tore it open. Inside were pebbles and a slip of paper.

Prince's rooftop. Destroy after reading.

Xandra immediately poured the pebbles out of her hand and placed them carefully onto the table. Then she lit a fire in the grate using her magic and tossed the note and envelope inside being sure to watch it turn to ash. She swept up the tiny pebbles and counted them. Nine. She guessed it was night's nine and tonight, but if she had to visit Rochan every night to find out, she could not complain. She wanted to be there now.

Xandra tossed a couple of the stones on the floor and then lifted her boots and shoved a few more in her treads before she scattered the remaining few under the bed. She slipped off her boots, the fire making her room a bit warm. She waited for her magic to regulate her temperature, then drew up toward the fire. Was Lord Diamond-Serpentine right about the volcanoes? She peered into the flames, but as expected, nothing. She closed her eyes homing in on fire and heat. The largest hotbed was right in front of her, then tiny blips in the palace, then mentally souring out above the land she felt and saw the hotbeds of volcanoes on the other isle. She tried to pull energy from the closer one…

Nothing.

Xandra concentrated on herself and the games. *What will happen?* She continuously thought over and over. Again. Nothing.

Xandra opened her eyes. The lord had spoken the truth: the volcanoes existed but were too far, too dangerous to go to. Staring at the flames, she pondered if she wanted the firebranding ability back. There would be a comfort in knowing— particularly if she would win Rochan and not be eaten by a naga—but at the same time, it was a relief not to know in case it was bad. The weight of the future on a Sapphirian was a heavy burden. Surprises and the unknown were so…normal. She pulled the fire back into herself, shifting through the ashes to make sure no part of the note remained. Then she studied combat to distract herself. If she could not see the future, she needed to prep for the final battle round—ensure she won. The books were helpful, and the styles of fighting were fast and powerful, while Fyr had heavier weapons that dealt worse blows. Lin would prove hard to beat. Xandra had watched her. She was strong, not as fast but still not slow by any means. A blow from her would send Xandra to the ground. Even though Lin was smart when it came to fighting—quick thinking and well trained in combat–she was not clever. She could be duped, likely to follow a feint and fall apart when angry. Hotheaded.

Xandra had refused to use her magic last round and wouldn't this next one unless necessary. She had not given any of her magical combat tricks away, so Lin would have no idea what Xandra could do. Lin, on the other hand, had given away she loved to do a wind blast. Combine that air with fire? It might go off like a bomb. Just like her and Rochan's magic combined became almost deadly.

Dinner was delivered on a tray, a steaming creamy tomato sauce that had an amazing aroma of spices with diced chicken and vegetables in it. It was called curry and was spicy and served with rice. Both were foods she had never tried before. The rice was bland but mixed with such a savory sauce it made a wonderful balance. The servant explained that the empress was staying in her chambers, and everyone was to eat in their rooms. It was not strange for Xandra to be excluded from dinner, but for everyone that seemed odd. With the wind beginning to whip around outside, maybe that was her having a mood. Rochan had joked about it one night, but maybe it was the truth.

The windstorm had stopped right about when Xandra finished her dinner. She was tired of reading, and the anticipation to see Rochan, the anxiety about what she was walking into was driving her mad. They liked using sun dials in Lyft, but they also had clocks. The one on her wall appeared to be broken, although she knew it was just her impatience to see the prince.

At last, she gave up waiting at half between eight and nine. Checked her appearance in her mirror, brushed her teeth for good measure, and straightened her circlet, pinning down some stray hairs. She took a deep breath before transporting to the prince hoping for two things: lip-lock time and for it not to be a trap.

The fact her priorities thought of one before the other was not a good sign if she wanted to survive.

22
MEETING

Rochan paced in his room. He was nervous. He found a note on his bedside table that simply said: *roof*. Nine pebbles were inside the envelope. He was worried about who it was or what they wanted. He longed to summon Xandra, but he remembered her discussion about her not being some savior, but a partner. He had to go at this alone if she was not given a similar note. He had to be strong, ready to fight the empress. She killed his father, and that anger reverberated inside him, stronger than the grief. He wanted revenge and freedom. He wanted to choose his own wife, destiny, and help his people.

Halfway between eight and nine, fire erupted in his room, and his heart leaped with surprise and elation. He pulled her into his arms and kissed her soundly. She returned the sentiment. He pulled her close, their bodies flush as tongues and lips tangled. How he missed her touch, her scent, the feel of her. Rochan was falling in love with her, and he did not care what might happen in the games. He would agree with any rebel or revolutionary who promised they would ensure this woman in his arms would be his for life.

He pulled away panting, realizing his mind was already marrying her, and his body wanted much more, way too much, of her than she could give him before marriage. "I'm sorry."

"Why?"

"Serious meeting about something with who knows who? We should focus."

She frowned, and it was adorably heart-wrenching. "I came early on purpose."

"Hopefully so we could discuss what might be going on?"

She bit her lip, and his eyes flittered down to her mouth. His lips crashed into hers again. He knew then that she had wanted time alone with him as much as she knew they had to discuss things. He let himself get lost in her lips for another moment or two before he yanked away and created distance.

"Please do not tempt me to our own destructions."

"So dramatic." She rolled her eyes, smiling. Then she sighed. "You are right. We must be careful and if I win, there will be plenty of time for kissing."

That idea sent his mind reeling into more than kissing. He realized for the first time that he had stopped thinking about his feelings for Xandra as wrong. They were natural and reciprocated. The empress knew nothing. She had taught him men were weak, disgusting, and full of lust women do not welcome. Xandra wanted to kiss him as much as he wanted to kiss her. It was pure between them, born of love and interest, friendship and adoration. Was there any feeling better than this, than love?

"You got a note too?" He inquired to break the spell between them. Then they admitted to getting similar messages.

"What will you do?" She asked.

"Depends on who is up there, doesn't it?"

"Who or how many?"

He huffed the air out of his lungs. "If there are many?"

"Rochan," she came over and placed her hands on his face. The use of his name with no honorific sent thrills down his spine. Every time she said it.

"Xandra," he said back trying to focus on anything but kissing her.

Her lips quirked. They were always in tune with each other. "Close your eyes and think." He followed her command, trying to relax as her hands smoothed down onto his shoulders. "What if one person was up there trying to convince you into rebellion. What would you do?"

He took in a shuddering breath at the thought and breathed out slowly as Dev taught him to control his emotions. The thought of Dev brought a sharp slice of pain before it boiled into rage. "I want revenge for Dev, to free Amma, myself…to be with you." His eyes shot open worried about her reaction to such an honest answer.

She wore a soft smile. "There is your answer. If there are many, your chances increase of success."

He pulled away. "No. It could be too risky."

"You are scared it is a trap?"

He stared her down. "More so that it is not."

"Why? Are you scared of her?"

"No." He turned away, angry she would think him that weak. Then he tamped down the annoyance because before the Fyrians had arrived, he *had* been terrified. The empress had not beaten him in a while. These games had distracted her as well as numerous meetings with her council. Perhaps they were displeased.

"Then what is?"

"I am afraid to lose you!" he blurted out.

She froze, her mouth open in awe.

"If she knows I care for you, she will kill you. She punishes in any way possible. Xandra, she just did so with Dev. Took my father from me. It was not just for freeing your family. That would be an arrestable offense, but it would normally go to trial. The council weighs in on that. I'm sure—although I'm not privy to the information, the council had wanted her to free them to prevent an inter-sphere war. She killed him to wound me, to punish me, to try to teach me what happens when you do not obey her."

"Then she is stupider than I thought," Xandra scoffed.

"Do not underestimate her intellect. She is brilliant but unhinged. Her actions are unpredictable."

"She made Dev a martyr. He is why these people, whoever they might be, are going to arrive—any minute—up there."

He shook his head. "You. They are up there for you." He touched her cheek.

She pulled his hand off. "Stop underestimating yourself, your power, and how much this sphere needs you. I am just a spark, but you are who they want in place of your mother, and Dev is the sacrifice that made them react. Did not you say Dev could read the future off the wind?"

Rochan nodded.

"We readers see our future disappear. Mine vanished right before I left to come here."

Rochan gripped her arms. He could not lose her too. He could marry no other.

"I think it is because my future is elsewhere. I cannot see the future here. The fire is not strong enough. I think I belong here, here with you. But if you do not grow a spine and demand your right to rule, your destiny, maybe we all do die. I have no clue what they will say up there, how you should respond, but we must be careful but open to what they say. I do not know who to trust so you must lead."

Rochan nodded. He was strong. Maybe Xandra was a crutch, but her confidence merely pushed his up and forward. She was urging him to see their future path: he was the future of Lyft, not her. She would be a consort if he had his way, an advisor, an ally, someone to assist him. But he would one day be emperor. Only if he claimed his rightful destiny. Otherwise, if the empress had her way, Lin would rule, and he would trade one abusive relationship for another. Oh, no, he would never let Lin lay a finger on him. He was no innocent little boy conditioned into it anymore. He would strike back anyone who would strike him here on out. Even the empress. He was no longer going to be the victim. He was the one who could talk to nagas.

"I am the one who talks to serpents."

"What?"

"She cannot."

"I know. I saw. You stopped them from attacking me. It is the same on Fyr. We Sapphirians speak to the draca. No one else can. That is why my family has been in power for thousands of years. Your mother should not be ruling."

Rochan nodded. "It is about nine."

She nodded, taking his hand. "You should be the one to take us up."

Rochan, not well practiced in windwalking, had to concentrate. She was right. Show up windwalking despite whoever was up there, knowing he was not allowed to train his powers to their full potential would be an intimidating surprise.

He opened his eyes to a gasping crowd. A crowd. As he took them in, he whispered to Xandra so she would know, "This is the entire council save one or two loyalists missing. Um…as you see with their spouses." Most had husbands but a couple had wives.

Xandra squeezed his hand, so he spoke. "This many of you is a surprise, I must say."

"And I must say that hidden power of yours is astounding," a woman came forward, Lady Serpentine, or Diamond-Serpentine if his mother stopped clipping off her husband's name. Her husband was with her.

Faking bravado because he was a bit intimidated, he admitted. "I am the one who speaks to the naga."

There were murmurs and staring at him that made Rochan uncomfortable.

"Let us make this quick to not be caught. We risk a lot by being here," Lady Diamond-Serpentine spoke. "Change is needed. The empress's crimes are piling up. Your Imperial Highness,"—not the right title but she was making her point—"You saw what happened to your father. No trial. You saw her try to tamper with the games to get rid of the one whom you care for, who suits you and this sphere best. The one who understands and would fight for equality for all. You saw her punish men for nothing, reward women for ruthlessness. You do not know the half of what she has done to the men on Isle of the Gods, merely for her bloodlust pleasure. Not even her wife knows that."

Rochan let go of Xandra's hand. "Do you have proof of all of this? That would stand up in a trial?"

"You would give the woman who murdered your father a trial when she gave him none?" Another woman asked aghast. Lady Pearl maybe? He mixed up names and faces because he was never allowed to attend a meeting.

"One who beats you? Beats your Amma?" Another dared.

Rochan growled, blasting them back. A few were unprepared for the power he hid within and slid across the roof and almost plummeted off the cliff the castle was built into. Rochan's room being at top of the highest tower overlooking the rocky terrain stories below meant certain death.

"Stop this pressure," Lord Diamond-Serpentine called out. "Let the prince think over things." He backed away from the crowd between them and Rochan and Xandra. "We can reconvene. Let my wife and I talk to them. Alone."

"I am not stupid," Rochan spat out. "I am not some battered child who cowers in corners either. I am a man with more power than any of you know. But if I start a new empire—as this is obviously the start of a conversation of doing so—I will cut out hypocrisy by being just. Murder for murder is not right. She will be judged by her peers because how many will stand by her side when the truth comes out?"

"She will bring in her supporters," a woman warned but Rochan did not bother to look at whom.

"And my future consort will bring fire upon them."

They gasped. Xandra took up his hand again. "My family came with a treaty, one the empress refuses to sign. Peace and an alliance among our spheres and aid to Water for another alliance. Not much is asked in return. Water's rightful queen needs soldiers. Lyft has many whom would jump at the chance of the freedom Water or Fyr could provide. Not even the empress's consort can get her to sign. She simply wants to control and punish. I agree this cannot continue. But let the games pan out. Let me win the prince. Then we plan."

Lady Diamond-Serpentine shook her head. "*If* you win. I am not sure she will let you live."

Rochan gripped Xandra's hand tighter knowing well the empress would make his future be what she wanted it to be. She simply allowed these games to occur to please Udaya. "If that happens, then you act. You make a plan. Leave us out of it. You must keep this woman alive, or I will not agree to anything."

Rochan would die without Xandra. He was that deeply in love. When he had admitted he would have no other, he exposed he was in love. Now, the thought of her back in Fyr without him killed him, but the thought of her gone forever was too much. These things he could not admit aloud, his weakness.

"If we do what we must to keep her alive?" Lord Diamond-Serpentine asked.

"Her and Udaya. Those are my terms for any usurping plans. You do what you will, but our further involvement will cause to much suspicion."

The crowd seemed to relax, realizing he was on their side, stronger than they supposed, and giving them the terms that solidified his commitment. He showed his weaknesses, but they'd be stupid to exploit them if they wanted his compliance.

"That is not a lot to ask. We can make that happen. We have had…things…in motion for a while, but with the Fyrian disruption and the games for your hand, we have had to hesitate and alter our moves. It will help if you keep this distraction up. The empress is not looking at anyone but the Princess of Fyr," Lady Diamond-Serpentine said.

The conversation seemed like it was coming to a halt when a pounding of feet came up the stairs. They started to panic but Rochan recognized the little feet.

"My servant."

Ansh climbed up onto the roof, his eyes wide. "Prince. Your mother is at the door."

23

COUNCIL

Rochan looked at the council on the roof above his rooms. They were caught. They looked to each other in concern. He asked, "Xandra, how many can you transport?"

"Never tried more than ten in my training but my father can move an army or a massive dragon."

The council whispered. "We have four here that can windwalk and assist the Princess. However, if we wait and you can get her talking…"

Rochan nodded and windwalked below into his chambers, grabbing his servant at the last moment. "Open the door."

He opened his balcony door and walked outside so the council could hear.

The boy announced the empress. Rochan turned, pretending to be shocked by her appearance. "To what do I owe this pleasure, Empress—"

"Drop the civilities. You know why I am here."

He did not have to feign his confusion here. "I do not. You never condescend to come to my chambers. You command my presence when it suits you."

"Until I heard of rumors of a girl in your rooms. I wonder who that might be."

"I am not going to deny my preference for the Fyrian princess. She is by far the superior of all the contestants thus far and has been raised by a monarch, taught to rule. But she is not here. Search my rooms if you would like."

"I was not asking permission." She glared at him and motioned her guards, four of them, to search his humble quarters—bedroom, sitting room, bathroom, and dressing room. The only place in the entire palace he was not watched.

Who had told her? Was someone up on the roof on the empress's side? Rochan's stomach churned. How would they know Xandra had visited him? After so many visits, now she suspected? The same evening the council planned to meet them? Was it one of his guards? The very men he had taught to read and gave every kindness to?

No. He did not believe her. She was trying to get him to fess up to something she suspected without evidence.

He had to distract the empress, bring her ire upon him, spare Xandra. He could not have avoided admitting he preferred Xandra at this point. The empress knew he did. If Udaya could tell, the empress could as well. His *mother* watched him closely—always—for flaws. Amma likely tried to convince the empress it was a good match, and the empress felt threatened by the Fyrian. Xandra was smart enough to vanish and not be caught, but still, he could not let the empress climb the stairs to the roof. But…despite her words earlier, Xandra might not leave him if she thought he needed saving.

"I think I would know better than to sneak a girl into my room. I could never get away with it. Plus, I'd hate to wonder why someone would do such a thing." He laid on his innocence thickly. If the empress did not know about Xandra's transporting powers, how could she explain her being in his room? She had no clue he had learned to windwalk either.

"Do not pretend you would not know why." The empress was getting angry.

He had to appease her a little but keep her attention on him and angering her was the easiest way. "I have an education in that subject and heard plenty of courtly gossip. I have had my share of girls throwing themselves at me. I am not a monster as you profess all men to be. I am pure as the day I was born. These girls? They are not. I am starting to question if that has anything to do with gender anymore or simply moral restraint."

Her mouth tightened.

He got daring, stepping closer to her. "I know you want me to fail. You always do. If I do not fail on my own, you set me up to do so. If I manage to succeed, instead of pride, you see a threat, and you beat me back into submission. I am bigger than you, stronger than you, and more powerful than you. You know this. I am the one who speaks to naga. I am done putting on a charade that you are better than me. Out of respect, I have not proven that. I am not stupid. I know showing that could start a riot, a revolution that would merely cause bloodshed." He rushed on because she was about to interrupt. "You wanted to squash me, kill me as you did your husband on his wedding night. I used to convince myself that you let me live because you cared, that deep down you loved me. When I became older and wiser, I thought it was simply you could not kill the part of yourself you saw in me—your flesh and blood. But it is just Udaya, my *real* mother that keeps me on this side of the sphere."

"Are you done?" the empress asked. Then she gave him the backhand across the face he had expected midway through the conversation.

"Yes, I killed that disgusting excuse of a what they would call a man whom my mother forced me to marry. I cannot speak to the naga as well as some, but I *can*. Enough to keep them at bay."

"With help. I had to stop them from killing the princess."

She slapped him again, with her palm this time. It stung more than causing deep, lingering pain, but her knuckles from the first hit might cause small bruises he'd have to get healed for appearance's sake. "Speak only when spoken to, boy."

He put his hands behind his back, locking one hand around his wrist to prevent himself from the instinct to defend himself. He wanted to fight back. Guards and all, he wanted to show her who he was, show Xandra. He could not act. There was a time and place to fight back, and tonight he would not gain any ground. He could only use words.

"No," he forced out. He would not only answer her. He had the council listening to her crimes so he must push forward. See what else she might admit to. "Then you poisoned your own mother. Why, for power?"

The empress's face scrunched up in unhinged rage, and he awaited an onslaught of pain. It did not come, his cringing enough for her to feel she had the upper hand. "Because she would force me into marriage again. I had plans. I had power. She was weak. Speaking of her regrets, nonsense of equality, the matriarchy ending, a government run by the *council* matching a royalty vote. How would a simplistic and self-serving group of people know better than me, descended from the gods? Why revert to a constitutional monarchy? It is an insult to my bloodline."

Rochan did not speak. He wanted to tell her she was not blessed by the gods because only those who spoke to the nagas were. He withheld his voice when he wanted to tell her Lyft began as a constitutional monarchy and it was his dream to return it to that one day. He refused to speak because he had heard no wind whipping above, no burst of flames. Everyone dared to stay above to listen. They heard it all and he would not jeopardize what they might do with the information. She had admitted to murdering two people and wanting her own heir dead. That was enough for a coup if they were brave enough. If she were imprisoned, the amount of people who could speak of abuse or their loved ones taken and murdered for their gender…

He could not get excited about freedom or a revolution. The council might be more cowardly than himself.

To break the silence of her glaring at him, he spoke, "The princess is not here, so what did you really come for?"

"To tell you that if Lin loses somehow—because she is a by far better warrior than your little *princess*—she will rule in your stead. I have chosen my heir, and I can rewrite laws to get rid of you, the pest who continually ruins my plans."

"Not without the council backing it, and the people's vote."

"I have that in hand, little *boy*," she punctuated it with another slap.

Rochan laughed. "You are angry. You are not ordering a servant but using your own hands. I learned long ago that means you are scared of me, needing to show me personally that you are supposedly better than me. You do not have the people at all. The fact there have been so many council meetings since the Fyrians arrived? So, you still have them in hand?"

She blasted him with her wind power, exasperated, on the verge of tears. He stood his ground, using his magic to stand fast to her wind magic attack, still hands behind his back.

When he opened his eyes, she was staring at him, mouth open in shock, eyes wide, with tears pooling. "When did you…how did you…who trained you?"

"No one," he said casually. He had to protect Udaya, a few helpful tutors, and Xandra most of all, but the one who taught him the most was gone. "Most of it came naturally. You decided to breed with someone who could talk to the naga, someone who was the descendant of the original queen who was in that position for being the most powerful, someone who looked like your wife with your romantic sentiments. I do not think you really thought through how powerful your wife is, nor how good her brother was at hiding his power in order to survive."

She landed a punch to his ribs, but he kept his hands clasps behind his back.

"Guards!" she shouted.

They had given up their search and were standing and watching. Two were his men and another four were not. He was going to get a good beating, perhaps almost die. He hoped everyone up on the roof would leave, stay safe. Maybe he could say something, a warning. If Xandra was up there, though, her fire "transporting" made a different discernible sound.

He would do his best to save the others and the woman he loved. "Six guards to punish me, beat me? Do you realize what it might look like if I cannot show up to the games, the ones for my hand in marriage?"

The empress glared at him. "Spare his face. Do not kill him…yet."

The men moved to grab him. Two of them forced him to his knees. The impact of tile to his kneecaps made him wince. It hurt enough.

"Nooo!"

To his horror, he recognized that scream. Xandra.

Damn her heart. Why would she risk everything?

She rushed down the steps from the roof, not transporting. Hiding that ability for a reason? Then he knew what she was about. Love blossomed in his chest. He could never leave her in such a situation as this. He would expose everything to keep her safe. He loved her, the kind of love old poets wrote about before his recent ancestors of the matriarch tried to enforce women marrying women and having men on the side for pleasure and progeny. Marriages of love regardless of gender should be the norm.

He realized something in that moment. He didn't *need* to marry her to survive. He *wanted* to marry Xandra. He had found her beautiful at first sight. Adored who she was as a person and wanted her in the ways he was told was wrong. She was his friend and partner foremost, and he loved her, but he wanted her too. That was what a marriage should be—all three: friendship, love, and attraction. He would rather die than live without her. How could he be mad that she felt the same? The fact she did was a warm balm to his soul despite the perilous situation.

"I see I was right," the empress purred, slicing through his moment of bliss. "Punish them both. Whip them. Ten lashes should teach them not to spend clandestine time alone. Whip them until they are pure. It will make her inept to fight, but we will make her presentable. Lin will win the prince's hand as she would have anyway."

Only one man moved forward to restrain Xandra, Rochan's guards and the other of the empress did not move. He was a man Rochan got in trouble for giving a name to when he was younger. The guard, Sanjay, glared at the empress behind her back, clutching his whip tightly, despite what Rochan had done for him. He could not let Xandra get whipped. Never. It would kill him. Why had she come down thinking she could spare him? He cared for nothing at this moment but to protect her.

"You cannot hurt her," Rochan growled.

"Why not?" The empress slapped Xandra's face.

Rochan reacted without thinking. He blasted the empress away, and she almost went off the balcony but her back caught the wall. He saw pain lace through her face and was pleased. Then his stomach turned. She liked that—to inflict pain and watch. He could not be like her. Her blood flowed through his veins, and here he was proving he was just as sick as she was.

Xandra laughed, surprising him.

He was ready to start a war, and the woman he loved was laughing. Xandra was clever, so he refrained from toppling his mother over down several stories into the courtyard to her death. The fantasy of doing so made him feel too much like her.

"Your Imperial Majesty, this might be a good time to remind you that my family has returned to Fyr, has told the King and *Queen* the state of things here. If I do not come home, or come home with scars from your whips, there *will* be retribution. My mum would murder for her children in seconds. We came here to make peace, to start an alliance to help a *woman*, a rightful queen, take back her sphere from men, from *illegitimate men* on the Water sphere. You have refused to even read it. You could not have. It favors women on all spheres, and yet here we are. Why?"

Rochan studied the empress's face as her lips shook, fumbling for a response. Xandra was right. The empress had not read it or listened to Udaya who had read the treaty over. Simply because the messengers were male. Rochan knew the empress was insane. He never wanted to admit it because she had birthed him, so what did that mean biologically for his mental state? If he admitted his mother lost her mind, would he not be brought down by the stigma? But hearing her now and knowing his rational thoughts, he saw the difference.

"Whip her! Twenty times. I want her unable to walk, let alone fight!" The empress's body shook with rage as she screeched the words.

No one moved. The soldiers frowned, not ready at all to act on it. The ones holding Rochan lessened their tight grip.

The empress shoved the closest guard using her wind and slammed him against the stone wall. She yanked his whip out of his belt and gripped the handle. "I will do it myself. And to show your mother and father I mean business, I'll start with your face."

Rochan struggled to free his arms out of the loose hold and blasted the soldiers holding him prisoner backward, slightly, to protect them from being blamed for assisting him which would cost them their lives. As the empress swung at Xandra, Rochan threw up his arm, the whip encircling his forearm, slicing through his shirt, a few times. He screamed out. The pain was excruciating as each leather strand did its damage.

Xandra threw up a circle of flames around them that burned the whip in half, only the handle remained in the empress's hand as she screamed for an attack. She was desperate and pathetic, a cornered animal. He could not believe in that moment he was related to her.

"Halt!" Someone shouted. He recognized the voice of Lady Diamond-Serpentine. The council could not do this now. It was too early to act. They had to let Xandra win. He had to marry her. But Lady was followed by Lord. The rest of the council, however, did not follow. What did that mean?

Rochan relaxed, only slightly, that this was not a coup moment, but two people sacrificing themselves. He was scared not knowing what would happen.

Xandra watched them as she gingerly unwound the other half of the whip from his arm, the pain throbbing in reminder. She held it by her side, ready to use it if needed, while her fire steadily protected them.

"What are you doing here?" The empress was trying to reign in her rage and worry because she realized they had been there for quite some time.

The lord spoke first, bowing deep. "I am sorry, Your Imperial Majesty. We asked for this meeting. It is my fault. As Lyft's head historian, I had not been given access to the prisoners as I had requested. I thought to get as much information as possible about the new Fyr we do not know about and a little about Water that the princess knew. We should update our books be educated as best as possible for allies or enemies, no?"

The empress crinkled her nose. "How much you talk, Serpentine. Control him." She directed the comment to his wife.

Lady Diamond-Serpentine spoke with confidence, "I facilitated this. And I was the one to interrupt this…*meeting*…you are having with your child. As part of the council, I will have to report your attempted attack to a royal of another sphere."

"Go ahead." The empress glared, trying to intimidate.

"It is my duty, what you swore me in to do." Then she leaned in close to the empress, her breath on her neck and her fingers dancing against the side of her breast. Rochan looked away realizing Lady Diamond-Serpentine was artful, and the empress was the one who was more victim to lust than him. "But please make it easier on all of us and leave. I made this meeting happen for my spouse and for all of Lyft to know what is going on elsewhere. That is important. If we went to the princess, you would stop us. If we met her in a public place, you would stop us. I would have asked if I knew you would be kind, but you have been angry as of late. I will simply explain the whole situation and how it was easily misunderstood."

The empress glared at Rochan. She did not fully believe it but could not fight it. Then she turned and left. The Diamond-Serpentines trailing behind her as well as the guards.

Xandra reached her hand over, not taking her eyes off the empress as she retreated, and yanked Rochan's sleeve back.

He winced and bit back a cry of pain.

She dropped her protective fire ring. Xandra sighed, looking at him. "Forgive me, but I am going to cause you pain to heal you." As soon as the words were out and before he could process them, flashing hot pain seared his arm. Then it was gone along with the throbbing whip pain. He opened his eyes to see his whole forearm smooth and uninjured. There were faint lines of white to prove it had happened. Scars to match the many he already had.

"I like this talent." To deal with the same amount of pain the blow gave to heal it in an instant was profound.

"I hope we do not need it often."

He kissed her soundly.

A guard cleared his throat. Xandra looked at him. "Sorry, Harsha."

"It is best I escort you in front of the empress to your rooms."

"Make it look rough, yeah?" she winked.

The guard smiled.

"You named him?" Rochan asked her astounded at her audacity, something he did daily in defiance.

She gave Rochan a funny look. "No. I made him choose his name."

Rochan grinned wide. As she was torn away from him, he kissed his fingertips and blew them her way. *I'll be back*, She silently mouthed to him.

This was an escape, a way too narrow one. But he heard the council leaving via windwalking. They had learned a lot.

Despite the danger, he could not wait for Xandra's return.

24

A CATALYST

Xandra waited in her rooms for ten full minutes, losing her mind, when the guard knocked on her door.

She opened it. "The empress has retired for the night. Be back before dawn. If I may be so bold…"

He was not used to being so, and she had to urge him on with her hands.

"Tomorrow you should rest up, sleep well in your own bed. This battle is everything."

She nodded not wanting to think about it. "I know." She placed a hand on his chest. "Keep reminding me of what I fight for. Always. If I manage to survive, win his hand, and live to have it. Harsha, you will be my personal guard—if you will have me."

"It would be the greatest honor." The guard went down on bended knee. Then he looked up with a small smile. "I read, from a book about Fyr the Prince procured for me—so I would be the best guard for you—and I think this is how I would vow my service to you as a guard?"

Xandra's heart soared. Someone who might have her back. "On Fyr, you would be my valet-bodyguard. You would vow to me that you would give up your life to save mine. But you would help me dress and wait on me and defend me. I am not sure if that role is for you."

"I think it is. I am not partial to any gender. I am not…"

"Speak. I do not understand."

"The empress took what makes men *men* when I was a child because I slipped on the floor and shattered a plate."

A eunuch. The empress was more than vile. How many of these guards were robbed of procreating because of one tiny mistake? Xandra wanted to tell him she was sorry, but that would be insulting. Instead, she took up his hand and shook it. "Vow to me you will be my guard and valet to take care of me every moment of my life until you decide to retire."

"I vow that, knowing I am being given the greatest honor."

He was too serious. Good for his job but not for their relationship. Back home, she saw how her parents' and aunt's and uncle's valets were more than friends, family.

"Not sure dealing with me is always an honor, but I'll take the compliment nevertheless."

Harsha squinted and tilted his head slightly, trying to make her out.

"I was making a bad joke. I am not always easy to deal with. I am troublesome at times."

He smiled shyly, "All the time?"

Xandra beamed back and briefly squeezed his shoulder in camaraderie. "That is more fitting. You are the only one allowed to put me in my place…and Rochan, but do not tell him that."

Harsha again hesitated. "A joke again? I do not like this one. I will protect you against him if it is ever necessary."

His loyalty was endearing and before she protested Rochan was not a threat, she hesitated. What was this sphere doing to her? She had to let Harsha be unbiased and do what was right for her.

Reluctantly, she nodded. In her heart, she trusted Rochan, but her life had always been run by logic. She needed an ally in all of this for *her*.

Feeling slightly like she was betraying Rochan, she nodded. "But," she took a deep breath. "I cannot ask you to protect me when I am in the arena."

"What if the empress orders your death after you win or lose? Can I intervene?"

Xandra took a deep breath. "No. You cannot win that. That is my battle. Anyone but my opponent or the empress herself when it comes to the arena. If there is an assassin, you can go ahead and defend me all you like. Will that please you?"

He nodded.

Xandra picked up a novel and handed it to him. It was a fiction novel she indulged herself in to let go of the studying and fighting in order to sleep. "This is something you are not used to. I hope you like it, but do not get caught."

He nodded and realized he was dismissed.

Once he was out the door and locked it, she transported to Rochan.

He was pacing, distressed from earlier.

He turned to face her. "I knew you would come."

She steadied Rochan's shoulders. Then she kissed him, which sent them into a tumult of lips and hands running along bodies until their kisses took on a fierceness that they both knew would lead too far.

Rochan panted and said quietly, "Can you focus, Xandra? The empress just attacked us, the council intervened, preventing me from full rebellion that would have gotten us killed. She threatened us. She is going to plan something, and I am terrified that it is something I will never come back from."

"Rochan," she tried to soothe, but what could she say? She pulled him closer, and his rigid posture relaxed in her arms. "What could she do with the council watching her now?"

166

Rochan's breath hitched as he touched her cheek, his dark eyes scanning her with so many emotions. "She took my father. Dev was biologically my father, but he also served as that male figure I looked up to and loved most. She will take my mother next, or you, because she knows how much I love you. I cannot hide it, even though I tried."

"Please do not hide it," Xandra whispered, her heart thumping.

Rochan leaned in to kiss her, but a sudden burst of wind broke them apart. She threw up her fire as protection. Rochan already had up a wind wall. The air from his power fed her flame and she had to pull back in the power before the room ignited.

In front of them, Udaya was on the ground, her eyes wide.

Rochan dropped his wall. "Amma, I'm sorry. You scared us." He helped her up.

"Your powers combined are very dangerous."

"We did not know." From Xandra that was the only apology the woman would get. She would not regret defending herself or the man she loved.

"What are you doing here, Amma?" Rochan asked. "The empress doesn't like when you windwalk either."

"It doesn't matter. You both have to leave. Do it tonight. Go to Fyr. There is no reasoning with your mother. She will not stop, Rochan. Serpentine is trying to *convince* her to spite me." The bitterness in Udaya's voice made Xandra catch on to the innuendo. Lady Serpentine was placating the empress through whatever means she could.

Rochan shook his head. "No. I'm not leaving you behind or our people to suffer from her insanity."

"She will not let the princess win your hand. If you win this final round, Princess, the empress will kill you. She has said it to me aloud. This is why we fought and why I am here." She met Xandra's gaze. "If you die, *that* will kill my boy."

Rochan's fists clenched as she gave him a loving look and touched his cheek.

"Promise you will go." Udaya looked at them both intermittently.

Xandra glanced at Rochan. His jaw set, fists clenched, and there was fire in his eyes. He was not about to run.

"No. I could foresee the future on Fyr. My own future disappeared. It means death or I live where fire does not rule. If I die trying to free your people, so be it."

Udaya's eyes shined as if in awe or ready to cry, taking in Xandra anew. "Well said by the woman who deserves to be an empress."

The compliment warmed Xandra, and she felt accepted as Rochan's choice.

"Rochan, I must go. I will do what I can to prevent what I can, but please. Have a plan, even if it is to escape."

Then she was gone.

Rochan sighed. Xandra took his hand in hers. "I meant it."

His eyes met hers. "I already know that you are the type of person who only says what she means. So, I will follow your example. I need you to escape if all hope is lost. I need you to go back to Fyr. I cannot bear to lose someone else." Feeling too much, he leaned his forehead against hers. It made her want to agree to anything.

"Compromise."

"Huh?" He pulled away slightly, examining her, his hands gently cradling her face.

"My parents are both very stubborn and willful—"

His lips curled. "That explains where you get it from."

"Stop," but Xandra laughed the flirty taunt away. "Seriously. They have to meet in the middle, like all the time."

"This is life and death, Xandra. What's the middle?"

"If I am mortally wounded. I will go back home. You saw me heal myself. I can do that, and my people will do even better to heal me. But only that. I will only leave if I am dying. Otherwise, I will stay with you. Always."

Rochan's lips crashed into hers again and again. Between kisses she managed to get out. "I…take it…you agree."

"Yes," he breathed into her mouth before intensifying their kiss, his hand pulling her way too close and then molding her body to his. She liked this more aggressive Rochan who gave into his feelings, no longer acting as if natural impulses were a weakness, that love was wrong.

Taking advantage, because who knew if they'd be alive in a few days' time, Xandra started to unbutton his Nehru jacket. His kisses moved from her lips and dusted down her cheek to under her jawline making pleasant chills creep up her spine.

Her hands moved under onto his linen-shirt covered chest, as his hands slipped across the bare skin of her back left exposed by the embroidered crop top. She had chosen these outfits for the Dhoti pants that let her fight and move freely not thinking about the band of flesh showing across her midsection. Apparently, Rochan was well aware of it now.

His touch only instigated more from her. She shucked off his jacket and pulled at his linen shirt until he backed away, his eyes wild, while she pulled the shirt off of him.

He yanked her to him by her bottom, making her yelp, his hands scooping her into him, against him, and she wondered if they would be able to stop this intensity between them before it went too far. The worst part was she was not sure if she wanted him to ever stop.

His hand moved from her back to her stomach, and she grew nervous about whether they would move upward or down. One slid up under her crop top and she embarrassingly moaned which made him claim her lips again.

She moved her hands from his sides she was clutching, slipping them toward his back to draw them closer together, when her fingers touched a rough patch of skin. The puckered up raised flesh was like satin ribbons surrounded by sandpaper.

Her hand froze.

Rochan went rigid and yanked away from her, breathing in pants, his eyes terrified.

"What…" she could not finish her thought aloud, now realizing what her fingers had found: scars.

Rochan's face crumbled and he backed away from her, scooping up his shirt.

"Do not." Her voice cracked in her pleading, making him hesitate. "Show me."

His expression turned sour. "Why?"

"I want to see what I'm fighting for. I want to see what that monster has done. I knew she had…*punished* you. I did not know how bad it truly was…how many times she had…"

His gaze was guarded, untrusting. His hands gripped his shirt hard in frustration, but he made no move to put his shirt on.

"I want to know every part of you Rochan, inside and outside."

He rushed over and kissed her, the shirt falling to the ground as he held her close devouring her mouth with his own.

Xandra might not be able to see the damage but could feel it, tracing her hands up his back she felt the lines of abuse as he shuddered in her arms, trying to pull away, but she pressed against him kissing his cheek and whispering, "Every scar, every line, marks the strength of a warrior who endured what he must until he could rise up and challenge those who keep him down."

Rochan shuddered more in her arms. Xandra had to do this, break the chains of his past to help him see he was more than it. It might upset him, but she needed him to be free. It was the only way they could survive. Thick lines interlaced all across his back, like a map of his trauma. Years of abuse it spoke, permanent scars, ones that could never be erased. One day, she would prove to him they were just a part of him by kissing every inch of him, but they had already played with fire when it came to how far their liaison was going. She did not want to get distracted, and she was going to marry before she fully acted on such impulses.

"Please stop," he choked out. His head was bowed, and she realized too late that he was crying.

She pulled his head into the crook of her neck, holding him as he took deep breaths to calm himself. She dared to run her hand down his back as if it were nothing, as if she did not feel his years of pain and abuse under her fingertips. On the second stroke she no longer did. It was just Rochan's back, the man she loved.

"I'm… It's disgusting."

Xandra held the sides of his face in her hands. "It is proof of her insecurities and her fear that you can easily overpower her. It is proof of her trying to rid of your strength, but that is not possible. Anything suppressed for a time will come out tenfold. You will lash out one day, Rochan. You can decimate her if you want to. Her fear and weakness, not yours. You are beautiful."

"Impossible. That's your role." He claimed her lips.

Xandra had to be the one to pull away. "I should go."

"No, please." His eyes pleaded with her, melting her resolve. He scooped up his shirt and put it on. "Stay with me. I want you by my side while I sleep. We will stay pure. Just to have you in my arms…"

It was a dangerous game they were playing, but such an innocent request. Nothing felt innocent between them. Still, she let him lead her to the bed and he pulled her down onto it, couching her to his side. She draped an arm and a leg over him, resting her head under his chin, on his chest, hearing his steady heartbeat.

He pulled a blanket over them and wrapped his arms around her under it, kissing the top of her head.

She fell asleep in his arms, never experiencing such comfort before.

He woke Xandra early. Rochan kissed her a dozen times before he insisted they part ways for her to focus for tomorrow's final match. He could not distract her.

There would be no rest for him. He was a ball of nerves. His fate was perched on the edge of a knife and falling to either side felt like life or death: Xandra wins, and his dreams come true with the council backing them and a revolution, or Xandra loses…

He hadn't even thought through what he would do if she lost. He would marry no other. His mother might banish Xandra. Rochan could not abandon his people. It would not be fair to flee and free himself when his people suffered under a deranged empress. Even worse, whether Xandra won or lost, would the empress be rash? Would she hurt Xandra?

Rochan dressed for the day. He slipped a sheathed katar in the waistline at the small of his back and slipped the jacket of his bandhgala over it. He preferred a more open neck, but he wanted to look strong, formal, a man of power. Dare he hope one day to be seen as the emperor? He wanted it more than ever now. He wanted to prove to his people he could liberate them, to prove to Xandra he was equally worthy of her hand as she was of winning his. More importantly, he needed to believe in himself, a luxury the empress squashed every time Amma or Dev had lifted him up. Dev sacrificing himself was a spark of revolution. Loss and hope started a fire in him to rebel. That day might be today. Amma had warned the empress might kill Xandra. He would do whatever it took for that not to happen.

Because he had one weapon the empress did not have, did not understand: love. Love made Rochan stronger. It fostered hope and made loss ever so painful, a pain he turned into rage. The rage gave him a thirst for vengeance.

He held in all these feelings as he checked his appearance in the mirror, smoothed the hair out of his face, and went down to breakfast. The empress and Amma were there, tension in their bodies and their whispers strained. They were arguing.

As soon as they noticed him, they stopped talking. The empress's cold eyes narrowed on him. Amma smiled but it was forced.

He sat down hesitantly, wondering if the empress was going to bring up last night. After Udaya asked perfunctory questions and told him he looked all grown up in his suit, the room went uncomfortably silent. They served his favorite:

potatoes, dosas, and roti. He could barely eat, only managing a few bites. Nerves turned his stomach to a boiling tangle of knots.

"Not hungry?" Udaya asked worried.

He shook his head. "Nervous."

The empress scoffed. "Why are you nervous? You are not the one fighting."

"I would rather fight than watch. At least the outcome would be of my own making. Instead, I have to wait and watch. Today, I find out who I will spend the rest of my life with."

"Lady Lin Quartz." The empress grinned over her cup of chai. It was a challenge.

The problem Rochan realized was once he made the gesture to stand up for himself, to defy his abuser, there was no going back. There was no way he'd let her push him down into submission again. Dev telling him to trust the flame caused the first spark of rebellion, the first Fyrians the kindling, Xandra's love the fire, and Dev's death created an inferno.

He would not yield.

"Or Princess Alexandra Sapphirian." He shrugged, not looking away from that cold and intimidating gaze.

She scowled and looked away first. "Trust me. Lin will win, so get used to the idea."

Rochan stood up having enough of her hate. "You know what? If that happens, maybe I will take a katar to bed with me on my wedding night."

The empress was up screaming as Udaya gasped. The cup of steaming chai flew toward his face. Rochan threw up his wind shield surprised as they were that it was strong enough to stop the cup, shattering it as if his magic was a tangible wall.

"What other power have you been hiding?" the empress growled.

Rochan smirked at her and windwalked to his quarters. Triumphant, he imagined the empress's face, her surprise, worry, rage. And her fear. He could show up with a weapon at any time and simply kill her in her sleep. He did not have the stomach for that, but the empress hardly knew him, never being a real mother to him. The happy feeling left him, and dread ran up his spine. The empress might take her rage out on Xandra or Udaya since now she knew he could stop her. Rochan could have always stopped her. He held the power in his abuse and the empress no longer did. He would not let her touch him ever again.

Today was the day Lyft would never be the same. He felt that in his soul.

Rochan bided his time until the final round by pacing. He could not relax, and his worry over Xandra in the ring against Lin grew exponentially. When he was summoned by two guards, he headed to the empress's box in the arena. He did not trust her. She had four of her guards there rather than the two that normally flanked her in public, so the feeling was mutual. Udaya was seated between them so at least he would not have to talk to the empress.

He bowed to them both and sat, fidgeting with his jacket, too aware of the katar pressing against the small of his back, the loud chattering crowd, and his future on the line. Udaya took up his hand to steady him and squeezed.

The empress sighed. "This will be over quickly. The princess has no wind magic. Lin is by far the best fighter in the battles."

"Perhaps the princess might surprise us," Udaya said diplomatically. "Plus, Lin is fifty points down. She needs to win and get enough hits. The princess just needs to win."

"That is your fault. You scored the date poorly for her and the princess so well."

"I scored it all honestly. Lin has no manners, poor comportment, and she and Rochan got along like oil and water. The princess and him are perfectly matched, and she was raised by a monarch, is intelligent, a great warrior, and beautiful."

The empress glared at Udaya. "Why do not you marry her then?"

Jealous. She was jealous of Xandra on top of seeing her as a threat.

"Nakano, all I meant was they would make beautiful babies. Lin, not so much. I would pray they would look like Rochan if he married her."

Rochan could not help but smile at the thought of a long future with Xandra with a few kids running around. He wondered whose powers they would get, whose eyes. He shut the romantic thoughts down. He was not at all ready for that, but it was something to dream and strive for.

He saw Xandra warming up, Lin doing so on the other side. Lin fought like a bull. Xandra like a tiger. She would lie in wait and then strike, making those strikes count. It reminded him of fables Dev had taught him while fighting. He grinned thinking of his father, and all that he had done for Rochan to mold him into who he was.

"Why are you smiling?" the empress demanded.

"Just thinking about tigers."

"Tigers?" Udaya asked.

"The fable of the Tiger Cub. Even a cub has claws."

Udaya gave him a soft smile. She knew Dev's pet name for him when he was little was Tiger Cub. She squeezed his hand.

"And you presume the princess hides her abilities just like that baby tiger?" the empress asked, her voice cold and empty. "You make me think of the fable of the fool."

"Fools presume. Sages know." Rochan glared at her. Xandra had not used her fire powers yet in battle, and Rochan figured she had more Fyrian fighting tricks up her sleeve.

The empress shifted in her seat uncomfortably.

The crowd cheered, screams echoing off the walls. Rochan did not let himself stand or lean over for a better view, desperately trying to hide his anxiety from the empress. The announcer said quite a few things, his power amplifying his voice through the air. All Rochan could hear was his rapid pulse in his ears. Both girls bowed to the empress box, but he only had eyes for the princess. Her eyes found his and she gave him a nervous smile. He gave her one back, not caring he was marking her as his favorite in front of a stadium of people.

He looked around to see who might've noticed. His gaze met the Serpentines who nodded, lady Serpentine adjusting a jeweled hair pin that glimmered in the light. The hair comb was actually a tiny knife. He searched the crowd for any other suspicious behavior, then spotted another council member staring at him. She opened her kimono to show a handle of a sheathed blade.

They were planning a coup.

He glanced at the empress, but she was eagerly watching the arena, anticipating the battle.

If Xandra won, the empress would lose it and give them opportunity. If Lin won, the council needed to intervene for his sake. With them, he had Lyft. They were backing him. It was happening. New nerves rolled over him, spiking when the gong was hit to start the battle.

Lin immediately leaped at Xandra using wind magic to lift her up and arc down in a stabbing motion. Xandra simply ducked, forcing Lin to stab the ground behind her. Then Xandra spun on her heel and stabbed her sword at Lin's back, slashing both sides of Lin's armor, scoring three points in the first few seconds.

Lin spun around swinging, but after the third slash Xandra had backed up quickly out of range. Lin tried several more moves, each one becoming increasingly more aggressive, losing all art form and grace of kalaripayattu principles. As each hit missed Xandra, Lin growled her anger out for all to hear. Each time, Xandra got in a hit for a point.

He chanced a quick look at the empress who was scowling.

Then Lin blasted Xandra back. Not ready for it, she fell to the ground. Lin leaped, her sword stabbing down toward Xandra's face.

He held his breath, his heart pounding.

She rolled away just in time and managed to use both swords to slash at Lin.

Udaya gasped. "She went in for a kill. Is this…not a game anymore?" Udaya whispered.

The empress smiled smugly. Udaya yanked her hand out of the empress's.

"I will stop it if it comes to that," Udaya hissed.

The empress glared at her.

"We will not bring on Fyr's wrath."

Rochan pretended not to hear. He watched Xandra with an anxious combination of fright and pride.

Lin spun her swords in tandem in an intimidating pose. Xandra did it right back, her style more graceful, in tune with her body, more aware of her opponent. She would be amazing at wind exercises.

Swords clashed, Xandra's blocking every swing from Lin. The crowd gasped as did the empress. "Where did she learn to fight our way?" He felt her eyes on him.

"She likes to read?" he shrugged, glee blooming inside. It was not a lie. She read voraciously. Not telling the empress he'd trained with her in his room and on the roof was merely an omission.

The empress squinted, not believing him. She could not prove he helped though. She only caught Xandra in his quarters once.

Swords clashed drawing his attention. Back and forth, they hit and blocked each other, dodged and feinted, almost as if it was just practice. They scored an even number of points, the scoreboard servants having trouble keeping up, but Xandra had scored ten points at the start, keeping her lead. It still meant Lin needed sixty and to incapacitate Xandra to win.

At one point, Lin started to smile. She had backed Xandra against the curve of the arena's oval right below him. He could not see Xandra's face to know if she was frightened.

Lin swung at Xandra's neck level, making his pulse spike.

She ducked, stabbing her swords upward as the crowd protested Lin's second attempt at killing rather than playing by the rules. They were to go for sparring points. Lin was going for blood. Murmurs of dissonance echoed throughout.

The official walked out onto the arena, but the empress waved her hand for him not to give Lin a warning. The empress was the fool. The people were unhappy, and she should've let the official warn for show.

Then everyone gasped, including the empress and Udaya, as Xandra turned into a ball of fire and appeared behind Lin, slashing her back armor repeatedly before Lin could spin around to defend herself.

As she spun, Xandra, looking furious, copied Lin's move to slice the girl's neck. Rochan's stomach plummeted. *Do not give the empress a reason to kill you.*

Xandra stopped her sword at the last second and tapped Lin's neck, before retreating, leaving a scratch. It was a message: I can kill you but choose mercy.

Lin glared and touched her neck where a thin line of blood pooled.

Then Lin went crazy. She rampaged and swung her swords at Xandra in a rapid pace that Xandra tried to keep up with before she had to transport away again. It was clear Lin was not a windwalker, for she did not follow. She thrust her power into an air bomb. Xandra returned it and in the middle of the arena, the fire exploded filling up almost the entire arena. Flames came toward the empress's box. It stopped a few feet from them.

The crowd screamed until Xandra pulled all the fire back toward her, containing it, protecting the crowd. Then she encircled Lin with it who was trapped and terrified—unable to windwalk, use air magic, or fight her way out.

The crowd was going crazy cheering for Xandra, but the empress did not call the fight. The poor servant boy doing Xandra's score was rapidly putting points up. The other boy had to help him.

"Nakano, you must call the fight."

"It's not over," the empress whispered. "The princess cannot keep the fire going forever."

"Lin cannot win. She is done. The princess is now forty points ahead and then had fifty to start. The entire arena knows it, darling."

Lin's face fell, and she knelt down, placing her swords down in the gesture of defeat.

Udaya tried again. "Look, even Lin knows it. She put her swords down in forfeit."

Rochan kept his face schooled, although he wanted to beam. The empress's glare was on him. She would not let him be happy.

Rochan looked into the crowd. Lord and Lady Serpentine were gone. So was the other council member he recognized. Something was afoot. Should he do something rash? Call the fight? Announce Xandra was to be his wife? Or did the council have it in hand and he could ruin their plans?

The empress stood, and she motioned her one guard over, the one she often used for windwalking.

Rochan would not let his mother lay a finger on Xandra.

He reacted.

Rochan appeared down below in front of Xandra. A collective gasp came from the spectators.

The entire arena went silent.

26
AN HEIR

Rochan appeared in front of Xandra. The arena went silent. Then he pulled her to him and kissed her. In front of everyone, he marked her as his choice. The swords dropped from her hands.

A split second later, the empress and her guard appeared in front of them.

"I will not accept you as winner." The empress's dark cold eyes bore into Xandra's, throwing a cold blanket over her triumph. Rochan was hers; he belonged to Xandra after the win. Not that she wanted to possess him like this ridiculous auction of his hand in marriage had promoted. She had saved him from this horrific woman. She would protect him, and he would protect her. She loved him. He loved her. It was what Xandra had fought for. Saving Rochan was what fueled her battle cry; the idea of being with him drove her on to win. The empress put her through all these trials. For what?

There were murmurs of confusion since the empress kept her voice low and threatening. The official came out. Xandra kept her fire going, seeing the scoreboard boys frantically adding more points still, no one telling them to stop.

"She has won!" Rochan said loudly, but his voice neutral.

"Shall I announce her as winner, Empress? She has scored beyond any chance of the other girl catching up with her. There is only a tiny bit of time left on the timer." He pointed at the large, thin hour glass's red sand flowing downward, the bottom full. Ten minutes was almost up.

"I decide who my successor is!" The empress screeched.

The man shrank back.

"You must." Xandra raised her voice to make sure the crowd could hear. "I have won, fair and square at every challenge you have thrown my way. *Your* competition, the one *you* created, I have won each round. But more importantly, I have already won the prince's heart. I will not leave here without him, and he will not leave his people. My only chance to secure the man I love was to win his sphere." The truth burst from Xandra. Rochan's shoulders were tense, his eyes glued to his mother.

"*My* people," the empress spat.

"The sphere belongs to no one, Your Imperial Majesty." Lady Serpentine entered the arena, with her husband, and was followed by the entire council.

"What is this?" the empress asked glaring them down.

"The council is simply doing its job. The Fyrian princess won your games, and we declare her the winner."

LYFT

A lone clap resounded from the stands. Everyone distracted looked over. Ahana stood in the third row from the bottom, clapping her hands loudly, a smirk on her face. The ladies around her joined in, their men, and then it spread like a fed flame around the arena. Ahana then started chanting "Xandra. Xandra." That took off like a wildfire and drowned out anything the empress tried to say.

Xandra stared at Ahana in awe. The girl placed her hands over her heart and then made motion toward her, a loving gesture, the move of a true friend. She was moved, and smiled, but had to turn her attention back to the empress and officials. She had to ignore the supportive crowd.

The official looked at the council, then the empress, confused. Then, he looked to Rochan, perhaps to be the tie breaker.

Rochan nodded, his eyes on his mother, glaring.

The official used some kind of wind magic to push his voice throughout the room as he had before. "The winner of the Empress Games is Princess Alexandra Sapphirian of Fyr!"

The crowd erupted with applause, and Xandra finally dropped her fire to let Lin free, but there was no time to process her success.

The empress was charging at them wielding two lightweight swords she had wrenched from her guard's sheaths. Xandra ducked and rolled out of the way just in time, snatching up one of her discarded swords. She forced the thought that she was fighting a madwoman out of her mind. *Focus.*

She blocked out the protests of the council, the crowd, the officials, and watched the empress carefully.

Rochan had Xandra's other sword and batted away the empress's next attack by inserting himself between them. The crowd gasped. There were shouts everywhere. Pride and love filled her heart. He was standing up to her, ready to battle her to save Xandra.

The empress growled as he batted both swords away. Xandra joined his side.

Rochan muttered, "Please. Stay back. I know how she fights."

Xandra wanted to protest, but she knew he was right. He cared too much to focus as well, and let his emotions rule him. He would mess up trying to protect her in battle. And he needed this. He needed to subdue his abuser.

Before she could retreat, the empress came at them again. They each battered her sword away.

Rochan gasped before saying, "Xandra, I do not think I can—"

"I know."

She handed over her sword to him and staggered backward to avoid the empress's next swing.

"My back, under my jacket."

Xandra lifted up his jacket and found the triangle dagger, a katar.

She spun around to have Rochan's back. The empress's guards were fighting the council who were well armed but not warrior-level fighters. Still, they had the numbers. This was more than her winning. This was a coup. If the council succeeded, she and Rochan would not have to deal with the empress, and he could rule.

But there was a threat looming, now barreling, toward them: Lin.

Xandra created a little distance between her and Rochan, drawing Lin away. With only a katar, she was at a major disadvantage.

"You really want another go? I won him in multiple ways." Xandra blocked Lin's crisscross of swords by jamming the katar upward. She remembered what it was, and its use from the books she read.

"I die if you do not die. The empress commanded me to kill you, or I am fed to the naga." She swung one sword and Xandra ducked. She thrust her weapon upward trying to disarm, but Lin jumped for an above attack and the katar missed the armor delving into the fractional gap. Lin went down with a wail. The katar was in her lower abdomen on the left side. The swords fell to the ground as she reached to remove the embedded weapon.

Rochan fell onto his back next to Lin, looking over at the girl, surprise in his features, then his eyes met Xandra's with relief. He had thought she had been wounded, and he got distracted.

Xandra grabbed Lin's sword as she heard a swish of attack cutting through the air downward. She turned and swung as she rose up. The force of her blow against the empress's sword—Rochan had disarmed one of hers already—meeting the inertia the woman had put into the blow flung the empress back a couple steps. Xandra's arm reverberated with the force of it. Rochan leaped up, attacking her, forcing the empress across the arena with wind magic and blows from his swords.

Wanting to help him but realizing she would distract him, Xandra bent down to Lin who had pulled out the dagger and pressed her hand to the bleeding wound. If Lin died, Xandra might have to go on trial and the empress—if she lived through this coup—might execute her. She also had never taken a life and did not want to start. Xandra moved the katar and other sword away from the girl. She forced her hands up under Lin's armor.

"What are you—"

"Saving your life."

"Why?"

"You are just a pawn in this who wanted to be an empress. I can save you, but you must swear to stick to the forfeit, swear I am the winner."

Lin nodded. "I swear. I am done. Just keep the madwoman from executing me."

"It will hurt like a—"

"Do it."

Xandra poured her healing magic into the girl too quickly not to ease the feeling of being burning alive, but Xandra was worried about Rochan who she could not see. Lin dug her hands in the sand as she screamed out. Then she said a weak thank you as she passed out.

Xandra picked up the katar and slipped it into her sword belt. Then she picked up Lin's swords and turned to see Rochan looming over an unarmed empress, the tip of the blade pointed at her throat.

She hurried over worried he would do it and worried he would not. The battles around them died down. The arena went quiet, everyone realizing there was no reason to fight if Rochan would win.

Rochan was panting, his eyes holding the empress's dark glare. Hate emanated from her. Aversion in his. After all she had done to him, he had every right to end her life, but what would it mean for him?

"Do it!" the empress seethed, pushing her neck toward the sword's point. Blood surfaced and started to weep down her neck. "You cannot. You are weak. Disappointing. A *boy*."

Rochan clenched his jaw. "You see what you want to. Your perception of the world is off because you lost your mind the moment you killed your husband. I am stronger than you. I easily disarmed you. I am wiser than you, not letting my hate control me. I speak to the naga, and you cannot!" He shouted it all loud enough for the crowd to hear.

Xandra touched his shoulder to stop him. He backed the blade away but kept her pinned down. Someone shouted, "Kill her." Another joined in and another, until the entire arena seemed to be chanting it.

"Rochan!" Udaya, the woman who was more of his mother than the empress, ran out. Xandra stood, swords ready, unsure if she would choose her son or wife. The woman adored Rochan and lost her brother to the empress's hand, yet she loved this monster after everything she had done. Xandra would protect Rochan as he protected her by coming to defend her. They were one and had each other's backs. No one else's. "Please. Do not." Udaya begged.

She pushed his blade away and put herself in between Rochan and the empress, facing Rochan as if to protect her wife foremost. Xandra gripped her swords tighter, and raised them up, ready to intercept any attack.

"Rochan, my dear boy. This is not you." She spoke low so the crowd could not hear. The kill sentiment faded into murmurs that rippled through the arena, unsure where things were headed, just as Xandra was. "You are all goodness, the light, the air I breathe. Not a death bringer, not a monster. You are Dev who is part of me, *not her*."

Udaya wanted Rochan to never become what her wife had.

The empress screamed in rage and agony. Udaya had chosen his side. She chose their son—not her wife. The empress's hand slipped down to her waist and unsheathed a small dagger.

Xandra acted quickly as the empress pounced toward Udaya. Xandra swung her sword downward.

The empress lunged at Udaya with her dagger arching upward.

Udaya turned around to face her wife at the same time.

Xandra froze. Her sword struck the empress's left shoulder, impaling her from the force of her attack. Xandra let go of the hilt.

The empress staggered back.

Udaya did not hesitate but lunged at the empress screaming, "For my brother!" She grabbed the sword's hilt. "For my son." She kicked the empress backward, the sword exiting the wound caused by Xandra. "May the gods judge you!" She stabbed the empress in the stomach.

They both went down, the empress pulling Udaya with her. The empress screamed as the point of the sword slammed into the ground, being pushed mostly back out. The empress grabbed the blade and yanked it out, dropping it into the sand from the pain.

Everyone froze, staring. Rochan had been immobile since Udaya had entered the arena.

The women wrestled, screaming at each other. Xandra gripped Lin's swords, ready in case the empress won in the scuffle, but also watched for openings where she could stab the empress again.

Udaya pulled away, and the crowd gasped. Silence filled the arena. She held up a katar, covered in the empress's blood dripping down Udaya's sleeve. "This is the weapon that killed the emperor on his wedding night and led us to this moment. After so much suffering, hatred, torture by the empress's hands, I regret giving her this means of escape from her marriage. Because I love her, I have set her free through the same weapon that demonized her mind. Rochan is the emperor. I command it. He is the rightful heir, and he shall choose his own empress, not some result of a cold, calculated game."

There was resounding applause throughout the arena. Servants fell to their knees and prayed, cried, or celebrated. It was all too much to take in. The guards who had defended the empress bowed in submission, placing their weapons down like Lin had. So much happy chaos.

Too late Xandra heard the empress growl. She was still alive! Xandra rushed over, sword in hand, but the empress was up and fell into Udaya before she crumbled to the ground.

Udaya fell back into Rochan's arms, the katar in her side. The empress fell back and lay with a creepily-satisfied grin. The gaping hole where the dagger had been bled profusely onto her abdomen; the shoulder wept with blood as well. Her movements had only hastened her blood loss, all in an attempt to kill her lover. The mental capacity to take someone you "loved" onto the next life floored Xandra. She simply stared at the monster as it bled out and lost strength. Not human.

"Xandra!" Rochan's desperate voice caught her attention.

She turned her attention to Rochan who was squatting down with his mother. Udaya lay back, wincing in pain, her one hand on the dagger embedded in her side, the other hand reached for Rochan's cheek.

"My beautiful boy. I am so proud of you. Rule with that kind heart. Be just."

"Amma." The pain in Rochan's voice prickled Xandra's throat. His pain was hers. She could not swallow. He looked at Xandra, tears forming in his eyes, tears that broke her heart. "You can heal her?"

Xandra would do everything in her power to keep this one shred of love for her prince. He needed family. He needed to keep that love Xandra had been overly blessed with, that Sapphirian brood she had felt was a nuisance—how lucky she had been. She had to keep Udaya alive, for Rochan. He deserved the sphere, Xandra's heart, but foremost, he deserved to keep a parent. "Move." Her tone was cold, but time was limited.

Rochan fumbled. "What are you—"

"Watch *that* one." Xandra pointed at the empress. "I am going to do my best to save your Amma."

"Guard!" Rochan called with authority to the closest soldier, one of the trusted men Rochan had outside his rooms.

Xandra was surprised how strong he was in the moment but focused her attention on Udaya's wound. She grasped the dagger. Udaya cringed.

"If the *former* empress moves, kill her," Rochan ordered.

"With pleasure."

Rochan asked him, "What is your given name?" He never knew?

"I do not have one," the soldier said dismissively as he pointed his sword to the throat of growling but pale empress.

"Then give yourself one."

Xandra ignored the rest of the conversation. "Do not move, Udaya. It will be painful." She yanked the katar out quickly and placed her hands over the bloody wound. "I am sorry for the pain I will cause you." Xandra pushed her fire into the wound, feeling the flesh burn and meld under her touch a tad slower than she had inflicted on Lin since safety was on her side this time.

She was yanked off of Udaya. Rochan's face was full of horror. He bound her arms as if she were a prisoner. "Xandra," he pleaded. "Stop." His breath came quickly down her neck, showing her his fear, his weakness: his heart, his capacity to love.

Udaya was in pain, but the wound was sealed. Rochan was wrapped up in his many emotions and did not understand. He was torn between protecting his mother and stopping Xandra in his confusion. "Look at me," she whispered.

Rochan spun her around in his arms. "Healing magic, remember? There is no time to wait for an elixir to dull the pain."

Rochan's eyes flittered over her face, taking her in, and he pulled her tighter to him, pressing his lips against hers again and again. After a third kiss, he pulled away and went to Udaya, cradling her head. She blinked half-lucid from the pain, but alive. Xandra had done it, twice after a battle and expending her magic.

A voice hissed, "Sapphirian."

Rochan's hand shot back to grasp Xandra's in his, for comfort, connection, or to stop Xandra from responding to the hissing voice—she did not know. Xandra squeezed it in assurance, and he let go. She knew he would watch and listen, but Xandra could see the empress was too weak to hurt her.

Instead of responding, she stood over the empress gazing down at her, her arms crossed but with a neutral expression. Someone so deranged would want to leave knowing she caused anger or pain. Xandra was determined to take that away from her if need be.

The empress tried to spit at her in spite, but mostly blood came of her mouth, weakly, landing back on her own face.

Xandra shook her head. "On Fyr, I had idolized you. A woman who grasped her own destiny? My mother did that in a much nobler way, so I had thought you had done it better, in a stronger way. Only after coming here and seeing how you treated my family, your own son, your wife, your people…you are not *someone* to idolize in any way. Not even someone to pity. You are a mistake in history that will forever be used as an example of what is wrong on an epic level. Lyft will heal from the wounds you inflicted. Just as Rochan's physical ones have. On coming here, my parents had warned me to observe. I did. I realized my sphere's definition of equality supersedes your poor version of matriarchy. Every horrid thing you built will die with you."

The empress's eyes opened wide, but her gaze was over Xandra's shoulder. Xandra turned around. Udaya was standing, Rochan half holding her up, her arm over his shoulder. This was the development that shocked the cold empress. Holding her sore wounded side, Udaya shouted to the crowd, "The gods of Lyft and the gods of Fyr spared my life! It is a sign that the spheres were meant to unite in peace through these two *royals*!"

The empress left the sphere to go where evildoers on Lyft go when they die, hearing nothing but cheering at her death and praise of an alliance she abhorred, knowing that her hatred and all its years of scheming would fade like her memory. At least that was what Xandra hoped.

Rochan fell to his knees, gaping at the sight of his dead coldhearted mother. Xandra knelt next to him as if they were giving respect to the dead. She whispered, "You must rise. Speak to the crowd. You, your Amma, and I must get out of here. Many are happy, but some will not be. Mostly, I am worried about a riot. You have to speak to them."

"I am no orator, no leader." It was hardly a whisper. She loved Rochan's tenderness and big heart, but right now she wanted to shake sense in him, bring out the fighter she knew was in there, the one the empress had tried repeatedly to stamp out, the man who just defeated his abuser in battle.

"You must be. It is your right. If you do not, Amma could be killed. So could I."

Rochan's eyes darted to Xandra's, his stare enraged at the idea. *Good.* She hit the nerve to pull him together. He could not lose those he loved who truly deserved his affection.

He stood. Xandra grasped his hand to support him. She could not transfer her power like some could on Fyr, like her mother, but she mentally wished him confidence by squeezing his hand.

He put his arms up in a motion to settle down, and people started to quiet. "My people." His voice was shaky. He cleared his throat and repeated it with strength this time. "Tonight's horrific events will forever go down in Lyftian history, but I beg you no more bloodshed. The entire sphere was not privy to what I saw within these walls. Know that the empress had lost her mind, sadly long ago. She murdered Dev Starsapphire and attempted to murder her own wife as you have just witnessed. Worst of all, she attempted to kill a princess from another sphere and tried to forever imprison two princes. Any of these actions alone was enough to cause a war. You have seen firsthand what can happen when fire meets air magic. Could we have survived that?"

He took a deep breath, letting them wonder before continuing, "The empress's crimes will be proven by testimonial and recorded. For now, I want you all to go home in peace. Stay in your homes and protect yourselves. I know not what will happen. Unlike the scheming empress, I truly can speak to nagas. I will

184

have them police the city to protect you all until we have a stable system of rule in place."

"You cannot rule!" someone shouted from the front row. Xandra instantly recognized her. Sashani, the girl defeated in the quiz round, shouted, "You are a boy!"

Udaya winced in pain as she raised her voice for all to hear. "I am the successor of the throne as the spouse of the empress and I—"

"You killed her. You cannot rule! I won. I am best suited for it. I am empress." Lin spouted.

Rochan's mother was weak and weary. She needed help before everyone tried to claim the empire.

Xandra took on her mother's dominant voice, proud for once to sound like her. "Who do you think you are? How dare you claim to win after I beat you? Look at the scoreboard! I saved your life." Then she switched gears to pander to the crowd as her father would, trying to seem as if she were meeting many gazes at once. "*I* was the winner as thousands of people saw in the arena, and in every round of this entire ridiculously unnecessary auction for a prince. I won him, but more importantly, I did it out of love. He is a person with choices and the heir to the sphere." Xandra looked at Rochan.

His eyes were wide, his chest heaving with breathy emotion. He would kiss the sense out of her in this moment if she stared back at him longer.

She tore her eyes away from him.

"You do not even have air magic!" someone protested.

Udaya spoke firmly. "Yes, a ruler of Lyft should have the power of air. The true winner of the throne before us is not a Lyftian with the power of air. But she is the winner. She and I, the new Empress Consort Princess Sapphirian, both wish for the prince of Lyft to take the helm."

Sashani spoke, "But—"

Xandra had enough of this girl. "Silence! Let me answer your other protests. He is male, but there was no stipulation to gender in the laws until an insane woman attempted to make her own. You claim Udaya has no hold on the throne, but did not the empress murder the emperor-to-be on their wedding night and claim the throne hers alone? There must be order and there must be change. Rochan is the smartest and most equipped for the task at hand. You witnessed the power of wind meeting fire. If the…Emperor Starsapphire chooses me to marry, there is nothing more powerful than those two elements combined. We are what Lyft needs right now, with the Empress Starsapphire helping the transition of power."

"Yes," Udaya said. She was leaning heavily on Rochan for support. "I will guide us, guide my son, to the old Lyft where all citizens had a say. Please, go. Go in peace tonight. Let us regroup and heal from this, and then we shall address the sphere with the path to a peaceful future."

Lady Serpentine shouted out, "The council will meet with the Emperor and Empress Starsapphire to discuss the next measures. Go in peace as all of your government asks."

Udaya retreated to a guard who helped her leave. Xandra was sure she had to be carried as soon as she was out of sight.

Rochan clasped her hand, weaving his fingers through hers, and whispered. "Naming me emperor and a Starsapphire? Ingenious. Anything to rid of her name." He glared at the dead body of the empress.

"I was raised in a court by the best parents, one who is an amazing orator and diplomat and the other so, so, so, good at manipulating and bending people to her will."

"You know you are staying, right?"

"Go home and miss all the fun? Never."

Then in front of everyone, he kissed her soundly again and without inhibition as if no one was watching. He pulled her body against his, from hips to chests, and plunged his tongue into her mouth. Hoots, awws, gasps, and whispers shook her out of the blissful moment.

Turning, too late, she saw the protester Sashani had grabbed an arrow and bow and was aiming right at her. The ambitious girl still wanted Rochan *and* to be empress. The arrow released.

Rochan threw his hand up as if to protect them, while Xandra tried to get her fire shield up. The arrow suddenly turned in direction and went upward until it pierced the crystal ceiling. The shards rained upon them. Rochan threw up a shield of air to bounce it away from them. People murmured at Rochan's power and quick reactions. Xandra was stunned herself.

"Arrest her for the attempted murder of the Princess of Fyr!" Rochan boomed. The guards immediately followed his orders. Sashani protested and tried to fight them off, but they incapacitated her as gently as they could and bound her in manacles. They led her away. "The same will happen to anyone who dares to incite a war with Fyr or make any attempt on the lives of the princess, my mother, or myself. Times are changing. Get used to it. The true emperor, the man who speaks to nagas, is here."

Lin walked up to them, a sword sideways in her hands, not in a way to attack. She went down on bended knee and offered it up.

Xandra looked at Rochan lost. He picked up the sword and looked down at her, and she up at him. "Speak," was all he said. He was emotionally spent, wanting to leave.

"I would like to repent my attack during and after the battle round. I was put under pressure to kill or be killed. I must earn my atonement."

Rochan glanced at Xandra. "She said as much in the arena." She would be compassionate. She would be wise. Her parents would expect that of her.

"What is it you ask of me by handing over your blade?" Rochan asked.

"To spare my life and in return, I offer mine up in service. I want to be a soldier, a guard, a protector. If you speak of equality, women can serve the empire, they can be true warriors and protectors."

Rochan sighed. "That is to be determined at a later point once our government is reestablished. It is not my decision yet to make. You have two choices. You can be imprisoned temporarily for your and our safety or chose a temporary banishment from the palace walls."

"I choose imprisonment."

"Why?" Xandra gasped, the thought aloud.

"I must be punished, Princess. I would like very much to earn your friendship, protect you, be your sparring partner maybe. You are such a great fighter. You could teach me Fyrian styles, and I teach you more Lyftian." At the last part Lin smirked. Xandra could not trust her, but she saw a bit of herself in Lin.

"That will take a long time to earn," Xandra said. "But I am not saying I am not interested."

"Of course. You are a clever fighter. I want to learn how you became that, how you adopted our style from books, how you wield the magic so well." She held up her wrists to the guards who chained her and took her away. Xandra saw the thirst of knowledge in her gaze. She reminded her now, once defeated, of her cousin Thomas. Had he not been her best friend growing up, she might not have put as much value in books, ones that taught her how to fight. Had she not rejected the feminine ways of Fyr and chased after her older brothers to have Aschen teach her how to fight, she would not be alive. Had Uncle Cobalt not taken her abilities seriously and continued her training, she might not have lived through all this.

Xandra's hand shook in Rochan's as Lin was led away.

"Are you okay?" he whispered, his own voice wavering.

"It's just she reminds me of my cousin who led me here, how everything happens for a reason. All my upbringing led me to this moment."

Rochan pulled her close. "Destiny wrote it."

There was an outpouring of cheers from the crowd, mostly of deeper voices because there would no longer be violence and hatred against the men. Scanning the front of the stands, a few women stood stoically silent but more clapped. It was not enough.

"You have to prove it to them, right now," she whispered. "Show them you speak to naga, that you are the rightful ruler. Many are happy but during my childhood I saw many who rebelled against a loss of power. Many women will be angry to lose control or fear men will overrule them. Some men could seek revenge too."

"What, summon a naga?"

She nodded. He took in the crowd and must have seen what she had. He took a deep breath, nodding. Then, he put his hands up in the air staring at the shattered glass ceiling, and shouted, "Khādati!"

Silence formed. Instantly.

Everyone looked around waiting, including her. There was a screech above and the broken crystal ceiling fell apart more, raining down on Rochan and Xandra. They had their powers up for protection; fire and air combined into a massive spectacle, a mini explosion shield. She pulled her magic back in to not harm the crowd under the overhangs who had been safely sheltered by the glass.

The naga slithered in on its air magic, majestic and still strange to Xandra. Its voice rang in her head, but the words were like another language, and she made it her new objective to learn it as soon as possible. She felt the sentiment of the first two encounters, but this time she could hear rumblings of a language. It moved through the air gracefully, but the people were either frozen or toppling over each other in horror to get to the exits in the back of the stands.

Rochan stared at the naga that circled them slowly, away from the crowd. It kept its eyes trained on him, listening to whatever Rochan was imparting to it in his mind much like she had been taught when her parents took her to meet the draca in the Firelands—well, she had encountered the Queen and DJ who resided intermittently on palace grounds prior. She noted the control he had over it.

He spoke a few more words in another tongue, maybe their language. The serpent picked up the dead empress's body carefully in its mouth and flew away through the gaping hole. Other nagas shrieked outside and then they faded away as Rochan stared up pensively, directing them.

Then he retreated. Xandra followed him, hurrying to catch up. She could see tears pooling in his eyes.

She dared to ask as a soldier opened a door for them. "What did that word mean?"

"Devour, to eat the empress."

"Rochan," her voice faltered.

"Not now. One day I will talk about her and all of this, but not today."

"I understand." She took his hand in hers, and they exited the bustling arena.

She would stay. Rochan needed her. And more importantly, she needed to be wherever he was.

"Do you want me to…?"

He turned once the doors were closed and they were alone except for a couple of guards. He leaned his forehead against her and let out a shaky breath. "I regret nothing. Get us out of here," he touched her cheek, his eyes meeting hers with emotional and physical need.

She transported them to his rooms and kissed him soundly until he cracked and started crying. She then held him close and told him soothing words about both of them being safe and free, how she would never leave him.

He stopped crying and then started kissing her in earnest. She slowed him down and held him close. "Let's just lie in each other's arms and think about tomorrow."

His lips pressed against hers. "As long as tomorrow means you will be here. I am yours to command. Stay with me, Princess."

She kissed him back. "I am not going anywhere. I am yours. I fought for you. You fought for me. Equality for you and me, and for all."

Rochan pressed a heated kiss against her lips. Then another and another. She pushed him away gently, touching his cheek. "We need to focus on the sphere. You and I are solid, but Lyft is not. Are you ready to marry or should we secure things first?"

The way Rochan stared at her and pressed his body against hers made her worry about his answer. If he asked her to marry him, she might do it—impulsively—and mean her answer. He devoured her lips again and again until he pulled away.

"I love you," he whispered on her lips.

Her gaze met his. "I love you too."

He kissed her gently, then rolled off of her and scooped her into him, his front to her back, a cocoon of love, friendship, and a promise of a future.

Xandra fell asleep loving the fact that her unknown future was of her making with the man of her dreams.

27
FYR

Rochan was nervous. Xandra clasped his hand, entwining her fingers in his—a loving gesture that emboldened him, made him feel powerful. How powerful would he be in Fyr though? If the wind did not speak to him as fire did here for Xandra, he would lose his confidence. He had faced a lot. After the empress's death, there was rioting and angry women who saw their power slip away, men wanting retribution for what his mother had done, but things were becoming peaceful. Udaya had temporary control to appease the women, and he was beloved as one of three saviors.

Rochan was rightfully supported as the successor who would take over but with hesitation. Slowly, he would take over roles so that no one would notice the transition in power—Xandra's idea. He was glad for it. He needed time to shed his old image and to gain confidence—his own and the people's—and he quite liked being able to live in freedom for a moment, with Xandra, enjoying the lack of full duty he'd need to overtake and healing from the abuse the late empress used to keep him suppressed. Freedom.

Two months since the empress's death was not enough time to heal his wounds or enjoy his freedom. But he was getting there. One duty at a time, Udaya ruling but asking his opinion, and Xandra helping him delegate behind closed doors—her idea again to make him look like the leader not her. He wanted them to be partners, publicly, but she insisted he needed to win them over and shine. Then only she would, but she would be demure about it. Apparently, her mother and father worked that way.

Xandra gave him a little smirk, her gray eyes full of glimmering excitement. "It will be okay. My parents are kind. My family will embrace you and love you. You will wish they would not. There a so many of them."

"I am worried what will happen here." It was a lie. He was terrified her father would intimidate him and force Xandra to stay in Fyr. He could not lose her now that all his dreams were coming true. He could not have it all. His late mother ingrained that in him. He was terrified he would wake up from this dream.

Xandra rolled her eyes. She knew him too well. "That is not it. Everything is fine. It has been two months since the empress died. I have been gone far too long without word. I must go back, and I want you with me. Sign the treaty yourself. Open trade with Fyr, and we can travel there once a year."

"Will that be enough? You will miss your family too much."

"Wait until you spend these two weeks with them. You will learn it is wonderful but also be happy to return to Lyft for the quiet and space."

He did not believe her. There was that twinkle in her gray eyes. She had missed them.

Rochan kissed her gently. "Shall we?"

She looked around the travel room and sighed. Surely, she would not miss Lyft, would she? In his heart he hoped she would. He did not want the comforts of her home to steal her away from him. He clasped the pouch around his neck with the double charged stone for a return trip to reassure himself he would be back, as Xandra used her free hand to pry open the pouch to get to the stone Dev had procured and Udaya had given them for escape.

They reappeared in a stone chamber. When Rochan opened his eyes, he saw a woman with a circlet on her head with the same eyes as Xandra and a man with a medallion who unmistakably was her father, an older masculine version of Xandra. The queen threw herself into Xandra's arms unknowingly breaking apart his and Xandra's handhold. Her mother hugged her fiercely and smoothed Xandra's hair after she let go. It was a beautiful affection that never had happened to him except in secret moments stolen with Udaya. He felt envious and then guilt washed over him. How could he take her away from all this love?

Before he could wallow in those feelings, the king addressed him. "Forgive my wife for not letting my daughter make a proper introduction. I am the King of Fyr, Alexander Sapphirian. I take it you are the Prince of Lyft?"

Xandra's mother let her go and Xandra wiped tears from her eyes before she launched herself into her father's arms and squeezed him. He chuckled and kissed her head, muttering sentiments of missing her.

Rochan stood awkwardly, feeling as if he should not be there, that he should leave them alone.

"I apologize, Prince Rochan, is it?" the queen spoke. That was when he noticed she was with child as the Fyrian royals had told the former empress.

"He is now Emperor Rochan, sharing rule with the Empress Dowager."

"Sorry. Pleased to meet you, Your Imperial Majesty." She introduced herself and then shook his hand.

He nodded, still finding the title strange. Udaya had insisted. Xandra had pushed too. It was only right he took on the imperial honorific the empress had refused him, had tried to kill Xandra's family over. It was like rubbing the "crime" in the ghost of the empress's face. Rochan pushed away his bitter feelings and thought about the future. He wanted to marry a princess and let her be a queen, shifting any kids they had back into royal titles, end the empire and form a kingdom again. He would make it his life's work to restore Lyft to its original glory.

King Starsapphire had a ring to it, since the first Queen was a Starsapphire. He would make it his life's mission to give the people more voice and power over their own lives.

The queen continued, "We almost lost hope, but your uncle had faith in you. Xandra. Then a couple months ago, your father saw your return in the flames."

"I looked in the flames every day and put all the details together. I figured out it would be this moment," her father boasted.

"He's lying." The queen rolled her eyes. "Every Sapphirian worked hard to piece everything together. That many firebranders working together pin-pointed your arrival down."

Rochan liked them. He could see Xandra's personality came from them both.

The king dramatically touched his chest. "You wound me, love."

Rochan could not help but smile at their blasé and lighthearted banter. It reminded him of private moments between Xandra and him, when she made him laugh and his heart soar from just being herself. She transformed his life.

The queen smirked, ignoring her husband's jest. "We thought it best only the two of us met you, to not overwhelm either of you, but it seems we could not reel in our excitement either. Let us retreat to the King's Room to calm ourselves."

Not able to envision where they were headed, he let Xandra transport him. The King's Room was an elaborate, ancient looking room with stone dragons carved on the mantle of the fireplace, crown molding at the ceiling, gold and silver adorned everywhere as well as leather and plush furniture. It was an ornate show of wealth in opposition of the clean, modern, colorful style of Lyft. It did not feel like his Xandra's personality. Just as she was not nearly as formal as her parents. She was not a typical Fyrian. Perhaps, she did belong with him.

Her father poured drinks, and Xandra insisted her father give Rochan more water with his. The drink was rank, tasting of medicine—no, more like poison. The king smirked at his wife. "He held his distaste better than you did that first time you tried firewhiskey, my love."

Xandra conspiratorially whispered to him, "They are always like this. Grossly cute."

Rochan could never imagine talking about his parents that way. He smiled and politely took a sip of what he realized was watered-down alcohol. He was not a fan.

The queen had no eyes for them but was gazing at the king lovingly as his gaze locked on hers that same way. "As will you be one day, my daughter," the queen said. She tore her eyes away and noted Xandra's blush. Her mother's eyes flickered to Rochan in understanding. Then she studied him.

Rochan went rigid. Would the queen forbid the match? Would she keep Xandra here? She seemed warm and kind, but it was clear she loved her daughter. Would she not wish to keep her with her always?

A conniving grin spread across the queen's face. "Oh, I'm tired already. Xandra," she laughed lightly. "Will you retire with me and catch me up on all that has happened while I lie down. Let your father and Rochan talk politics and treaties, and I long to hear about what Lyft is like."

Strange. He thought Xandra would be in on these talks. As if sensing his trepidation, Xandra clasped his hand. The king's perceptive gaze noticed it. Rochan grew nervous. Her mother knew their feelings for each other and now her father. He swallowed hard.

Xandra met his gaze and nodded, her eyes promising him everything he needed: safety, acceptance, and kindness. He was safe. She would never leave him with her father otherwise. There was trust between them, deeper than he even could have with Amma, considering the years she had let terrible things happen to him.

Too quickly, her mother and she transported, leaving Rochan momentarily surprised by the queen's white fire.

The king took a swig of his drink, looking at Rochan anew. "May I address you as Rochan?"

He nodded. He still could not speak. The man was obviously kind and warm, but Rochan was highly intimidated.

"You may call me Alexander."

Rochan nodded hoping he had the audacity to drop the honorific.

The king sighed heavily. "I would not let her go to a man who loved her less."

Rochan's eyes met those bold, eerie blue ones. How did he know the depth of Rochan's love? Even Xandra did not, for it was hard to express the abundance of feelings inside oneself when he had never been allowed to show it outwardly.

"I was once you, a boy in love who found himself thrust into power. It will be difficult for you at first, for a few years, but you will need a supportive partner by your side."

Rochan was not sure if this was a test or what the king was actually saying. Was he giving Xandra permission? He relaxed. The king would not take Xandra away from him.

"My lifemate was that for me when I needed her most. She still is. Xandra is young, but she is strong. Unlike her sisters and female cousins, she is my warrior daughter. I am not sure if she has told you, but her future disappears on Fyr. She was destined to strike out on her own in another sphere. Much as I will miss her,

I know she will be the best ambassador for Fyr on your sphere if you will permit her that station."

Such a position would keep Xandra by his side, but Rochan wanted more.

Finally, he mustered the courage to speak. "I agree she would make a great ambassador, and I will examine who would suffice for an ambassador position on Fyr. But King Alexander," one day, I wish Xandra to be much more than merely an ambassador. I want her to be my empress. May I ask her?"

The king smiled softly—a bittersweet grin. He softly said, "Love. Flame. Draca."

"What is that?"

The king's eerie glistening eyes met Rochan's. "A Sapphirian motto, a recent one. It means that we royalty are unstoppable if we have love, our power, and our dragons. I am guessing my daughter has all three?" He raised his glass, so Rochan raised his to drink. "You do not need my permission, but I am glad to know your intentions are noble."

Rochan tried to push the memories of kissing and cuddling the man's daughter from his mind. The man had so many children, he must know how Rochan felt about his daughter. That made Rochan even more nervous.

The king took a sip of his drink. "I do have some stipulations if this alliance were to happen."

Gods of air, he wished Xandra was here with him; Rochan would hand over the sphere for her hand. She would be the one level-headed enough to stop him.

"Do not worry," the king's tone grew gentle. "The princes you freed were very forthcoming with what things were like on Lyft, and they explained your help in their freedom, and my daughter's plans at that time. I take it the empress is unseated for you to be able to be here?"

"She is dead. My other mother is keeping the peace until I slowly take over."

He nodded. "I am sorry for your loss."

"It was not…it was…" Rochan had no idea what to say about the death of the empress. She was his mother but his abuser.

"I understand. Not quite to the extent of what I think you likely had to withstand, but my father had been an unloving, controlling brute. You still love them and miss them—part of them at least." He stared at the fire in the grate, but he might as well have been looking into Rochan's soul.

A silence grew, so Rochan broke it. "What are your stipulations, King Alexander?"

"I wanted to make sure the empress was out of power, with no hopes of returning, of course. I could not let my daughter go back otherwise. I also want the treaty signed. My daughter must be allowed to come home and have family members come see her. Water desires our aid as well. We must be united to prevent tyranny on each other's spheres. The three spheres should seek universal peace."

"What of Earth?"

"They have given up their magic for technology. Every day, they destroy their planet and the earth magic with it. We cannot help them now."

Rochan thought about the spheres and the treaty terms. He needed to negotiate. "I agree about open travel between our spheres and trade, but I am not sure we are in a position to give Water aide."

"You would be surprised how many people are unhappy in your sphere."

Rochan's stomach dropped. He was offended but did not dare speak out. He held his tongue hoping the king was going to elaborate on what he meant.

"I inherited a mess. I assume you are dealing with the same. Selling it as a new start to the many unhappy males wanting retribution could be a way. Some of them will just want to be away from the bad memories, the sphere itself."

So, King Sapphirian did not mean to offend, and what he said made sense. "It would take me time. I would only send volunteers."

"I would not ask otherwise. The same for my people. We shall write it into the treaty. Now that the treaty talk is out of the way, can you tell me what my daughter has done?" The dread in his voice and understanding of his daughter made Rochan laugh. A calm ease rippled over him. The visit would go well, and he had permission to marry his love if she'd have him. With Xandra by his side, Rochan would be unstoppable.

28
A TREATY

When Xandra finally was able to leave her mother's chamber to go down to dinner, she stopped by Thomas's room to update her cousin about events on Lyft. His room was empty. It would have to wait until after dinner. It would be better for him to see Rochan again and hear about how he had inadvertently set Lyft on its path to freedom. If he had not messed up, Xandra would not have followed and met Rochan.

She found her father and Rochan laughing in the King's Room. She hardly got to see that beautiful wide smile of perfectly aligned teeth. No wonder, considering recent events on Lyft, but still a pang of jealousy ran through her. She wanted that smile bestowed on her, not on one of her father's lame jokes.

As if Rochan sensed her, he turned, and that joyful face met hers. He was up and over to her, offering his arm. She remembered his hesitancy to do such a thing as politely make contact when she had met him. Glad he had overcome one of his mother's cultural boundaries, it made her heart full. Perhaps there was hope he would become a just and kind emperor yet, erase the shadow of his mother.

"Why are you smiling?" Xandra teased him.

"Peace, treaties, and agreements. What could be better to unite our spheres in harmony, forever?" Rochan's dark eyes twinkled, and she could not help herself but to lean up to snag a short kiss. It almost sounded like he was alluding to marriage. Xandra did not feel ready, but to be asked by Rochan would be the best moment of her life.

Her father cleared his throat uncomfortably. Rochan backed his body away from hers, still letting her hang on his arm as he sat her down next to her father. He seated himself across from them. Ugh. He was more than proper. Marriage was way off the table then. That was okay, as long as she was allowed to return to Lyft. Her father explained the treaty terms before Rochan signed.

Xandra's heart did a flip-flop and picked up its pace. She saw the lines in there of authorizing a permanent ambassador on both spheres, as well as royal approved travel between each. Lyftians could go to Fyr and Fyrian to Lyft. If she could go back and forth, she might not have to make a choice. She could get back to Rochan. She would immediately demand that her father make her an ambassador.

Her father cleared his throat. A knowing smug look was on his face. She wanted to challenge that look for she knew it well. But the raising of his brows beat her to the point. He knew all. Of course, he did. He was intelligent, shrewd, and she was his replica in almost everything. How strange it must feel to look back at his old self, a boy who had loved an Earth girl who was able to save his people and break his curse. Probably as weird as it was to see her future self in his features. Would she be seen in the future as the savior of Lyft? Only if she went back could she instill a positive legacy like her father, her mother. She had to go back.

Rochan signed, followed by her father. They signed a second copy that Rochan rolled up to take to Lyft.

"Before we head to dinner, there is something you need to know Xandra. I did not want to mar your homecoming—we were just so happy that I foresaw your return. It's Thomas."

"He was not in his room."

"No." Her father let out a breath.

Dread filled her.

"He's on Water. Hence the need to get these troops there to get him back home. Your cousin seemed to believe he needed to redeem himself and stole your Uncle Cobalt's self-appointed mission."

Xandra felt many things at once: worry over Thomas, fear she would never see him again, and disappointment she did not get to say goodbye. Then pride came through. "Dad, please do not rush to get him. He needs to carve his own destiny. His future vanishes off Fyr, so maybe Water will be his new home. He would make a good ambassador."

Her mother sent a servant with a note for her father, likely urging them to dinner. He smirked when he read her note, stood up, and burned the note in his hand tossing the ashes into the fireplace. Not a note for their children's eyes. Rowland found one when they were younger and was scarred for life from what he'd read. Xandra did not want to know what her lovesick fools of parents wrote. Before her father left the room, he stopped and looked at them both with a stern expression. "I expect you at dinner in ten minutes."

They were alone. It felt…planned. What was her mother up to? Had her note instructed her father to leave them alone? Why?

Xandra looked at Rochan quizzically. He avoided her gaze.

Did he plan on returning to Lyft without her? Did her father not approve of him? No, she would not let them dictate her life. "Shall we go to dinner?"

Rochan fidgeted. He was nervous. "No, not yet." Whatever he'd say, she would not like it. She had to prevent it.

"I do not care what you have to say. I do not want to hear it."

Rochan's eyes darted up to hers. They were full of shock and pain.

"I am going back with you, and I do not care what you and my father might have agreed to. I will not give up what we have done in Lyft. Surely, you can make me an ambassador or some title where I can have a way to help your people."

Rochan's face went through a transformation as she rushed the words out. It ended in a wide grin and a glimmer in his eyes. He walked over to her touching her cheek endearingly.

How wrong her statement was. Rochan was hers, and she was his. No one in all the spheres in the universe would come between them. Not even her father, who wanted to keep her safe in Fyr. She would be in his study if he drafted her return to Fyr into the treaty.

"No." Rochan shook his head laughing lightly. "I cannot make you an ambassador, and I cannot marry someone who lives on Fyr while I am on Lyft. The title I wish to see you have is empress."

Xandra's jaw dropped and she froze, her heart doing the opposite—racing wildly. "Whaaa…?" was all she could stupidly get out.

Rochan pulled her up into his arms, his forehead resting on hers, their eyes so close they multiplied in her vision. "I want to marry you, Xandra." Then he leaned his mouth down until their lips met. She kissed him with all the emotions in her mind, with the energy of her pounding heart.

When she pulled away, she gasped. "Rochan, I do not know if I am ready." She ruined the moment. Sure, some still married in Fyr at sixteen, and in Lyft, they tended to do the same—in the days before the empress. She did not want to hurt him though. "We are young, your empire is in tatters, and there is so much we could do before we settle down and have children."

Rochan blushed and stared at the floor. How could they marry when he would never have the confidence to accept his feelings and urges as what they were: natural. She was the one who had to make the moves, instigate their relationship—all because of what his mother had done to him. It would take time for him to see himself as her equal, to realize she would always be kind to him, that love was not conditional and not about obedience. He had to grow up, just like her.

"I did not ask you, Xandra." Rochan smirked. "I was asking for an understanding. I'm not ready either."

Xandra smiled. "Engagees is what my land calls that. Engaged."

"Then we are engaged?" he tested out the word.

Xandra threw her arms around him, pulling him close. She peered up into his eyes. He was happy, and so was she. It was enough. She would enjoy the time with her family and return with Rochan to Lyft. They would rebuild his sphere and when the time was right and they both were ready, they would marry. She could not wait for the day, and yet she could. She loved him with all her heart, but relationships take time. Now, she and Rochan had time to create a sphere of their own.

Love. Flame. Naga.

EXPLORE MORE OF THE STORY!

COMING 2026

A CELESTIAL SPHERES NOVEL

WATER

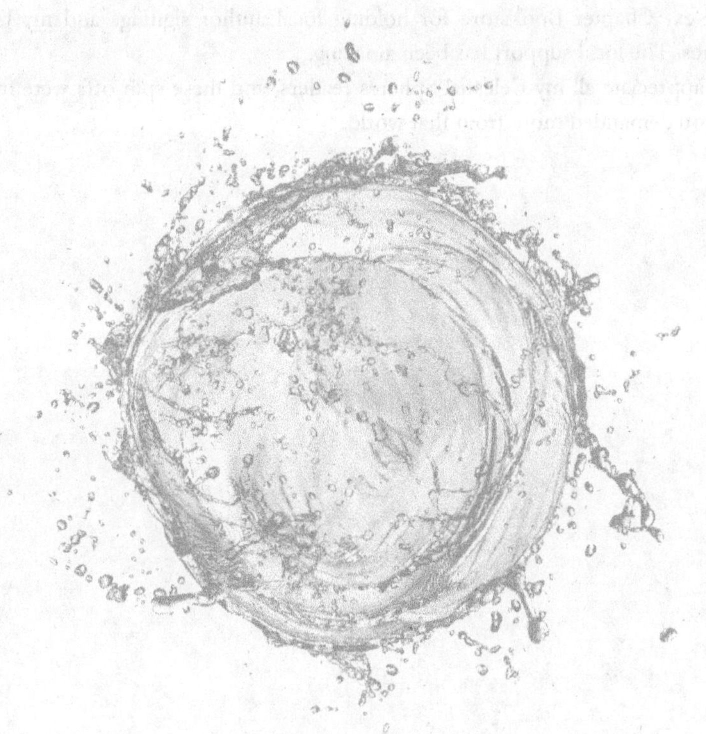

ACKNOWLEDGMENTS

I'd like to thank the Carolina Forest Authors Club for their critiques that made me realize I was immediately overcooking a book again from the start. Thank you, sensitive readers, CJ Carson and KR Galindez, for your insights. Huge thanks—as always—to Authors 4 Authors for believing in my visions and polishing them until they shine.

Thank you, my besties and family, for all being there, always, especially when I get into the zone and drop off the face of the Earth to write. You are always there for me when I resurface. Thanks to Carey for helping me at events and having great ideas for displays and much more. Special thanks to the husband for all he does to allow me to be a good mom, work full-time, and fulfill my writerly dreams.

Shout out to my local author friends for the ongoing support we have fostered in our close-knit community. Thank you WFXB FOX TV for having me on your Carolina AM show and for continuing to invite me back. Also, thank you Our Next Chapter Bookstore for holding local author signings and my book launches. The local support has been amazing.

I appreciate all my Celestial Spheres readers, and these spin-offs were made after you demanded more from that world.

About the Author

Lisa Borne Graves is a YA author, English Lecturer, wife, and supermom of one wild child. Originally from the Philadelphia area, she relocated to the Deep South and found her true place of inspiration. Her love for all literature led her to branch out from the academic arena to spin her own tales. Lisa has a voracious appetite for books, British television, and pizza. Her inability to sit still makes her enjoy life to its fullest, and she can be found at the beach, pool, or on some crazy adventure.

Follow her online:

lisabornegraves.com
TikTok: **@lisabornegraves**
Instagram: **@lisabornegraves**
Facebook: **@lisabornegravesauthor**

ALSO BY LISA BORNE GRAVES

THE IMMORTAL TRANSCRIPTS I

QUIVER

What would you do if you could live forever? Could you hide it from the one you truly loved, especially if her life depended on it?

Thanks to his dysfunctional Olympian family, Archer Ambrose finds out firsthand how difficult this can be. He never falls in love but bestows it on others—until he meets Callie.

When Callie Syches moves to the Upper East Side to prepare for her father's impending death, she doesn't expect to meet the boy of her dreams. She also never believed her father's harebrained theory about myths, but her uncanny ability to "see" uncovers godly secrets Callie can hardly fathom.

With an immortal family demanding absolute obedience, how far will Archer go to protect his love from the storm the gods will unleash upon them?

In this reinvention of Cupid and Psyche, experience an electrifying series where familial and romantic bonds are at war, and knowledge could mean the end of everything…or a new beginning.

books2read.com/quiver

Authors 4 Authors Publishing

A publishing company for authors, run by authors, blending the best of traditional and independent publishing

We specialize in speculative fiction: science fiction, fantasy, paranormal, and romance. Get lost in another world!

Check out our collection at https://books2read.com/rl/a4a or visit Authors4AuthorsPublishing.com/books

For updates, scan the QR code or visit our website to join our semi-monthly newsletter!

Want more romantic fantasy? We recommend:

KISS OF TREASON

by Brandi Spencer

Two forbidden lovers share the rare gift to heal others with a kiss—but at a cost.

Odelia's life has been a lie. When the queen tries to remove her from the palace, Odelia uncovers the truth. Now she must decide whether to forsake her people or embrace a destiny that would pit her against the current heir to the throne...her best friend. Though her only hope of avoiding a civil war lies in winning his heart, revealing her secrets too soon could cost both their lives.

And a kiss might not be strong enough to save them…

books2read.com/kisstreason

www.ingramcontent.com/pod-product-compliance
Lightning Source LLC
Chambersburg PA
CBHW010735100726
47899CB00009B/3063